Whimsey: A Novel

Kaye Wilkinson Barley

Dedication

To my parents. How lucky I was to have been raised in a small town on the Eastern Shore of Maryland. Even luckier was having Alan and Hazel Wilkinson as parents. Thank you for a home that always welcomed friends and family with a wide open door and wide open hearts.

Thank you for nurturing the imagination of this little girl and for always saying hello to her imaginary friend whenever she came to dinner. No one had a lovelier time growing up than I did.

To My Donald. Where to begin? You're the one person who believed in me from the very beginning, and finally convinced me to believe in myself. The one who has always encouraged my every endeavor – even the most outrageous and hair-brained . We have always managed to laugh; through all the ups and downs and through all the curves life has thrown us. I wouldn't change a thing, love. You are my heart. Just like we said on May 11, 1986, "the best is yet to be."

Acknowledgements

Special thanks to Earl Staggs, who has encouraged me to write since the day I met him. This book would not have happened without him. He held my hand and walked me through the birth, growth and release of Whimsey. If I had had any idea how much I didn't know about writing a novel, there's no way I would have attempted the arduous, fun, heart-breaking, joyous task of turning out a book. I am now, after two plus years of work, enormously proud of Whimsey. I've done what I started out to do – it's the book of my heart. But only the first one – I have a big heart and I think there are still stories to tell living there. Hopefully, what Earl taught me during this one will serve me well in future efforts. If not, the fault is in the pupil, certainly not the teacher. I love ya Earl Darlin'. And I promise to keep you supplied with Dolle's Peanut Butter Fudge for as long as the three of us are around.

And to Judith Greber who has been the cheerleader everyone needs in their corner. I find myself saying, no matter what I'm doing, "What would Jude do?" Sadly, I don't always get it right, but I will keep on trying. What a mentor. What a lady. Everyone should be as lucky as me.

To Celia Miles and Nan Dillingham who were my first editors for the two regional anthologies I will always be proudest of. Celia's words "you were born to write" will live in my heart forever.

To Evelyn David who invited me to write my first blog. Mercy. Who knew it could lead to this?

My thanks to all the writers throughout all the years who have taken me to magic places.

My endless thanks especially to the members – writers, readers, reviewers, and booksellers - of the mystery community who have welcomed me with open arms. I continue to believe you're the most generous and giving tribe a person could have.

To brave first readers who gave me invaluable advice regarding Whimsey. Margaret Maron, Louise Penny, Judith Greber, Hank Phillippi Ryan, Nancy Martin, Kathleen Prater Taylor, Luan Stauss, Vickie Fennell Smith, L.J. Roberts, Jill Harman Smith (who also happens to be the brilliant cover artist of this novel) – Thank you.

To all the wonderfully delightful wicked women I've been blessed to have in my life, beginning with the women in Cambridge, Maryland. We started out as childhood friends, and here we are a whole lotta years later. Still dancing the night away whenever we get together just like we did at The Carousel in the 60's. We are one extraordinarily lucky bunch. Next up – the Wicked Women of Atlanta – I love you and I miss you every day. Some of us had some wild rides. We may never want to do it again, but oh Laws, let's never forget 'em! And, the Wicked Women of Boone – thank you for opening your arms to me when we arrived in this magic town 16 years ago. And all you adorable Wicked Women who live in my computer at DorothyL, Facebook, Picture This!, Meanderings and Muses, Jungle Red and all the blogs and places I love to hang out – you guys, what can I say. Anyone who hasn't discovered their own community in the big wide world of the internet has no idea the strength of those friendships. A special shout out to my friends at Picture This! – you guys are one of the brightest spots in my day, every day. ILTG!

       To all of you who have stuck with me and encouraged me – Thank you. I could not have done this without you. From the bottom of my heart, thank you.

CHAPTER ONE

Atlanta, Georgia

February

Emmaline Hamilton Foley lifted her head from the pillow and glanced at her clock.

11:00

AM or PM?

Looking toward her window was no help. The shadowy dark skies could as easily be morning gloom as evening gloom. She had vague memories of falling into bed just as the sun was beginning to cast a pale sheen across the sky.

After spending another night working until dawn, it wasn't surprising she was still in bed at 11:00. But was the work any good or would today bring another round of disappointment? Would the jewelry designs she worked so hard on last night look cheap, shabby and amateurish in the light of day when her mind was clear?

Stretching her long lean limbs and yawning loudly, she rolled out of bed to make her way to the kitchen for her morning wake-up.

She caught a glimpse of herself in the mirror hanging over the dresser.

Not pretty, Emma. Not pretty at all.

She raked her fingers through her thick mass of silver hair. Hair her mother's side of the family had been blessed -or cursed- with since forever.

Today I look old enough to have actually earned this hair. She leaned closer to the mirror and inspected the tiny lines around her eyes. Were they getting deeper?

A strong cup of coffee first. Then I'll look at the designs. Today will be a good day. The designs will dance and shimmer. She crossed her fingers and looked upward. *Right?* She gave a nod. *Right.*

As the coffee brewed, she checked the fridge for cream. *No cream. Great.*

She crossed the room to look out the window of her condominium , taking in the view of downtown Atlanta she faced day after day. Busy Peachtree Street directly below and miles of expressway just a few blocks in front of her. Concrete bridges and loops going in circles and cloverleafs. Cars speeding by in all directions as far as she could see. Today the view was overshadowed by a dreary gray sky and a cold icy drizzle. How had she ended up here?

"I used to wake up happy. Hopeful. Who have I turned into? Where's the real Emma?" Emma closed her eyes and shook her head. "And if I'm going to continue talking out loud to myself I need to get a cat. Or a parrot."

She turned away from the window. *I need to get out of this place. At least out of this sad ugly excuse of a home.*

There are beautiful homes in lush green spaces in Atlanta and they're lovely. Why am I still in this horrid sterile box twenty-eight floors up overlooking nothing but expressways, for God's sake? I could go to one of those quiet old leafy side streets off Peachtree that no one outside of Atlanta even knows exist. I could buy one of those wonderful funky old homes in Inman Park. One that's full of character and charm. Why haven't I done that?

"It's because you're too lazy to get yourself moving, girl. Face it. Apathy has become your permanent state of mind."

Emma went rigid.

"Madeline?" she whispered.

"Yep, it's me. Surprise!"

Emma shook her head. "I've lost my mind."

"Oh, you have not. Don't be ridiculous."

Deciding to charge right in in order to figure out what the hell was going on and if she would need to check herself into the psych ward this morning Emma sat down in order to carry on a conversation with Madeline who was, or had been, her imaginary best friend when she was a little girl. Long since gone.

"Madeline. Mm, good to see you, only, of course, I can't see you since you're imaginary, but, um, you've been gone for an awfully long time. What brings you around?"

"Simple, Emmaline. You need me. You've been in a bad place for a while now and I'm here to help you get things back together. And this way you won't have to worry when you talk to yourself 'cause I'll be here. We can talk just like we used to. And you won't have to get a cat or a parrot. God forbid."

Emmaline sat back and stared into space. She remembered the long conversations she would have with Madeline and how they would argue. Even then Emma knew Madeline was "just pretend," and it didn't matter. When her older brother Jonathan was off doing other things, too busy to pay attention to her and her parents were traveling she would get lonely. Aunt Zoe was great, but sometimes she wanted someone she could tell secrets to and she knew Madeline would keep those secrets forever.

As she grew older and Olivia entered her life, Madeline began to fade away. Emma had a real life friend to take Madeline's place. But, truth be told, she'd been missing Madeline a little bit lately. Maybe this could be a good thing.

"Well, okay. I'm glad you're back. Just don't try to boss me around like you used to or I'll get that cat. AND the parrot."

"Lord A Mercy, you are in a bad spot if you're willing to put up with a flea ridden bird that can't do anything but repeat every word you say. Ugh."

"Oh, Madeline, you haven't changed a bit. Just hush." Emma shook her head, poured her coffee and walked through the living room into her office and turned on her computer to check her email.

While her computer was loading she sat down at her work table and picked up a bracelet she had worked on the evening before. Tears started behind her eyes. It was another piece that had good intentions but fell way short of

4

being what it could be. She tossed it down in frustration and anger. Turning her back on it she returned to her computer.

Scrolling through and deleting junk, passing over messages she would open later, she stopped at an address she didn't recognize - "zoeham."

Whoa! Surely not! Had Aunt Zoe decided the Internet wasn't evil after all?

She opened the message and saw that Zoe Hamilton, her mother's sister, had indeed discovered the Internet and judging by the length of this note, was as comfortable with it as her old Remington typewriter.

Emma reached over to ease a pillow off the loveseat and placed it behind her back, leaned into it and propped her feet up on the small needlepoint footstool under her desk. She smiled and sipped her coffee while she read.

"Good Morning, Child! I'm guessing you're surprised to see a note from your adoring Aunt Zoe. Truth be told, I'm pretty surprised to be writing it! I decided (well – with a bit of nagging from you, your brother and the rest of the free world) that it was high time I learned how to use this cute laptop your parents gave me for Christmas. I do recall Zelda gave me specific instructions to 'get busy getting with it,' or something to that effect. I believe it may have been her way of nudging me into this Age of Technology when I was quite content living in the Age of Aquarius.

However, to prove I am not a total curmudgeon, I will admit that once I got beyond being scared to death and more than a little intimidated, I have grown to love my little laptop. I'm even considering getting one of those small tablet things. Have you tried one yet? Olivia, is never without her snazzy little iPad and I covet it. (shhhhh, you're not to tell!).

After y'all left after the holidays, I was getting a case of the blues missing everyone, so I signed myself up to take a basic computer class at the community college and took to it like a duck to water! Now I'm even thinking about starting a blog. Or, are blogs now passé?

I have tons of news, darling girl, but actually I would rather share it all in person. I have to come to Atlanta to take care of some business - which I will explain in full when I see you. I will, of course, plan my trip when I know you'll be around and when it will be convenient for you to show your old auntie around the big city. Since most of my business is going to necessitate my being downtown, Buckhead and Roswell, I plan on making a reservation at the Ritz in Buckhead. That seems to be most central to where I'll be having meetings. Actually, I may insist some of the people I'm meeting with come to me. I can always plead the old lady card. Heeeeeee.

So as not to sound too mysterious or like a little girl with a big secret, I will tell you that it has to do with the shop and some plans I have, but I want to discuss them with you. I trust your instincts and your honesty, as you well know, and a fresh perspective on something I'm tossing around in my head will be welcome.

Check your calendar, Emma Dear, and let me know if there might be a few days (probably 3 or 4, possibly 5) that you'll be free. I don't want it to be all business! Some shopping and fine dining are always fun, of course! And expected! Olivia plans to come with me. Your brother is, I think, looking forward to a few days of Bachelor Fatherhood. Jonathan and the children always plan grand adventures whenever Olivia leaves Whimsey for a day or two. Max and Abby and Jonathan are as noisy and raucous together as you, Jonathan, and Olivia were when you were that age. And almost as precocious!

Chat soon, m'dear, and very much looking forward to seeing you.

Xxoo

Auntie Z."

Emma leaned back in her chair. "Wow." She swiveled her chair to face a wall where a four foot by four foot collage hung filled with color and images and what at first appeared to be a hodge podge of *stuff*. Upon closer examination, that stuff was actually carefully arranged, although artfully placed to look random. A grouping of ephemera depicting an expansive beach scene. The sea and the sky in shades of blues, greens and greys varying from the deepest hues to the softest hint of shades done in water colors and egg tempera. Clouds and sea foam done in textures of cloth and paper. The sandy beach adorned with some real sand, shells and sea glass. Off in the distance were familiar looking houses dear to Emma's heart. Tucked away in a corner was a small bottle appearing to have washed ashore. Only a very curious, or very observant, soul would notice the small piece of paper tucked into the bottle – a personal note written to Emma by her Aunt Zoe. The collage was a representation of her home - The Island of Whimsey.

Well, now, Emma wondered. *What on earth is going on here? Since when does Zoe Hamilton let me, or anyone else, know ahead of time that she's planning a visit? For as long as I've been alive, she's just acted out her whims and expects the rest of us to follow along without question. And we have. Quite happily 'cause it was always an adventure.*

Emma spun her chair away from the computer, tipped it back and sipped her coffee.

Zoe Hamilton owned a small, upscale shop on the island of Whimsey. Over the years, it had evolved from a cute little store selling mass produced decorator items to a high scale shop known for its eclectic mix of more unique pieces. Anything unusual enough to capture Zoe's attention was more than likely going to find its way into her shop. The items ranged from large pieces of hand-crafted furniture, art and sculpture to tiny sterling antique thimbles.

Emma, along with others, had been encouraging her aunt to make the move completely away from the expensive bric-a-brac, sit-abouts and pictures made only to match the furniture, to those items she truly enjoyed hunting out, displaying and selling.

Maybe she's finally decided to make the change from shopkeeper to gallery owner. I'll see about all this right now.

"And, maybe," said Madeline, "she's coming here to talk you into moving back home to Whimsey where we both belong."

"Oh, Madeline, do hush. We are *not* moving back to Whimsey, and that's final and you know why. It's not just because my designs suck. Do you want to take a chance of

8

running into Eli? Or that weird witch Reese Prescott? I don't think so."

Emma took her coffee to her favorite overstuffed chair, grabbed the phone and called the number that had not changed since she was a girl.

CHAPTER TWO

One week later, Emma walked into the lobby of the Ritz Carlton Buckhead and immediately knew Zoe and Olivia were close by. She would recognize the earthy deep throated laughter of her friend Olivia anywhere. As she approached the lounge, she spotted her aunt and her best friend sitting at the bar with their heads thrown back in laughter. She noticed a number of other appreciative eyes watching the two women, both of whom were beauties.

Olivia was the same age as Emma, both were tall and slim. Olivia had fair skin and the reddest hair Emma had ever seen. When they were little, she often questioned her mother about why she couldn't have red hair like Olivia's. When they were in high school, there was one disastrous attempt with a bottle of red hair dye bought in secret at the drug store. That was not a happy memory, and now Emma just coveted Olivia's hair from afar. The two of them had cut a striking picture while growing up. And still did.

Zoe was also tall, but at 5'8", an inch shorter than Emma and Olivia. At the age of 59, she carried herself in a manner that could only be described as regal, wearing her thick silver hair piled in an old fashioned Gibson. She wore black silk pants topped with a dramatic black and white abstract pattern tunic, accented by ropes of pearls and black jet designed and crafted by her father, Benjamin Hamilton.

They spotted her as she started their way, and Olivia hopped off her stool, ran to Emma, and threw her arms around her. After some squeals and giggles, Emma turned to see Zoe with her arms wide open. She walked into her aunt's arms and they embraced quietly.

After Zoe drew away, she looked closely at Emma. "Hmmm, we have a lot to talk about, I do believe." She patted a barstool, "Hop up here, darling child. We're waiting on our table and in the meantime, we'll allow all the nice gentlemen here to gaze upon the beauty of three women from Whimsey, what say? And we shall talk."

And talk they did. Through a drink before dinner, through dinner and through coffee after dinner.

Dinner was filled with back and forth chit-chat, questions and answers, catching up on the family and extended family, along with friends on Whimsey. There were interesting happenings and fun anecdotes to be shared. Whenever Emma tried to steer the conversation toward Zoe and why she was here, Zoe would wave her hand, smile and reply with "Later, child, later."

When the three women were served their after-dinner coffee in a quiet corner of the lobby, Aunt Zoe finally disclosed her plans, "You know I've wanted to change the shop into something more. I've wanted a gallery for years, and now I think the time is right. I want very much to showcase the talent of Whimsey. Many of the locals have made names for themselves, and many others are on the verge. Why should another gallery in another city benefit from the art and magic of Whimsey when I can keep all the artists together in a way that will benefit each of them rather than a dealer who has only profits in mind? Whimsey could possibly lose many of its young artists if they feel their only chance for recognition and monetary reward will come from the big galleries in the big cities."

Emma nodded in agreement, "It sounds lovely, Aunt Zoe. I know this has been a dream of yours for a long time and is in keeping with what Great Aunt Elizabeth hoped for when she bought and developed the island. The shop, however, isn't nearly large enough to do what you want. And there's no way you could ever enlarge it so you can house the art of everyone on Whimsey. What do you intend to do exactly? Knowing you, you have a plan already in place."

"You're right, of course, Emma – on both counts. I wouldn't even want a place as big as we would need for that. Instead, what I intend to do is enlarge, but only enough to display a small number of permanent exhibits, and the rest will be rotating exhibits. Rotation taking place every six or eight weeks."

Olivia reached over and touched Emma on the arm, "Oh, Emma, wait till you see the plans and drawings. You'll fall in love with it all, I promise."

Emma nodded, "It's going to be stunning. Have you lined up your permanent artists?"

Zoe nodded, "Most of them. I have one more artist I want to invite. That's why I'm here. Will you allow me to represent your work, Emma?"

Emma felt hot and cold all at once, as though a large glass bell jar had been placed over her head. She couldn't answer because she couldn't breathe.

Zoe placed her hand over her niece's, "Emma? Emma, darling? Are you all right, child?"

Emma shook her head.

Olivia took her other hand, "Sweetie, what is it?"

"I can't. And please, let's not talk about it. Just . . . I can't. And I really have to leave now. I'll talk to you both again before you go home. Please don't worry. I just really need to leave, but we'll talk soon. I promise. When I'm feeling better. I'm suddenly not feeling well at all."

Emma left quickly without looking back, had the valet bring her car and drove home on auto-pilot. When she got back inside her condo, she poured a glass of wine with shaky hands and sat on the sofa. As she knew would happen, the phone rang. It was Zoe wanting to make sure she had gotten home safely. Emma assured her she had and apologized for running out so abruptly by pleading a sudden illness she thought might be an onset of the flu.

After what felt like hours, her hands finally stopped shaking, and she realized she had tears on her face. She drank her wine while wiping the tears away. How could she tell her aunt and her best friend that her talent had deserted her? That her jewelry designs lacked imagination and originality. They weren't any better than some of the jewelry being turned out on an assembly line. Pretty little things that were fine for mass consumption, but would never be viewed as art.

She couldn't allow Zoe to put her work in her gallery along with artists and artisans who truly deserved the honor. She would look like a fool. Everyone would know her work was there only because she was Zoe Hamilton's niece and not because it deserved to be. Emma knew this gallery was going to be something special. Spectacular would not be over-stating the success that was in the wings. Zoe's collages, which sold in the six figure range, displayed by themselves would make any gallery's reputation.

Emma went into the kitchen and poured herself another glass of wine. When she went back to pour herself a third glass, she picked up the bottle and brought it back into the living room with her. Sometime during her conversation with the wine bottle, Emma passed out.

She was still on the sofa when the phone rang the next morning. When she finally shook herself awake enough to answer it, the old-fashioned answering machine she refused to part with clicked on.

The voice on the other end of the line was firm and quiet. A voice belonging to a woman not to be ignored or brushed off, "Emma, it's Olivia. You may have convinced Zoe you felt suddenly like you were struck with the flu, but not me. We have to talk. Whatever is going on with you can be fixed. Have I ever failed you? Wait - don't answer that. That little incident was years and years ago. Not important anyway. Zoe and I are going to ride in like the cavalry used to do in those old westerns we loved, remember? We're going to come by and pick you up at noon. It's just after 8:00 a.m. now, so that will give you plenty of time to take a hot shower so you won't smell like Mad Dog 20/20 when we get there. I do know you, girlfriend, so I know you've put away a bottle of wine before passing out. I've only known you to do that one other time. It wasn't worth it then either. But today, we talk it through and we fix it. See you at noon. Love you, Emma." And she hung up.

Emma took the receiver away from her ear, looked at it, shook her head and started laughing. *Sometimes having a best friend this pushy makes me crazy. She's right. I need to talk to them about this. This is one time Olivia's not going to be able to fix things for me, and she and Zoe deserve to know what's going on. But not right now. Not yet.*

She sat quietly thinking for a few minutes, and then heard a voice.

"They're not going to let you off the hook, you know."

Emma closed her eyes. "Madeline, hush."

But she knew Madeline was right. Her first thought was to hole up until Zoe and Olivia left. But that would never work. The two of them were stubborn enough to wait her out and wily enough to coerce her doorman into letting them inside her condo.

Pacing and running her hands through her hair, she remembered a cabin in the North Georgia mountains she had visited with a friend who was also a jewelry designer and craftsman. They'd shown their work in many of the same shows over the years and become friends. Quickly grabbing her address book, she found the number for the Grebers and called, tapping her fingers against the phone impatiently until someone answered.

"Jude? Hi, it's Emma? What? Oh. Sorry. I didn't realize it was so early. Listen - do you and Bob still have your little place in Ellijay? Is it rented right now? Cool! Can I rent it from you? I'm not sure - a few days. Oh. Really? Well, that'll work. I don't mind keeping an eye on the workmen and overseeing things for you, but I still want to pay you some rent. Okay - we can hash all this out another time. Yes, of course I'll be out of there by May 1st,

I don't need the place for that long! Well, you know, I just might. Do you still have the studio behind it? Is it okay if I make use of it? Of course I will! I solemnly swear to clean it all up and make sure it looks exactly the same as you left it. This is great! Wow. Look, I can't talk now, I want to get up there today. That way I'll be there when your workers arrive tomorrow to start the remodeling. No - I will not get in their way, I promise! If you don't mind me using the studio, that's where I'll be spending most of my time. Okay, gotta run. I'll call you later today once I've gotten in, and we'll iron out all the details. How's that? Cool! We'll chat in just a few hours, and Jude, thank you."

She hung up the phone. *Wow. This will work. I'll just have to straighten it out with Olivia and Aunt Zoe later. Once they hear and understand, I know they'll forgive me. But, oh boy, they're both gonna be mad as hell today. I have got to get moving.*

She grabbed her suitcases out of the closet and starting tossing things into them.

"Wheeeee, road trip!" squealed Madeline.

"Oh, Madeline, hush, silly," said Emma. But found herself grinning when she said it.

When Olivia and Zoe arrived at Emma's condominium, the doorman told them Emma had already left with her car loaded down with suitcases, but she had left them a letter, which he handed to Zoe.

Olivia watched as Zoe read the letter, slowly put it back in the envelope and looked up.

"She's gone."

Olivia shook her head in confusion, "Gone? Gone where?"

Zoe shrugged, "She didn't say." She turned around and started out the door. "Let's get out of here."

As they walked back to the car they had hired, Zoe handed the letter to Olivia.

Once they were seated in the car, Olivia read Emma's letter.

"Dear Ones - I haven't disappeared forever, but I will be gone for a while. I just need time, and something else I didn't realize I needed until this morning - distance. I promise to be in touch. Don't worry!

Love you both to the moon and back,

Emma"

Olivia put the letter down in her lap and looked at Zoe and saw the tears streaming down her face. She reached over and took her hand.

"It's going to be all right," she whispered quietly. "I promise."

The drive from Atlanta to Ellijay normally took just an hour and a half or so. Because of the rain with intermittent sleet as she got closer to the mountains, Emma knew it was going to be a long slow trip. Trying to find a radio station to keep her company didn't seem to be the answer. She had some serious thinking to do.

Aunt Zoe and Olivia would finish their business in Atlanta and they would go back to Whimsey angry with her. Angry and hurt.

The thought of these two women upset with her was almost enough to cause her to change her plans, go back to Atlanta and explain everything to them. And then make plans to move back home to Whimsey, where her heart would always be.

Whimsey. Just the thought of it deepened the pains in Emma's Heart. Whimsey. Where there was genuine magic and where extraordinary talent soared to heights unknown anywhere else. Emma's grandparents, Benjamin and Lillith, as well as her parents, Zelda and Scott, experienced it as did everyone Emma grew up with.

Everyone with the good fortune of being part of Whimsey benefitted when Emma's great aunt Elizabeth bought an island more than fifty years ago and made it into the incredible place it became.

Everyone. Except Emma.

CHAPTER THREE

In The Beginning

Savannah, Georgia - 1949

Benjamin Hamilton and Lillith Calhoun met in Savannah in 1949. Lillith was 19 and Benjamin was 21. Their story became part of family lore and Whimsey history and one family members loved to tell.

The two met through the newly formed Society of Savannah Arts while struggling with their respective careers. Lillith was a painter, Ben a jewelry artisan, and both dreamed of being able to earn their living doing what they loved. At the Society's first showing the evening before, Lillith sold only two paintings. Although the buyers had not presented themselves, Lillith was sure one had been her Aunt Elizabeth, and the other quite probably her father.

Lillith's hope - along with the money her parents had given her to fund one year of artistic struggle - had hit bottom, and to top it off, her father requested her presence at supper that very evening.

Lillith tried get out of the dinner by saying she'd made plans to meet up with Ben and the Society show organizers for supper so she wouldn't have to field questions from her parents regarding her sales. Questions she was certain they already knew the answers to. Had she sold anything? Were any galleries interested in handling her work? Did she realize her year was almost over? Did she remember their agreement? Yes, yes. Of course she remembered. If she wasn't standing on her own two feet at the end of the year, she would be expected to move back home out of the small apartment her mother referred to as "that dump." Move back home and start taking in students. If she couldn't make a living selling her art, she would, instead, teach it.

On this, her parents would not budge.

Dinner that night was, however, surprisingly non-confrontational. Lillith wondered what was up, and worried that they were perhaps going to renege on their agreement and force her home immediately.

As Ruth, their long-time maid, brought in coffee, Lillith's mother Edith turned to Lillith's father, "Well, Wallace, I suppose you better tell her."

Lillith stiffened when she saw her father's hands fidgeting with first his napkin, then his moustache, then his ear. Not good signs.

Finally, Wallace cleared his throat and said, "Lillith, your Aunt Elizabeth has asked to see you."

When Aunt Elizabeth "asked," it didn't mean what it would mean to a normal person.

This was a demand for an audience.

Wallace Calhoun walked Lillith to Elizabeth's house the following morning. During the short walk, Lillith's attempts to glean information from her father about what this was all about were met with mumbles, shrugs and a shake of the head.

"I don't know. You know my dear sister Elizabeth. She speaks, we listen. And then we do what she says."

"But why?"

"Because it's hell to pay otherwise."

Lillith couldn't hold back the snort. When she glanced up at her father, she could see him trying to hold back a chuckle as well.

A second later, they were both laughing out loud. People crossing the street pretended not to notice the usually somber Wallace Calhoun apparently losing it in public. It should be noted, this sort of behavior was frowned upon in the somewhat staid neighborhoods of Savannah. While southern eccentricity and outrageousness were generally accepted, and, for the most part, embraced, the citizens of Savannah preferred it be kept behind closed doors. "If it ain't pretty, don't put it out on the front porch" was a philosophy most lived by. And expected the rest of the city to do the same. Otherwise, you might be mistaken for a Yankee. Heaven forbid.

"Yes, but now you'll have hell to pay with Mother."

"Oh, well. Nothing new there."

And once again, they were both overcome with loud, raucous laughter.

"You know, Lillith," Wallace said after he'd regained his composure, "your laugh is one of the best things about you. You have an inner joy I hope stays with

21

you forever. And you don't try to bottle it up in order to appear sophisticated and above it all. I admire that about you."

"Well, I'm not sure where it came from. Not Mother so much, and usually - you're a bit more, ummmm - serious."

"Yes, one has an image, after all."

"Pfft."

"Lillith, I know you and Elizabeth get along well, and I truly have no idea what this summons is all about. But, I caution you, be sharp and aware and don't let her bully you - even in that sweet southern passive-aggressive way she has, which she's turned into an art. I don't want you walking out of there wondering what you agreed to and why. She's a canny one. Your mother and I are a bit concerned about what she might have up her sleeve."

"Oh, I'm very aware, Father. Not to worry. Some might say I inherited a little of that trait from her, after all."

"Hmmmm . . . "

As they approached the house, Ben and Lillith noticed Elizabeth rocking on the front porch, surrounded by small square tables, one on either side of her and six more scattered randomly across the porch.

One table held a large silver pitcher beaded and frosted with water droplets, along with four crystal glasses sparkling as the morning sun glanced off them. Elizabeth's luxurious bounty of silver hair, for which she was somewhat famous - and of which she was infinitely proud - sparkled almost as brightly.

Elizabeth Calhoun was also proud of her trim figure and worked hard to keep it by walking a brisk five miles every morning regardless of the weather. She was a familiar sight along the streets of Savannah as her long stride carried her swiftly through her morning routine, apparently indifferent to the admiring looks cast in her direction by the men of Savannah. And equally indifferent to the less admiring glances from the women. At 5'10" tall, Elizabeth Calhoun rarely had to look up to anyone which suited her personality quite nicely, but was off-putting to most others. This, too, suited her quite nicely.

"Welcome! Come join me for a glass of Rupert's delicious lemonade. We even have fresh mint from the garden. I do dearly love fresh mint in my lemonade, don't you?"

"Elizabeth, good morning." Wallace said. "What, pray tell, are all these tables doing out here on the porch? Have you moved out here permanently now?"

Lillith's eyes nearly popped out of her head when she spotted a stack of Samuel Eli Whimsey novels on one of the tables and scooted over to quickly drop her shawl over them.

"Oh, Wallace, always the comedian. That is, I suppose, what prompted your lovely Edith to fall head over heels in love with you."

She cast a look under her lashes as Lillith gave a decidedly unladylike snort.

"Lillith, my dear, you are looking the picture of health and happiness, I must say! Lovely to see you. Sit, sit. Both of you. You must share some of this lemonade with me on this glorious morning. Smell that mint - heavenly, isn't it?"

"Aunt Elizabeth, why *are* all these tables out here? I've never seen your porch so cluttered. Aren't you worried about the neighbors talking about how your standards are sliding?"

"As if! Very funny, Lillith. You know I've never given two hoots about what the neighbors or anyone else has ever thought about me - let alone what they've said. Gossip serves no purpose. You'll do well to remember that, m'dear."

Lillith thought to herself this was a bit of an understatement seeing as how her aunt had been gossiped and talked about for as long as Lillith could remember. There were always stories flying around the city about where Elizabeth may have been the two years she was gone from Savannah without a word to anyone. There were also the whispers about a past husband, or possibly lover, since no ring was ever seen on her hand. How else would she have become so wealthy? No single woman could possibly amass the wealth Elizabeth Calhoun so obviously was in possession of. Not even the brilliance of her brother's financial acumen would have bought this house in such a prime Savannah setting.

"As far as what all this clutter is about, it's just a gorgeous day. One entirely too lovely to be spent inside. Soon enough, the Lowcountry humidity will drive us all inside to wilt, so I decided to spend as much time during the next several days right here on the verandah. It's just as easy for Rupert to tend to me, as he is so wont to do, out here as it is rambling around in this monstrosity of a house. Speak of the devil!"

Rupert, a tall distinguished-looking black man about the same age as Elizabeth, showed up as if on cue. He stood next to Elizabeth bearing a large platter with the tallest cake imaginable.

"Anna thought you might all enjoy a slice of her coconut cake to go with your lemonade," he said. "Best coconut cake in the county, if I do say so myself."

"Well, Rupert, you didn't bake it. Your lovely wife did, for heaven's sake."

"Well, Elizabeth, how do you know I didn't give her my recipe?"

"Ha! As if! And, mind your manners. It's Miss Elizabeth to you, sir. Are you getting disrespectful in your old age?"

"I've always been disrespectful. After forty years, you should know that."

They exchanged a quick grin between them, something old friends would do rather than an employee and servant.

Rupert sliced and passed around generous slices of his wife's famous cake and made a smooth exit off the porch while humming quietly. Lillith could have sworn she saw him wink at her aunt as he left.

Wallace picked up his glass. "Elizabeth, I see an extra glass over there. Are we expecting someone else for cake and lemonade this morning? By the way, isn't it a little early for cake?"

"Wallace, who made up the rules about what we're allowed to eat when? Do you like the cake?"

"Delicious!"

"Well, would it be any better in two or three hours?"

"Certainly not!"

"Then eat up, dear brother. Enjoy! Didn't some famous woman once say, 'Let us eat cake?'"

Wallace looked at his sister with clear fondness and shook his head, "Not exactly, sister, but I get the point."

"Aunt Elizabeth, I've been admiring your shawl. It's new, isn't it?"

Elizabeth looked down at the shawl she was wearing, which was woven in many shades of yellows, gold and amber with a few sparsely spaced stripes of pinks of varying shades, "It is, and isn't it stunning? I'm in love with it."

Lillith reached over to feel it, "Mmm, silk. And handmade. Where on earth did you find it?"

"A friend of mine made it. A very dear friend, actually. I'll tell you all about that sometime, but not right now. You know how antsy your father gets when our attention isn't placed squarely on him."

Wallace unbuttoned his vest buttons and leaned back contentedly in his chair, "Oh, pshaw. I'm not the one in need of the spotlight in this family, dear Elizabeth."

"Well, rather than arguing with me, please feel free to light up that cigar you're daydreaming about, brother dear."

"Sister! I don't know what you're talking about!"

"Pshaw yourself! Edith isn't here so she'll never know. A man who works as hard as you deserves the pleasures of a good cigar. Besides which, I'll enjoy the fine fragrance. Here. Have one of these."

She picked up a humidor from the table beside her, opened the lid and extended it toward him.

"Elizabeth, where on earth did you come by these? They're outrageously expensive and extremely hard to come by."

"Oh my, not to worry, I have my ways."

Elizabeth winked at Lillith, reached out and patted her knee, "Dearest, if you don't have plans for this afternoon, might you spoil your dottering old aunt with a few minutes of your time after your father leaves?"

Lillith snorted. "Dottering? Pfft!"

Elizabeth looked at Lillith and rolled her eyes, "Lillith, you must break that habit of yours. Snorting is not a trait our society finds acceptable in a lady. As endearing as it may be, I'm afraid it reflects poorly on your family."

Lillith raised a heaping forkful of cake to her mouth, "Yes, well . . . ."

Wallace stopped unwrapping his cigar to say, "Lillith, on this I agree with Elizabeth - those snorts are unbecoming. Not to even begin to mention how they send your mother into vapors."

Elizabeth grinned, "Oh, the vapors is it? Well, we can't have that."

Lillith swallowed a mouthful of cake, "To answer your question, dear old dottering aunt of mine, I would be quite happy to continue our conversation here on this lovely verandah of yours. Now as far as the problem, as you two seem to find it, of my so-called snorting. I'm not aware I'm doing such a thing, but I'll certainly attempt, in the future, to be more ladylike in order to please you both. Along with my mother, of course. The vapors must be a terrible trial to endure, after all. However, dearest auntie, might I remind you of your earlier statement regarding the fine citizens of Savannah. I believe you declared never having given two hoots about what they thought, or said, for that matter. Or did I perhaps misunderstand?"

After a stunned silence, Elizabeth and Wallace looked sternly back at Lillith, who returned their gazes with a smile and innocent eyes as she sipped her lemonade.

And all three of them fell into peals of loud, happy laughter.

"You are a fresh young woman, niece. Don't you know you're supposed to do what we elders say, and not necessarily, what we do?"

"I'll try my best to remember that," Lillith murmured in reply. "Might I have one more small sliver of Anna's cake, you think?"

"Why, of course, my dear. And, Wallace, do have Rupert wrap a slice for you, along with one for your lovely bride."

Twenty minutes later, after saying their good-byes to Wallace, the Calhoun ladies settled back and propped their feet up on a bench Lillith pulled over from the other side of the porch.

"Ah, much better," Elizabeth said as she lit up her own cigar now that Wallace wasn't around to scold her. "Why sit with our feet on the floor, ankles crossed ever so daintily, when we can prop 'em up. Better for the circulation."

This prompted yet another snort from Lillith.

"Lillith! You did it again! I cannot imagine what your beau, the handsome Mr. Hamilton, thinks when you make that noise through your nose."

Lillith spun around, mid snort, eyes wide, and stared at her aunt.

"Well, of course, I know about Benjamin Hamilton. You don't take me seriously enough, my dear, when I tell you I have my ways."

Lillith watched as Elizabeth bowed her head to take a sip of her lemonade, watching the wrinkles around her eyes and mouth grow deeper as her smile widened.

"Auntie, you are the evilest of the evil. An imp to the nth."

"Yes. Yes, I am, my dear."

And they both fell, once again, into hearty laughter.

"And here's your young man, now."

Lillith spun around the other way to see Benjamin walking their way, a big grin on his face.

"Lillith, love. Hello! Do close your mouth, my sweet. Can't have you swallowing any bees now, can we?"

Lillith felt as though she was on a ride at the fair and getting a bit dizzy from twisting to one side, then the other. She watched as Ben walked over to plant a kiss on Elizabeth's cheek. And as Elizabeth smiled up at him, she realized not only that they knew one another, but knew one another quite well.

"Umm . . . I didn't realize the two of you had met."

"Oh, my dear, yes, yes. Your Benjamin has been a friend of mine for many years. I knew his parents quite well and was close by when Benjie was born."

"How odd that neither of you mentioned it."

"Well," Ben said, looking somewhat sheepish, "at first, it didn't seem all that pertinent. Then Elizabeth and I thought we'd just let things take their course."

"Let things take their course . . ."

"Aha!" Elizabeth said. "Rupert! I see you've brought more lemonade. Thank you, my friend, and if you haven't eaten all Anna's cake all by yourself, my niece has expressed a desire for another slice, if you please. And I feel sure our friend Ben might enjoy a piece also."

As Rupert departed, muttering and grumbling about how his cake was dwindling, a silence fell upon the porch.

Elizabeth leaned towards her niece, "Lillith, let me put an end to your pout. There was never anything meant by neither Ben nor myself by not mentioning our friendship. At first, as he said, it just didn't seem pertinent. Ben and I knew one another. Then you and Ben met. How were either of us to know your meeting would blossom into what it has. After a while, the opportunity to mention it just seemed to be awkward. As this meeting has shown, we were right about that, if nothing else. So. Now we all know that we all know one another. It is what it is. The simple fact of the matter, my dear, is that while you may think your friendship with Ben is a secret, it is not. You forget what a small town Savannah is at heart, after all. Furthermore, if you had been paying attention, you would have surely known that, of course, Ben's family and yours would know one another. But. Love does make one blind, and perhaps even somewhat dumb, so you're to be excused."

Smiling happily, Elizabeth looked from one to the other and took both their hands, pointedly ignoring the frown on her niece's face.

"And I must say, I think the fact of the two of you is quite lovely, and I couldn't be happier. Now, let's have that cake, or Rupert may whisk it right back away and eat it himself. Then I have a story to tell you."

After what seemed like a very long time. Elizabeth looked squarely at Lillith and Benjamin.

"This may seem strange to you both. I beg your indulgences. The story I want to tell you, and only you, needs to be told in the proper manner. And the proper manner needs a good deal of time. Lillith, if I send Rupert to your parents' home with a message that you'll be staying for lunch, would you do that, please? And you, of course, Benjamin. The two of you need to be together when I tell it."

Glancing at one another, the couple agreed.

"Aunt Elizabeth, please. You're not ill . . . ."

"No, no. I promise you, child, I am not ill. And after this evening, I'll feel better than I've felt in my entire life."

Ben and Lillith exchanged another glance as Elizabeth rose from her chair and skipped - skipped! - across the verandah to the front door, calling Rupert as she went.

Lillith watched in amazement, "Was she skipping?"

Equally amazed, Ben said, "Skipping. Yes. Yes, I believe she was."

"So that's what skipping is really supposed to look like."

CHAPTER FOUR

Lillith and Ben relaxed over their lemonade and coconut cake while they waited for Elizabeth to return.

Benjamin swallowed his last forkful and turned to Lillith, "How did your dinner go with your parents last night? I hope it wasn't as difficult as you feared."

"No, actually. I think their plans to try to make me come home were derailed by Aunt Elizabeth's request for an audience."

"Odd. All these family conferences and requests for your presence happening at the same time."

"Yes. And a bit disconcerting. Seems everyone might have a plan for my life - although, so far, they aren't sharing what those plans are. Nor are they asking what my plans might be. It is, after all, my life."

They settled into a companionable quiet as they each pondered what might be coming and if it would derail the life they both hoped for.

Ben was the first to notice that someone had joined them on the verandah.

Quickly rising, he extended his hand.

"Sir? Benjamin Hamilton. And you might be?"

Standing before them was a tall slim aristocratic elderly man in a perfectly tailored formal suit, holding a top hat. A handsome gentleman sporting a well groomed somewhat large and intimidating silver handlebar moustache which perfectly matched his thick mane of silver hair.

The stranger accepted Ben's handshake, "Good evening, young man. Samuel Eli Whimsey, might Miss Calhoun be at home this evening? I apologize for my unannounced visit, but I find myself unexpectedly in your fair city. Miss Calhoun, a long and dear friend, being the lady she is, has often asked that I drop by when I happen to find myself close by."

"EEK!"

Ben and Mr. Whimsey both jumped as they were startled by the shriek coming from Lillith.

"Samuel Eli Whimsey!" Lillith exclaimed. "I know you! I mean - I know who you are - I mean I've read - well, no, certainly not - I have not read - wouldn't dream of it - but, well . . . ."

Mr. Whimsey threw his head back and laughed, "So my infamy precedes me."

Flustered, Lillith said, "So, you are - I mean, that is you, you're the . . . ."

"Yes, I'm afraid I must admit. I am, indeed Samuel Eli Whimsey. The same Samuel Eli Whimsey you fear me to be."

"And you're a friend of my Aunt Elizabeth's?"

"Actually, my dear . . . ."

"Oh, but you can't be. My parents will die when they hear."

"Well, Lillith, dear, let's not tell them," said a voice that was unmistakably Elizabeth's.

"Whhaat?" whispered Lillith.

"I said let's not tell them." And Mr. Samuel Eli Whimsey tore off the silver mustache and silver wig, revealing Elizabeth - with that rather famous long silver hair of hers billowing around her head and shoulders.

Looking at her guests and the shocked expressions on their faces, she laughed, looking from one to the other. Finally, she heard a quiet chuckle from Ben and a nervous titter from Lillith.

"Rupert, I think now's the time for the brandy, don't you?"

"Oh, yes, ma'am," Rupert said from the doorway behind Lillith and Ben, "Got it right here waiting for this moment."

"Shall we sit, children? And I'll tell you a story."

Once they'd all settled into their chairs and Rupert poured the brandy and left, Elizabeth said, "So the two of you now know my secret. I am Samuel Eli Whimsey. The writer of those books over there on that table that you attempted to hide from your father with your shawl, Lillith. Which was just what I needed from you to determine whether you had read them or not."

"Read them? Why, they're perfectly scandalous! I inhaled them! Each and every one of them. I can hardly wait till the next one."

"And what do you think of all that, Benjamin?"

"I like them too, Elizabeth. I have to prod Lillith to read them faster so she can pass them along to me once she's done."

"Well, Heavens to Murgatroid! If the two of you don't beat all. What a perfect couple you are, and will be, I dare say, for many happy years to come. A sense of humor and the ability to make one another laugh is far too underrated.

"I'm very glad you both have enjoyed them. The next one to be released in the series will be the final one. Lord and Lady Barlow have had more than enough adventures to last a lifetime. They're beginning to get a little long in the tooth, shall we say, to continue gallivanting around the world and engaging in the sexual athleticism they've been doing now for the past oh so many years. It's beginning to become a little beyond believable. They'll be retiring. If at some point, Mr. Whimsey decides the public might be ready to read more about them as a tired old retired couple, well then, we shall see what happens."

"Oh, no, Aunt Elizabeth, please don't do this. I can't bear the thought of not having any more adventures with Simon and Beatrice."

"Oh, pshaw, Lillith. Don't be silly. It is always best to leave a party while everyone is still having fun. Besides, I'm going to be much too busy with a new project. I won't have time to write more Simon and Bea tales. I'm sorry."

"What are your plans, Elizabeth?" Ben asked.

"Children, I think you're going to enjoy the second part of this story even more than you did the first part. It will concern the two of you, after all, and your futures. You will, I believe, forgive me for dropping your literary heroes and moving on."

Elizabeth took a sip of lemonade before continuing, "First of all, I am weary of having to hide who I really am. It should be perfectly acceptable for a woman to write anything she wants to write. If she's good at it, which I obviously am by the looks of my bank account, she should be applauded for it. It's hypocritical for me to hide behind the name Samuel Eli Whimsey writing books both men and women enjoy. They're not really scandalous books. They've only gotten the reputation for that based on what dried up old women say because they need a little excitement in their lives. The only excitement their society finds acceptable is gossip. And that is a sad commentary. I guarantee you more than one of those ladies has a collection of Mr. Whimsey's books stashed away somewhere and enjoy them behind closed doors. Harumph."

"Aunt Elizabeth, I thought you had become financially comfortable through the investments Daddy made for you."

"You're quite right, m'dear. Your father is a very smart man. And he has, indeed, made me quite comfortable, as you say. But, I've made myself quite wealthy all on my own with my books. Richer than anyone, including your father, knows about. The gossips who've been guessing about the money all these years have no idea. Apparently, I also inherited a little of that same money sense from our father your father did. I've made

37

some wise investments on my own which have allowed me to pursue some things I'd rather not everyone know about. Some projects that have helped women escape from marriages harmful to themselves and their children, for example.

"And now I'm ready to move on, in a full time capacity, to broaden those efforts. I want to build a spot that is more welcoming to people of the arts - men and women. A spot where they'll be able to bloom. So often, artistic efforts are stifled due to financial constraints. People do, after all, have to have money to survive, but why shouldn't they make a fair wage by bringing beauty into society instead of being treated as though their efforts and creations, while appreciated up to a point, are undervalued and underfunded.

"You commented earlier, Lillith, on this lovely shawl I'm wearing. This shawl was made by Rupert and Anna. Together, they spin fiber, dye it and weave it into some of the most glorious cloth you've ever seen. But what are the chances of them ever being paid a fair price for their art? None. Not a whit. So we keep it a secret and sell the shawls and clothing they make under a name other than their own. This sort of thing just has to stop. I want Rupert and Anna recognized for their art. I'm going to do what I can to see that happen.

"I intend to set up a place where, through my funding, a few artists, artisans and various creative sorts, are able to live for one year doing nothing but honing their skills and getting an inventory stocked up so they'll be able to start making a living by selling their work. The plan, as I said, will remove the binds that now tie women to their homes without allowing them the freedom to do other things - like being creative in the arts. It will also remove those binds from our black citizens. In repayment, the people who are helped by my efforts will be expected to put some of their money earned from their fruits of labor into the project to help the next group. Etc. Etc. That's a short and simplified version of my plan. A more comprehensive plan was drawn up by an attorney I've known for years who has proved quite trustworthy with my secret existence.

"I've made arrangements for the two of you to meet him so he might explain all this to you in a way which you won't find quite so startling coming from your odd Auntie Elizabeth."

Elizabeth seemed pleased with the looks on the young faces before her. Ben was looking at her in awe and adoration. Lillith looked a little like she might have been struck dumb or lost her mind, with her mouth hanging open in an unattractive way.

Ben asked, "Want to give us a hint, Elizabeth?"

Elizabeth cocked her head and gave it a few moments thought. "I've bought an island."

"WHAAAT?" Lillith cried out.

"An island?" Ben said, "What island? What do you intend to do with it?"

"It's a small island, mostly unknown and forgotten, located only a few miles east of Savannah. It's never even had a name of its own. It is rich in indigenous plant and animal life and absolutely perfect for what I have in mind."

Warming up to the story, she continued with what she had in mind. She intended to have some clearing done on the island so she could build a home. A large home. A home she would move into to oversee the rest of the development, a small community including a few stores from which the inhabitants would be able to purchase staples and allow the merchants to earn their keep. All initially moved forward by funding by Elizabeth. "The community will grow, of course, but the growth will be carefully overseen and will be a slow progressive process based on needs of the island's inhabitants. All of this will be explained to you by my attorney. Patience, please."

Lillith and Ben looked at one another for several long moments.

Lillith reached out to take Ben's hand, and they both turned to Elizabeth, "And what can we do to help?"

"Lovely! Oh, my dears, you have no idea how I was hoping to wrangle you both into my dream. It can be quite perfect now, I have no doubt." Elizabeth raised her glass and nodded her head gently, "Let's have a toast, shall we? To us. To the two of you. And to the Island of Whimsey."

And so began the Island of Whimsey, founded by Elizabeth Calhoun in 1949.

And, too, began the partnerships.

Benjamin and Lillith were married.

At Elizabeth's invitation, they moved into the large home she had built on the island, and their work began.

The three of them started getting the word out to friends in the arts, along with friends of friends. Slowly, people began showing up to meet with Elizabeth, Ben and

Lillith to hear their plans. The thoughts of living in a sort of Utopia were pleasing, of course, but they all recognized there were practicalities that needed to be considered. Only with a great deal of commitment and hard work would this community come to be.

With natural charm, a strong conviction in what she was doing and a will of iron, Elizabeth Calhoun oversaw the building of the island. She chose a cadre of professionals in whom she placed great trust to help and because she was a fair woman, they all responded in kind. Her dream became their dream. And because they worked hard together, enduring the hard times and getting through them together, strong bonds were formed, and the Island of Whimsey became a community in all true senses of the word. The community was planned out with the future in mind, including a large section at one end of the island for the necessary community services - a school, a doctor's office which would grow into a small clinic, a post office and a police station.

What Whimsey did not have would be easily reached by the ferry Elizabeth was keen on building at the other end of the island, not far from the town square.

CHAPTER FIVE

Ellijay, GA

The month Emma had been in residence, her little mountain get-away had not proven to be as quiet as she'd hoped. The cabin was small with nowhere to escape from the noise and confusion of the extensive remodeling going on.

The studio behind the cabin became her haven. She was impressed with the equipment Jude had in it, which she'd mistakenly assumed would include only the most basic jewelry crafting tools. Not only was there a full range of basic equipment, there were things Emma found to be immediately intriguing. Specifically, a high temp oven and a centrifuge.

Emma had not done any jewelry casting since she graduated from the Savannah College of Art and Design. Her designs, although somewhat bold, were not bold enough to warrant the heavy pieces attained by casting. It might be time, she thought, to venture into this technique. The time here in Ellijay was stirring her creative senses, and she thought some of the new designs might evolve into pieces she could be proud of. But it was also proving to be slow going.

Emma stepped into the cabin only long enough to turn up the heat so she'd be able to work comfortably when she returned, but first needed to go into town for groceries.

She drove slowly on the curvy mountain roads. It being February in the mountains, the expected icy winter weather was wreaking havoc on traveling even the short drive from the cabin into town. The slightest hint of ice was enough to have practically everyone heading to the grocery store to stock up on essentials in case they were unable to get out for a couple days. She was relieved to find a parking space on Main Street and made her way gingerly to a small café, hoping to settle in with a quiet cup of coffee and maybe one of those delicious apple turn-overs the owner made from scratch.

Quiet was one thing apparently not in the cards for Emma this morning as she was jolted with a screech causing her to stumble as she was stepping off the curb. The stumble caused her to fall flat on her bottom in a pile of wet slush. If that wasn't bad enough, someone fell on top of her and knocked her backwards.

Emma slapped at whatever tackled her, furious when it laughed. Then she realized it was saying her name.

Putting her arms down, she tried to see what was on her when it took her hand and helped her into a sitting position.

"Well, hey there, girlfriend. Fancy meeting you here."

Now it was Emma's turn to shriek. "Alex! Alex, oh my God. What . . . why . . . Help me up from here!"

Alex pulled Emma to her feet and they hugged, danced in a circle and laughed and cried.

"Oh, Alex, it's so wonderful to see you. Let's go in the cafe and have coffee, okay?"

Alex, grinning from ear to ear, nodded her head, "If you promise to quit slapping at me."

Emma laughed, they linked arms, and together they ran, slipping in the icy slush, across the street into the cafe.

They settled in a booth after hanging their long, very wet coats inside the door, then held hands across the table and grinned at one another.

Finally Emma said, "Alex Swinney. You are as gorgeous as ever. You were too beautiful when we were growing up on Whimsey, got even more beautiful while we were at SCAD, and now look at you. Runway model material, at the least." Emma smiled to herself remembering how the boys had fallen all over themselves over Alex when they were growing up. Her smooth creamy cocoa skin and high cheek bones came from her African-American heritage. Her startling green eyes were from the Irish on her father's side of the family. The combination resulted in dazzling beauty. Alex's mixed heritage meant nothing to the folks on Whimsey Island, where racism and religious or ethnic prejudice did not exist. To those boys enamored with her beauty, she was just *Alex*.

Emma sat back and drank in the vision of one of her oldest and best friends. Growing up, they, along with Olivia and two others, had dubbed themselves "The Wicked Women of Whimsey." After graduation from Whimsey High School, they all attended the Savannah College of Art and Design together, but had gone their own ways since. They had, of course, kept in touch and seen one other sporadically, but even their best efforts had not allowed a single occasion for them all to be together since college.

And now, here she was sitting across the table from one of them. Alex. Regal as ever with an air of aloofness

44

along with mischief in her eyes. And short spiky hair. With pink highlights. How could anyone look that intimidating and aloof with pink streaks in their hair?

Alex laughed, "Emma, you m'dear, should take a look in the mirror. If there's someone at this table who should have been walking down a runway instead of sprawling on their back in the middle of Main Street in Ellijay, Georgia, in the sleet, ice and snow, it's you."

With that, the conversation flood gates opened, and the game of playing catch-up began. They had coffee and turn-overs and more coffee. The next thing they knew, the shift had changed, and a new waitress was asking if they cared for lunch. Without batting an eye, they ordered bowls of hearty home-made vegetable soup with steaming cornbread slathered in butter.

Emma had seen Alex recently enough to know she had moved back to Whimsey a couple years ago in what was to be a temporary stay. She went home to help her father take care of her mother, Mrs. Swinney, when she was diagnosed with Alzheimer's. She ended up staying after her mother's death. Now she was living with her dad in the home she had grown up in and continued using the weaving studio in the very spot her parents had taught her to weave as a child. The very same studio her great grandparents, Rupert and Annie Jackson set up in the home they built when they moved to Whimsey back in 1949. When it became apparent that Alex shared her mother's love and talent for weaving, Mr. Swinney added on and enlarged the studio so that it was large enough to hold all the supplies and looms Alex needed to fill orders that came from around the world. The studio was filled with the spirits of the family of weavers and the stories they had shared and passed down while spinning and weaving on this same spot of land over the span of six decades. Emma, along with her brother Jonathan, her parents and Aunt Zoe spent many enjoyable hours there talking about their daily lives as Alex and her mother turned skinny little fibers into items of great beauty while her father watched on with great pride, a smile on his face. Now, Emma knew in her heart, he was watching Alex work on her own and felt blessed to have her home.

"So your dad is doing okay?" Emma asked.

Alex nodded, "He is. And boy oh boy, is he going to love that I ran into you. Girl, what are you doing here?"

"I'll tell you, I promise, but I'm dying to hear more about you first. Last time we talked you mentioned you were seeing Jack Singleton. Is he still in the picture?"

Alex leaned back and her face seemed to take on a glow, "He is, indeed, very much in the picture. Emma, that man has stolen my heart. I couldn't leave Whimsey now for love nor money. We're talking about getting married, but don't want to rush things."

Emma nodded, "No. No reason to rush things. You've only known one another since we were all babies, after all."

They both hooted loudly which had the lunch crowd in the cafe looking over at them. Most of them couldn't help but laugh along, moved by the pure joy the women exuded.

"Have you gotten the man to actually leave the island yet?" Emma asked with a wicked grin. It was a long-standing joke that Jack Singleton never left Whimsey for any reason other than an occasional trip, which usually lasted a shorter time than originally planned. Jack didn't see any reason to leave. He loved Whimsey with every fiber of his being and wasn't shy about saying so.

"Girl, I only have so much power, give me a break!" Alex said. "We might make an occasional trip into Savannah for dinner, but that's about it. There's always a boat that needs work. You know how he is."

"Oh, yes, I know how he is." Emma said as she buttered another piece of cornbread. "I also know those boats you speak of are some of the finest being built today. There are but a handful of boat builders like Jack around now. It's an art that's dying. Some people, sadly, would just as soon pay a cool few million for one of the manufactured versions."

"True enough," Alex agreed. "But those who buy Jack's know they're getting more than just a boat. They get a work of art, as well as a part of Whimsey along with a bit of the Whimsey magic to sail the seas with them."

Alex grinned from ear to ear, "When are you moving back?"

Emma cocked her head to one side, "Moving back?"

"Well, yes." Alex sobered a bit, "I mean, hmmm. I'm sorry, Emma. I just assumed you'd be moving back home now that Zoe is finally getting the gallery plans into motion. But I guess you don't want to leave your studio in Atlanta, and, well shoot, there are plenty of ways to get your work to Whimsey from Atlanta. I mean, gee, there's the postal service and UPS, and, jeez, I'm babbling and I'm not even sure why."

When Emma didn't answer, Alex placed her hand over hers, "You're not coming home to Whimsey, are you?"

"No." She shook her head.

"Want to tell me why?"

Emma shook her head again, "No. Not just yet anyway."

"Is it because of Eli?"

Startled, Emma drew back and looked at Alex, "No. Why would you ask that?"

"Oh, honey, I'm sorry. I thought maybe . . . ."

Emma interrupted her, "Hey! You need to tell me what on earth has brought you to the North Georgia mountains! Girl, *what* are you doing here?"

Alex told Emma about the fiber arts workshop she was involved in with a group of eleven other women. "We're all lovers of our art, of course, and fiber arts has become one of the in things for all the people who are moving out of the big cities back to what they hope will be a simpler life style. Since Atlanta has gotten so big, Ellijay actually now has a sizeable population of folks living here who drive into the city every day to work. But they're able to live the quiet small town life they love rather than stay in the big city. Part of the simplicity they're seeking includes spinning and weaving, so we gals come where we're invited, and we teach folks what they want to learn. It's fun for them and fun for us. And it's another effort to keep some of the arts alive, vibrant and growing. The workshop actually ended yesterday, but one of the women in our

48

group has family here, so we all agreed to stick around an extra couple of days so she could visit. We're supposed to leave tomorrow, drive to Atlanta to the airport and take off in different directions till the next workshop. We do a couple of these a year, and they last a week. But if the weather prevents us from leaving, we're okay. The rest of the group has taken over the bed and breakfast down the street." Alex smiled at Emma, "And now, m'dear, in case you think I'd forgotten, it's your turn. What are *you* doing here?"

"It's no secret really." Emma paused, "Well, actually it is a secret. Alex, I'd very much appreciate it if you would keep this between us. Please don't tell Olivia or Aunt Zoe we bumped into one another."

Alex frowned at Emma and shook her head, "Girl, something about all this is just not right."

Emma dropped her head into her hands, "Alex. I promise you I'll explain everything. I promise. But I can't right now. It's not as mysterious as it sounds, but I had to get away from Atlanta, and it happened that Zoe and Olivia were there when I made a quick get-away. All this will make loads more sense later. But for now, I'm using a friend's cabin as a place to get my act together. Something I've needed to do for a long while now. Since before Hunter died, truth be told. And that's what I'm doing. Getting my head screwed on and working on my designs."

"I'm sorry, sweetie," Alex said as she took Emma's hand again.

Emma nodded, "I'm going to be okay, Alex, but it's taken me a while to even realize I wasn't okay. Does that make any sense?"

"Totally," Alex said. "Emma, you spun out and rushed into a marriage that wasn't ever going to be the kind of marriage you deserve." When Emma started shaking her head, Alex raised her voice a tad, but gently said, "Wait. Let me finish. Those of us who love you saw what you couldn't see. But we wanted you to see it on your own. We knew you would. We just didn't know the bastard was going to go get himself killed in a stupid car wreck in another country and leave you behind to feel guilty. If we had, we would have done things differently. Like kill him ourselves." When Emma gasped, Alex rolled her eyes. "Emma, have you lost your mind? That was a joke. Granted, it was in poor taste, but it was a joke."

The waitress came over to ask if they wanted anything else. They both shook their heads no.

"I think, Emma, you need to get some things out and off your chest or you're not going to get beyond what's hurting you. This run to Ellijay you've made may help some, but you're going to need to let go of the anger and the hurt I see in your face. If you don't, once you go back to Atlanta, you'll be right where you started."

Emma straightened her shoulders, "The hell I will."

The waitress came to their table, "You ladies are more than welcome to stay as long as you'd like, but I wanted to let you know the forecast for ice is sounding pretty bad. If you're planning on driving out of town, you probably need to think about doing it in the next hour at the latest from what they're saying on the news."

"Oh, Laws," Emma said as she thanked the waitress and stood to leave. "We better settle up and get going. I don't want to hit bad weather on my way back to the cabin. I need to get to the grocery store quickly and get home."

As they walked to the door, Emma said, "Wait just a sec. I want to buy some of their delicious coffee beans to take back to the cabin. Want some?"

Alex snorted as she laughed, "Lord a Mercy. Some things never change. You have always been the biggest coffee snob around. No, I think I'll pass on the beans, but thank you."

"Well, there are worse things," Emma said as she started walking towards the gourmet coffees.

"Yes, yes. You're right about that."

Emma and Alex said their good-byes, and Emma promised to give Alex a call on her cell as soon as she got back to the cabin to let her know she had arrived safely.

Emma walked gingerly to her car and drove slowly home on roads that were icing over rapidly. She experienced one bad spin-out before she got home which left her shaken.

She was happy to see the workmen were gone when she pulled into the driveway. She walked into the cabin, welcoming the warmth. She dropped the bags of groceries on the floor just inside the door, tossed her coat on the sofa, struggled pulling off her wet boots on the way into the bedroom, not wanting to take the time to sit, and threw her clothes off onto the floor in disarray. She was chilled and still shaky from the drive home and didn't want to mess with the groceries. She wanted a nice hot bath with some bubbles.

Once she was settled back enjoying the warmth of the bath, she started thinking about her conversation with Alex. It had stunned her when her friend had brought up

Eli, but it surprised her even more when she brought up Hunter.

Since Hunter's death, everyone tip toed around the subject as if it were taboo. Emma had said nothing to make them feel otherwise. No one really knew the whole story. Emma didn't intend that to change. Ever.

After her bath, Emma changed into her one of her favorite at-home outfits – black leggings and a soft almost threadbare white oxford cloth shirt. Normally, a bit of a clothes horse with unerring fashion sense, she preferred comfort above all else while at home and shopped for the soft loose fitting shirts in a men's store. For a while, she had worn Hunter's shirts, but had bagged them up with the rest of his clothes after his death and donated them to a local homeless shelter. She briefly thought back to a white oxford cloth shirt she used to wear a long, long time ago. One that had belonged to her first love, Eli, but he had broken her heart, too. Now she chose to wear shirts with no history other than the bag it came packaged in.

She walked over to the doorway, picked up the bags she had dropped there and put the groceries away. She pulled out the new coffee beans and French press she had bought at the cafe and was looking forward to settling in with a cup of fresh coffee. She suddenly felt lighter, somehow, and began humming an old Willie Nelson tune.

As she approached the counter, she spotted something that made goose bumps pop up on her arms. There, sitting on the counter next to the old percolator was a crayon. A red crayon. Brand new, never been used, in a color red more specifically known as crimson.

"Uh oh," Emma said. "Great Aunt Elizabeth, are you here?"

A shimmer of light moved into Emma's line of vision. "I am. I'm just here for a minute. I wanted to bring you a new crayon. Just think of it as an old family tradition. And, Emma? I want to tell you not to worry, child, everything is going to get better soon. I promise." And the shimmer disappeared.

The fact that Emma's Great Aunt Elizabeth Calhoun had died a year and a half ago at the age of 102 didn't seem to have stopped her from dropping by now and again. It always spooked Emma a little, but she was beginning to get used to it. Even so, she was a bit unnerved by the fact that her great aunt had managed to find her in this cabin in Ellijay. *I need to ask Aunt Elizabeth exactly how she does that, if ghosts have built in GPS or something. But in the meantime, I need to get to work.* She smiled as she picked up the red crayon, tossed it in the air, caught it, and put it back on the counter with a pat. She vaguely remembered a family story about her grandmother Lillith suddenly one day "finding her crimson." She didn't recall the whole story, but it would come to her.

There's just something energizing about a new red crayon, she thought with a grin.

"That's my girl," said Madeline.

CHAPTER SIX

Emma arrived back in Atlanta on May 1st with a sizeable stack of new designs. She had crafted a few of the designs in silver, but knew they needed more work before they would be what she was trying to achieve. They were, however, far superior to the work she had done before taking her sabbatical in Ellijay. She much preferred the word sabbatical to the phrase "running the hell off to the mountains like a coward for whatever crazy reason," which is how Olivia referred to it whenever they talked on the phone.

Emma had finally called her aunt and her best friend after bumping into Alex. Olivia was furious, but at least didn't hang up on her, which had been a strong possibility.

Her Aunt Zoe had been more forgiving, but it took a while and several phone calls during the months Emma was gone before she heard the hurt beginning to leave her aunt's voice.

Emma refused to tell her the whole story, promising only to explain everything when the time was right. Preferring to say she needed to get away was as far as she would go. She did allow that she was working and had come up with some new ideas, all of which were still perking in her mind and taking a while to come together.

When, during one of their phone calls, her aunt told her she had planned a trip to Atlanta, Emma felt a tug of annoyance. She was not going to be pushed.

"Emma, I can feel that little mood change over this phone line." Zoe said. "You are not the only person or thing in Atlanta, you know. And I do, after all, still have a business to run. A major transition is involved in closing it, letting my suppliers know, and making plans for it to be a gallery I'll be proud of. So, child, you're going to just have to get over yourself. This has nothing to do with you. The decorators and wholesalers I've worked with in Atlanta for the past oh so many years deserve more than an email telling them I won't be using them any longer. I've made plans to come. I've asked Olivia to come with me to help. I made the plans while you were on your 'sabbatical' and had no idea when you might be returning to Atlanta. I intend to keep those plans. If you would like to get together one night for dinner while Olivia and I are there, so be it. If not, I'm sure we'll manage without you."

Emma sat back in her chair, took the phone from her ear and stared at it. She was stunned. Her aunt had never raised her voice in anger or spoken to her in a harsh tone in her life. It was then she realized how badly she had hurt her. The hurt might be easing, but Emma could see it was being replaced by anger. Much deserved anger, from her aunt's point of view.

"Aunt Zoe, I apologize," Emma said with sincerity. "I've been thoughtless, and I have a lot to make up for. I know that. And I would very much love spending some time with you and Olivia. Now, tell when you'll be arriving."

Emma was still feeling positive about her work, believing the muses had returned during her stay in the mountains. She was, at the same time, feeling pragmatic about it. She had been hoping for a quick little miracle after her dry spell, but realized instead of wishing for miracles, she needed to change her mind-set and get to work. She also needed to get rid of the anger she had been carrying. If she was unable to shed it, she would have to channel it. She was getting there, but she still had issues to deal with, and she would. She felt stronger and more in control than she had in a very long time, more like her old self - the self she had missed and welcomed back. The self she knew was capable of getting back on track and turning out some pieces that any gallery would be proud to carry - in time.

"I think we're gonna live after all," said Madeline.

"I believe you may be right," replied Emma.

Two weeks later, in the lobby of her condo while waiting for Zoe and Olivia, Emma realized instead of dreading their visit, she was excited.

When a black limo pulled up outside the door and the back window rolled down to reveal Olivia's smiling face, Emma couldn't help but laugh out loud as she got in the car.

"What on earth is with the limo? Have you two women lost your minds? I could have driven."

Zoe shook her head and laughed gently, "What, that little yellow bug of yours? Oh, no. As cute as it might be, it's teeny! I think this will do much better for the three of us. We have quite a few places to go, and this will help things along quite nicely, I do believe. This way we can just relax and not worry about the traffic. Atlanta traffic scares me to death, to be honest. And, we can have a nice visit. I have missed you, child."

Emma nodded, "I've missed you, too." And then she turned to Olivia, "And you - even though you've spoken to me horribly over the phone."

Olivia nodded, "Did I? As horribly as you would have spoken to me if I had gone running the hell off to the mountains like a coward for whatever crazy reason? You think?"

Emma dropped her head and stared at her lap for a few seconds. When she looked up at Olivia, her face was hard, her mouth set in a firm tight line, "Practiced that line, haven't you? Don't think I don't remember you saying that exact same thing to me more than once already. Don't judge me, Olivia. I've apologized. More than once. If that's not enough, tell me please, what else it is you expect me to do."

Emma was surprised to see tears spring into Olivia's eyes. "I'm sorry," Olivia whispered. "I was scared you might not come back, and I've been worried."

Emma felt tears in her own eyes. She nodded, "I'm sorry, too. Please just give me a little more time. Please?"

Olivia nodded.

In an attempt to lighten the mood, Emma said brightly, "So. When we last talked, you told me a great deal about Jonathan and the kids, and I loved hearing how well they're all doing, but you haven't really said much of anything about your work. I want to know how that's going. At Christmas, you told me you thought you might have a chance at a big commission. Have you heard anything yet? You don't usually do commissions, do you?"

Olivia's eyes started sparkling as she nodded her head vigorously and bounced in her seat. "Yes! Yes! I got it! You're right, I don't usually do commissions, and I've never had any desire whatsoever in doing portraiture work. What she wants is more a depiction than a portrait, and her ideas seem to mesh with what I love doing. We reached an agreement that I would paint what she wanted, but I would paint it my way – none of this 'oh, no, no, no – that blue in your painting doesn't match the blue in my antique Oriental rug.' Of course, it's not the kind of money Zoe can ask for and get for her work, but it's darn close."

Emma grabbed Olivia in a hug, "Oh, honey! This is wonderful. I am so proud of you. You were meant to be a star, and it sounds as though you are on your way! None of us ever doubted it would happen. You were already on your way to making a name for yourself before this big commission."

Olivia grinned from ear to ear, "You know, I fought leaving the island and going to the Savannah College of Art and Design at first, but it was the best idea you ever came up with, Emma. If you hadn't badgered all of us to go, there's just no telling what we would be doing instead. But, moving back to Whimsey after graduation was the next smartest thing I did. I don't think I could paint anywhere else. It's not just talent, although I know I have that. And it's not just the education, although I'm happy to have it, of course. But there's more. It's the Whimsey magic that makes it all come together. No one will ever convince me it's not."

Emma shook her head and moved one finger back and forth, "Oh, no and pafooey. You didn't want to leave Whimsey to go away to school because you wanted to get married. To my brother. And the reason you were in such a hurry to get back to Whimsey after graduation was because you wanted to get married. To my brother. I'll be the first to admit, y'all are just magical together, and that's the truth. But, the magic of your work is you. It comes from you – your heart and your soul, sweetie. Never doubt it."

"Why is it so hard for you to admit to the magic that is Whimsey, Emma? You know it's there. Earlene and her crazy little band of pixies are all the proof most of us would ever need. I don't doubt my talent, but I know the magic makes it a little more special. I know that." Olivia sat back, cocked her head to one side and studied her friend.

Emma put her hands over her ears and shook her head, "Oh, Laws – I am not going to talk about Earlene the wicked little pixie."

Zoe had been sitting on the seat facing them, being unusually quiet. But she couldn't help but laugh out loud at the look on Emma's face when Earlene's name was mentioned, "Okay, we'll not discuss Earlene, who I think is, a darling little pixie with maybe a hint of wicked."

Emma rolled her eyes.

"Now, about this evening," Zoe invited Emma to stay the night at the hotel with her and Olivia. "We have a suite with two bedrooms, a living room, a small kitchenette and two baths. One of the sofas in the living room pulls out to make a queen sized bed, or you can climb in with Olivia. Why not stay? There's always an extra toothbrush or two available in these hotel rooms."

Emma considered it for possibly a full nanosecond before agreeing. It had been a good day, and she didn't want to put a damper on it by spending another lonely night at her condo.

She also felt this was the perfect time to explain to Zoe why she was unable to accept her invitation to be a part of the new gallery.

"Perfect! It'll be fun," said Zoe. "And now here we are in Roswell. We're going to visit a few of galleries and shops here. I want to pick up a few small things, but mostly I need to start letting some of the dealers here know about the new gallery before they hear it through the grapevine. And, I need to tell some of the wholesalers I've been buying from that I'm discontinuing the shop and won't be making any more purchases for retail decorating. What I want the two of you to do is scoot around the corner and pay a visit to my friend Vanessa. She's just opened a new boutique, and most of the clothing she's selling are her own designs. They seem made for tall women such as ourselves. I'll meet you there in a little while. She promises we'll fall in love with everything in the shop."

CHAPTER SEVEN

Loaded down with new clothes from Vanessa's shop, along with several shopping bags of accessories, the three women dropped everything in a heap when they entered Zoe's hotel suite at the Ritz. Exhausted, and not up to freshening up for dinner out, the women agreed with Zoe that room service sounded like a grand idea.

Kicking off their shoes, they each dropped into big overstuffed chairs with matching ottomans, propping their tired feet up for a respite while waiting for their meals to be delivered.

Zoe took the lead, "Emma, darling. Do you want to talk about what upset you so when we were here last? I confess to being concerned and baffled. Today you seem fine, which I take to mean you have worked things out in your own mind. I hope you feel you can share whatever has been bothering you."

"I want to talk to you both about this, yes." Emma blew out a breath. "I really can't participate in your new gallery, Aunt Zoe. And because I knew you both would have good arguments in an attempt to change my mind, I've brought something to show you. This will tell you all you need to know." She handed each of them a piece of jewelry.

As each of the women looked at what she had handed them, she saw recognition and understanding in both their faces.

After a while, Aunt Zoe put down the brooch she had been handling, turning it over and studying it. "It's nice. But, that's all it is. Nice."

Olivia was handling a heavy gold bracelet, and unable to look at Emma.

Emma picked up the brooch, "So. There you have it. My designs are 'nice.' That's it. Until I find my own magic again, I can't allow you to put these things in your gallery simply because I'm your niece."

"No. And I wouldn't. I would never embarrass you by doing that. I know you're capable of more. I've seen your work. It was coming along wonderfully. You were growing and becoming more assured with your work, becoming known for your designs and making a splash in the artisan jewelry design community – a community not easily impressed, by any means. What happened, Emma?"

"I honestly just don't know." She turned to Olivia, "And, if you tell me moving back to Whimsey would help, I will have to bonk you on the head."

Olivia raised her head, "But . . . ."

Emma raised her hand, "No, don't say anything. I've said it all to myself already. I'll just keep working and something will click. I'll get back on track and maybe, eventually, I'll be able to join you in the gallery. Having the gallery as a goal may be just what I need to get my mojo back. This might be good enough for mass retail, but it's certainly not of the artistic caliber I was doing and need to be doing again in order to be a part of the new gallery. I will tell you, however, I truly did turn a corner while I was in Ellijay. These pieces were done before I went up there. The designs I did while I was there are quite good. The pieces themselves are not coming out as well as the designs, but they will. I'm still tweaking the prototypes. I'll get there. But. It's taking a while."

Zoe looked Emma in the eye, "I want you to know that I believe in you. But you're not the same Emma I helped raise. You seem bound and determined to be miserable. You're throwing away opportunities many people would be damned happy to have but never will. Do you know how many people would so love to have family that loves them? How many would give whatever it took to have a home to go back to when things were rough? Not only are you blatantly ignoring these things, and hurting those of us who are trying our ever-lovin' best to share them with you, you're allowing yourself to become so mired in your unhappiness that you've throwing away gifts God gave you.

"Why, in heaven's name are you staying in Atlanta? A place you have no ties, when everyone you care about is still available for you to be with? To live near. To share your life with. Living in a concrete box with no one, not even a cat, to talk with in Atlanta makes no sense. None. I'm asking you point blank – why are you still here? Why won't you come back to Whimsey? When any of us have asked you this, you've given answers that aren't answers. Don't you think it's time to answer that question truthfully? Don't you feel as though we, who love and support you, deserve an answer? Have you even answered it for yourself?"

Stunned by her aunt's words, Emma fell back in her chair. She glanced over at Olivia and saw that she was stunned as well. "You're angry." Emma said with a look of bewilderment.

Zoe came over and sat on the ottoman next to Emma's feet and took her hands in her own, "Child, I'm sorry. I don't say these things to hurt you. But you have allowed sadness to overcome you and to override the important things in your life. This makes me angry, yes. Because I love you and believe in you and know how very talented you are. And this sad person you've become is just not you. I want the real Emma back. And, Emma, I think maybe if you trust Olivia and me enough to talk to us about all this, it might help."

Olivia sat on the arm of Emma's chair, reached in and smothered her in a hug, "Oh, sweetie. I think maybe Zoe is right. Do you want to? Is the time right?

Emma wiped tears from her face and sat very still. After a while, she shook her head, "I don't know if I can. There are some things I'm working through. But this helps. This tough love thing of yours, Aunt Zoe, is a new one on me. Wow."

Emma got up and paced around the room, walked over to the window and stood staring out for a minute or two. She turned to face the two women, "Um, do you think maybe we can we make a pot of coffee using some of those new beans I bought today? I'm going to need strong coffee if you guys are gonna be beating up on me." She tried giving them a grin, which came out pretty weak.

"And maybe some Kahlua?" added Olivia with a small grin of her own. "I think I spotted a bottle in the kitchen."

Zoe got up and headed to the kitchen, "Sounds lovely. You get your beans, Emma, my sweet, and I'll make us some coffee."

There was a knock on the door. Room service had arrived and the three women sat down to a smorgasbord of Tapas – appetizers and side dishes of this and that.

While they ate, Emma explained how she seemed to go into a downward spiral as soon as she heard about Hunter's death. In retrospect, she was now able to see that she was in worse shape than she realized, and the spiral had actually started much earlier. She came very close to telling them the full story about her marriage and how Hunter's death affected her but knew she wasn't ready to talk about all that just yet. She wasn't sure she ever would be.

"So. End of story. That brings us to where we are right now, ladies. You, Aunt Zoe, getting ready to open the gallery of your dreams. And you, Olivia, beginning to capture the attention of the art world in a huge way. And me getting ready to slowly descend into the world of mass manufactured costume jewelry of the cheapest sort. I can't blame my design failures on anything except myself. I've lost my passion in my work. And, in my life. Honestly? I'm well on the way to hating who I've become."

A quiet came over the room. Emma lowered her head into her hands and wept silently. She wept for herself and all that could have been. She wept for who she had become and for all the wastefulness on her part. She wept with the loneliness of missing her friends and family and the loveliness of Whimsey.

"I want to come home," she whispered quietly.

"Oh, child." Zoe came to her, took her in her arms and rocked her as she had when Emma was a small girl and had taken a tumble on her bicycle. "And you shall."

Emma and Olivia and Zoe talked and talked until the beginning of the rising sun started shining through the windows.

Zoe walked to the window, "Oh my, would you look? I don't recall when I last watched the sun rise."

Olivia and Emma joined her at the window and put their arms across each other's shoulders as they watched the sun come up.

Olivia turned to Emma, "Well, lovely as that was, that's nothing like what you'll see at home, missy. I remember how much you love sunrises. Seems to me I remember you got some of your best ideas sitting on the beach by yourself at dawn."

Emma stared at the sky, transfixed, "I am an idiot," she whispered. "That is exactly where my best designs have always come from." She turned and looked at Olivia and Zoe, "From nature. Always. How could I not remember that? Even this sunrise, pale though it is compared to a Whimsey sunrise, makes me feel something powerful and moving. It's a feeling I used to be able to use in my designs. Lately, even in Ellijay where I almost recaptured it, I've been brushing it off, forgetting how magnificent it can be. I'm an idiot."

Zoe said, "Emma! Child. Why, you look like a different person."

Olivia nodded, "You do. Look at yourself. You're glowing!"

Emma laughed quietly and shook her head, "Who knew it could feel so good to realize you've been an idiot. Wow."

66

Zoe placed an arm around each of the women, "Let's all get some sleep. I am much too old to be up watching a sunrise with no sleep. To bed. We'll get up in just a few hours, have a bite to eat and get on about our day. Okay? We'll talk then."

Emma and Olivia nodded in agreement, both yawning, stumbling toward their bedroom.

CHAPTER EIGHT

For the next two days, although Emma had checked in with Zoe and Olivia a few times by phone, they hadn't seen one another since the day they'd watched the sun come up together. She had assured them she was fine, working hard and accomplishing lots. Since she sounded happy, they believed her and agreed to leave her alone for the time being, provided she would meet them for dinner the night before they had to leave for home.

The three women had an enjoyable dinner, and anyone looking at them would see the shared love amongst them. They looked at one another in the eye when they talked, laughed and smiled at one another often, giving loving touches as they spoke to one another.

When it was time to leave, they found themselves being escorted to the door by the maitre de, the waiter and the wine steward, all of whom seemed sad to see them leave, but happy to have been graced by their presence at dinner. Each wished for patrons more like these three attractive, smiling women.

Emma said her good-byes in the lobby, hugging her aunt and her friend and promising to keep them informed about her plans. Promising to get home to Whimsey as soon as possible.

A few weeks after her dinner with Zoe and Olivia, things were falling into place for Emma as she prepared to move back home.

Emma was, indeed, getting her mojo working again. She was sleeping at odd times, usually falling asleep at her desk or worktable while drawing up new designs or while crafting them. But she was happy. The amount of sleep she was getting was, apparently, enough to keep her healthy and alert because she was clear eyed and energized. She arranged to have the small family owned restaurant around the corner from her apartment building deliver meals because she knew she would forget to eat otherwise. That the meals were delicious was a plus. That they were healthier than what she would whip up for herself was a bigger plus.

She was also using a studio she had borrowed from a colleague for casting some of her designs. After becoming reacquainted with the high temp oven and centrifuge in Ellijay, they had become crucial to her work. And the work was good, but it still wasn't good enough. She was, however, feeling confident that she was heading in the right direction and would eventually have the break-through she needed.

She received an offer on the condo within a week of putting it on the market. It seemed there was a high demand for furnished places in downtown and hers was bought by a local high powered corporate attorney's office to use for visiting clients who would prefer keeping a low profile while in town.

Her plan was to leave Atlanta on September 1st.

The realtor assured her the client was happy with that.

Things were falling into place so perfectly, Emma realized later she should have been suspect. Something had to happen to upset the applecart.

CHAPTER NINE

A week later, Emma had spent the day at the studio doing a lot of casting. She walked out feeling as though she was walking on air.

The new pieces were going to be original, dynamic, and the boldest things she had done. It would take a woman with a huge amount of self-confidence to be able to wear these pieces and carry them off.

She just couldn't seem to be able to find the right stones. She wanted tumbled, polished natural stones, but everything she had paired with the heavy silver pieces just weren't working.

On her way home, she realized she was hungry but her dinner delivery wouldn't take place for a couple hours. Reading her mind, Madeline piped up, "Let's stop for pizza! The Peppy Pepperoni sounds good."

When she pulled into the parking lot of the Peppy Pepperoni she could smell the garlic before she opened her car door.

"Yum. Heaven," she said and her stomach growled loudly.

"You really need to feed us more often than this," said Madeline.

"Oh, do hush, Madeline," replied Emma.

As she crossed the parking lot, she caught a glimpse of someone, shook her head, and said, "Nope. Can't be." But she looked again to be sure.

It was.

There he was.

Eli Tatnall.

Tall and rangy, his dark hair a little longer in the back than it should be, he still had the same trim beard and the same clear gray blue eyes she knew saw things most people missed.

Emma's breath caught, and her heart started racing.

How can this be? How can he be here, in Atlanta? And how can he still make me feel this way?

As she turned around to go back to her car, she heard him.

"Emma?"

She stopped. Then she started moving again toward her car, but he was right next to her.

"Emma. I can't believe it. It really is you. You haven't changed a bit. You're as beautiful as ever."

Without pause and without thinking, Emma slapped him, got in her car and drove home.

What was he doing here?

Eli Tatnall stayed on the island after graduation. His life continued just as it had been, helping his father, Ethan, run the ferry and helping his brother, Ethan, Jr., with construction work and cabinet making. And he studied photography under Emma's mother, Zelda, who had recognized an early talent. Emma knew his work had become fairly well known regionally, and he was able to make a good living from it. Enough that he was able to entertain his other curiosities in a multitude of things. Some of those things had apparently brought him to Atlanta.

When she got home, she was shaking so badly she dropped her keys when she tried to unlock the door. Once inside, she dropped her keys again, then dropped herself onto the sofa.

Then she laughed.

Oh. My. God. I just slapped Eli Tatnall. The Eli Tatnall who was my first boy friend. The first boy who kissed me. The love of my life. The boy who broke my heart. The reason I married Hunter Quinn. And I slapped him! A few years too late, but I slapped him. Boy oh boy, Olivia is never going to believe this one.

Emma put her head back on the sofa and the memories washed over her.

Emma's best friend growing up, besides "The Wicked Women of Whimsey," was Eli Tatnall. Their families were best of friends, often spending weekends and summer vacations together. Eli and Emma learned at a young age they could trust one another, and a strong bond formed between them. By the time their senior year rolled around, it was natural progression for them to attend the prom together. The night was marred by words from a classmate, Reese Prescott, who had imbibed a bit too much cherry brandy. Reese asked Eli to dance with her, which he graciously did. As Emma watched, Reese began to inappropriately move against Eli, embarrassing him and making a spectacle of herself. Eli extricated himself and attempted to quietly walk Reese back to her date, only to find him passed out drunk in his car. Reese insisted Eli take her home, and she promised to show him a good time. Emma's brother Jonathan stepped up and told Reese he'd be happy to see her home since he and Olivia were on their way out. Reese pitched a fit and caused a scene by loudly telling Emma that while she was off playing college girl in Savannah, she would steal Eli out from under her nose.

The prom incident was never mentioned again, but Reese held tight to that grudge. Whenever Emma came home and happened to bump into Reese, the air would turn frosty as Reese relayed what great times she and Eli were having together in Emma's absence. In her naive trust of Eli, Emma brushed it aside, sure that Eli would never hurt her that way. But during a weekend trip home that came about on the spur of the moment and unannounced, she saw Reese and Eli together. They were in Eli's truck, parked at the end of Main Street at the dock. Reese had her head on Eli's shoulder, and his arm was around her shoulders. They didn't see her, and Emma quickly turned away and ran home. She didn't tell anyone about what she had seen, and she didn't call Eli to let him know she was home. She held the hurt in her heart, feeling it break into smaller and smaller pieces day by day, year by year until it finally hardened itself against any future hurt.

Hunter Quinn was the first serious relationship she had after Eli. The boys she dated while she was at SCAD were mostly just friends, and she focused on her art in such a way that she didn't miss not having a boyfriend. She had

The Wicked Women to do things with and never lacked for a date when an occasion called for one.

Emma married Hunter knowing in her heart she didn't love him as she should. But she didn't think she was capable of that kind of love again. She had given her heart once, and there was no more to give. She though what she and Hunter did share would be enough to make a good marriage. It may not be the happy marriage she had witnessed between her parents, who still acted goofy around one another, but it would be enough.

Sadly, she learned she was mistaken. It had not been enough, and now Hunter was gone forever.

Her thoughts turned to Eli more often than she liked. Usually, she was able to bury herself in her work and forget about the boy whose smile could set her soul to dancing. She had seen him, of course, every once in a while when she would go home to Whimsey for visits, but she was able to maintain a breezy, friendly attitude with enough reserve to keep him at arm's length.

He asked many times what had happened, and her only response was that it was just a childhood crush they had both moved on from. He insisted he had not moved on, but Emma never gave him an opportunity to discuss it because she knew whatever he said would be lies. He didn't know she had seen him with Reese.

While drifting in memories, she was brought back to earth when she realized someone was knocking on her door.

"Maybe it's the pizza guy," said Madeline. "I'm starving to death here.

"Oh, Madeline, hush. We never called for pizza."

"Oh? And whose fault is that, Miss Smarty Pants?"

As Emma approached the door, she could have sworn she smelled pizza.

How odd. But when she looked through the little peep hole, there stood Eli Tatnall. With a large pizza box in his hands.

Eli knocked again. "Open up, Emma, or this pizza is going to get cold."

Furious, Emma flung the door open. "Who do you think you are just showing up here bearing pizza as though nothing ever happened all those years ago when you broke my heart by messing around with that hussy, Reese Prescott?"

"Whoa! What?" said Eli, looking dumbstruck.

"Nothing. Never mind. I didn't say anything. What do you want?"

"Um. Can I come in?"

"No. Put the pizza down and leave."

Eli shook his head and chuckled, "No, no, that's not how this is going to go down, Emma." He looked around. "Who were you talking to before you opened the door anyway?"

"Nobody."

"Aha! Madeline your evil twin is still around, huh? You know, you're probably the only person on God's green earth who ever gave their conscience a name."

Emma's face reddened. She put her hands on her hips, "How did you find me?"

"Oh ho, I am one smart private eye guy, I am. After you left - quite the exit, by the way - I looked you up in the phone book. Asked the pizza guy where on Peachtree this place might be, then looked on the mailboxes in your lobby to get your apartment number. Good thing I'm not here to murder you, huh?"

Emma felt her lips twitch and turned away, afraid she might laugh. No one had ever made her laugh even when she was furious. Except Eli. Damn him.

"So. Are we going to eat this pizza, or what?"

"No. I am going to eat the pizza. Just put it down. You have to leave."

Eli shook his head again, "Nope. If the pizza stays, I stay. Kick out the pizza guy and the pizza goes. Them's the rules. Besides, Emma, you just dropped a major bombshell and the least you can do is explain it to me. Seems we have entirely different memories of who broke whose heart all those years ago."

Emma was furious, "I'm hungry. Come in."

Eli bowed, and handed Emma the pizza, who unceremoniously dropped it onto the coffee table in the living room, opened the box and grabbed a slice.

"Now, Emma, you were raised better. Shame on you." Eli picked up the pizza box and walked into the kitchen. He opened cabinets until he found plates and opened drawers until he found silverware. "You get napkins and I'll bring us our supper. In the dining room."

"I don't have a dining room."

"Oh. Pity. Well, here at the kitchen table then. No, no, not paper towels, Emma. Napkins. Real ones. I know you have real napkins."

Emma opened a drawer, snatched out two linen napkins and threw one of them at Eli, then sat down at the kitchen table.

"Got any wine?"

She just looked at him. He was grinning. From ear to ear.

"In the fridge," she said with a clenched jaw.

"Wine glasses?" he asked innocently.

"Oh, for Pete's Sake . . . ."

"Temper, temper, Emma. Never mind. You stay seated. I'll find them." And he did.

Emma's mind was humming and she started muttering under her breath. "Now what? Do we just sit here across the table from one another like all these years haven't passed with us at odds with one another? And him not knowing why? Or rather, pretending to not know why. Have I lost my mind? WHY did I let that fly out of my mouth about my heart being broken? Oh, God, I wish he would just leave. But not with the pizza. I'm starving!"

"Emma? Are you talking to yourself? What are you muttering about?"

"Excuse me, but I was not muttering."

"Well . . . ."

"Eli, why are you here?"

"I'm in Atlanta meeting with a client. I do photography shots for advertising, and one of my clients owns a chain of restaurants here."

"No. Here. In my apartment. Why are you here?"

Eli signed and pushed his chair back, "Emma, when I saw you at the pizza place, all these memories came whooshing back into my mind. All at once. It was like my whole life went flashing by, and you were by my side through the whole show. When I told you you hadn't changed, I meant it. The only thing I could see was how beautiful you are, and all the good things we were to one another for so long just came back to me. I wanted to hug you and hold you close. And then you slapped me."

"No." Emma shook her head.

"Yes. Believe me, I got that part right," he said as he rubbed his face where she had slapped him.

"Not that. I remember that. I meant 'no' we are not going to take this walk down Memory Lane."

"Emma . . . ."

"No."

She stood up, "You need to leave."

"Emma, look, I know you're coming back to Whimsey. Everyone knows. Everyone is thrilled about Zoe's gallery and that you're all coming back. We're going to be running into one another on a regular basis. Don't you think we need to come to some sort of truce?"

"Truce? You want to come to some sort of truce?"

Eli was looking a little unsure, but continued, "Well, yes. For lack of a better word."

Emma walked to the door and opened it, "I want you to leave."

Eli stood and Emma could tell he was angry. His jaw was set in that way it did when he was on his way to losing his temper, which didn't happen often.

"I'm leaving. But, Emma, sooner or later, you're going to tell me what the hell happened. You just left me high and dry with no explanation, and you've treated me like some stranger ever since. You've gotten this thing about keeping a person at arm's length down to an art. Truth be told, I'm sick of it. I've spent years trying to figure out what happened. I've wasted a lot of years thinking about you and getting nowhere. I'm ready to move on, Emma. Maybe having you back on Whimsey will help me get over you and do just that. Man, I sure hope so." He walked out the door, closing it very quietly behind him.

Quiet was not good. Door slamming Eli was okay - he would get over that. But quiet Eli was deadly serious and not something he'd be likely to be getting over anytime soon.

Wait a minute here! Why am I worried about how mad Eli Tatnall is? I'm the one with the broken heart here! Emma picked up the dishes from the kitchen table and starting throwing them into the dishwasher. *Then why am I feeling so confused all of a sudden?* And she sat down in the kitchen floor and cried like a girl whose heart had been broken. Again.

Over the next several days, whenever Emma would go to the studio to work, she would stop by The Peppy Pepperoni. Most days she told herself she wouldn't, but she couldn't help herself.

She had no idea what she would do if she saw Eli. She didn't know if she would even let him know she was there, but she couldn't go by without stopping. By the end of the week Madeline the evil twin was screeching - "Nooooooooo - not pizza again tonight. Noooooooooo."

So sometimes she would get stromboli.

It was obvious the pizza guy behind the counter remembered who she was and looked a little nervous when she came in the first time, like he thought she might be there for the sole purpose of slapping someone. But over time, when she only ordered food to go and didn't assault anyone, he became a little friendlier. She asked if he had seen Eli since that day.

"You mean the guy you slapped?"

"Yes. Him."

He shook his head, "Nope. Haven't seen him."

She had the feeling he wasn't being quite honest with her. "Well, if you do, would you let him know I asked about him?"

He cocked his head, "Sure. But you're not planning on coming back and beating him up or anything, are you?"

Emma's face colored, "No. Just want to ask him a question."

He nodded, "If I see him. Sure."

The end of August finally rolled around and it was time to go home to Whimsey. Emma had not seen Eli since the night he'd left her place so angry.

"Finally!" squealed Madeline. "We're going home."

"Finally," Emma whispered back.

CHAPTER TEN

Emma left Atlanta well after rush hour, ecstatic that she'd never have to drive during another one. Never experience the craziness she compared to the demolition derby car smashes she'd seen in the movies. Never again have to feel as though she might be risking her life every time she pulled onto an expressway. If another driver didn't try to run over her or run her off the road at least once a day, she could be fairly certain of having at least one obscene hand gesture tossed in her direction.

But no more.

That life was over and done with.

She was going home.

She had planned it so she would arrive in time to catch the last ferry from just outside Savannah to the island.

After driving onto the ferry, she hopped out of her little yellow VW bug, linked her hands behind her back and casually strolled over the ferryboat operator.

"Hey, you," Emma said. "Is this boat ever gonna leave or are we just gonna sit here all night."

The man she was speaking to gazed straight ahead for a few seconds before turning to face her. When he saw who it was, he threw his head back and laughed the laugh she had loved since she was just a tiny kid.

"Emma, darlin'! Come give this old man a hug."

Emma ran into Ethan Tatnall's arms and he spun her around. He put her down on her feet and stepped back. "Let me look at you, girl." He grinned and shook his head, "Now why didn't you let us know you were coming?"

"I wanted to surprise you."

"Well, you sure did that. Is Zoe expecting you?"

"I told her I'd call her when I got to Whimsey, that it might be tonight, or it might be tomorrow."

"Good, good. Then you can stay at the house tonight. Lou will be over the moon to see you, and I know the two of you will have lots to talk about. How 'bout I give her a call and let her know? And she can call Zoe. That way Zoe won't be looking for you tonight."

Emma looked down at her feet for a second, "Will Eli be there?"

Ethan shook his head, "No. Eli moved out some time ago. He's moved into that little house he and Ethan, Jr. fixed up. You know, the one my grandfather used to live in."

"I always loved that little house. I thought Ethan, Jr. was living there."

"He was. But he and Bay got married, you know, and decided they were going to need a bigger place. I think they're in a hurry to start a family. Eli has always loved that house, so he jumped at the chance to move in. Fixed it up real nice. So, what say? Can I talk you into staying at our place tonight?"

84

Emma smiled real big, "I would love that!"

So that's what she did. Hanging out at the Tatnall house was always one of Emma's favorite things to do. Spending her first night back home on Whimsey with the two of them seemed just right.

As did sharing a meal of shrimp and grits, a specialty of Lou's. Begging, as always, for that elusive secret ingredient she could not quite figure out. And Lou, as always, swearing there was no secret ingredient.

While sitting around the old pine table in the kitchen in front of a fire, Emma answered all the questions Ethan and Lou had for her and caught up on all the Whimsey news. The mood was as close, comforting, and as loving as it had been when she was a little girl.

Neither Ethan nor Lou had changed a whit in all the years she'd known them. They and their two sons, including son Eli, who had been named for Great Aunt Elizabeth's nom de plume, Samuel Eli Whimsey, were part of the large group of friends and extended family she had grown up with. Ethan, with his thick shock of salt and pepper hair which always seemed to be in need of a haircut along with his broad smile and weathered complexion, looked like the stereotypical "Old Salt" associated with men who made their living on the water. Lou was her same tall, slim, quick-moving self, giving the impression of constant movement even while sitting. Lou Tatnall had more energy than any one woman had a right to, especially one who was nearing 60 and had raised two rowdy sons. The large rambling house appeared not to have changed in all these years either.

Emma realized she had drifted off from the conversation while she was daydreaming and looking around the Tatnall's kitchen. "I love that the two of you haven't changed one thing in this house. There's nothing more comforting to me than coming in here knowing it's going to be just like it was when I left. Especially this wonderful old kitchen. Hard to believe there's an entire business run out of this kitchen, in addition to all your family meals."

Lou and Ethan shared a look.

As Ethan began to laugh, Lou got the giggles and the two of them proceeded to get as hysterical as two thirteen-year-old girls. Emma sat staring at the two of them, wondering if she had suddenly grown a second head or something equally as amusing to these two old friends, who had clearly lost their minds.

Ethan wiped his eyes and pointed to a door on the back wall of the kitchen, but then got tickled again and couldn't get up.

Emma, feeling left out of the loop and getting a bit grumpy about it by now, walked over the door and opened it.

"Whoa!"

Now Emma could not quit grinning herself as she walked into a big white state-of-the-art kitchen. It could be the designer showcase for Wolfe and Sub-Zero appliances, complete with two stainless refrigerators, two stoves with double ovens, and two convection ovens sitting side by side on the far wall. There were shelves along one long wall, from floor to ceiling, holding a huge supply of baking ingredients along with more shelves along a second wall holding what looked like hundreds of bowls and baking tools. A marble counter top took up the third wall. A wooden chopping block the size of Texas took up some of the center space. All topped by two massive hanging racks filled with copper pots and pans.

"Surprise!" shouted Lou, hopping up and down with excitement.

"Like it?" asked Ethan, leaning back, his hands in his pockets and a smile on his face.

Emma was speechless until she turned around to see her friends' faces glowing.

"So *this* is Granny Lou's Whimsical Kitchen!" Emma turned in circles, her eyes wide. "You total fraud, you! You've let me think for years that you did all your baking in that wonderful old kitchen of yours!"

"And I did. For a long time. But it got to be too much."

"She got real famous, you see," Ethan added. "Couldn't keep up. Had to hire some help and teach them. Then they were falling all over one another."

"Ethan, Jr. built this," Lou said, "Him and Eli chipped in to buy the equipment. Ethan, Jr.'s wife Bay set up an on-line bakery, and we've been shipping fancy croissants of all kinds around the world ever since. We've even incorporated. Can you believe it?! I'm the CEO, Ethan's President - you know, like that. And, of course, we've been able to pay the kids back."

Lou turned and walked back into the old kitchen, "But, you know, all the family cooking's still done in here. And we all still eat 'round this old table. Ethan's grandfather brought this table with him when he moved to

Whimsey and started the first ferry, and it's always been sitting right there. Probably always will be. So, really, nothing has changed. Well, not much."

Emma returned to the worn old table and sat. She listened to all this with her mouth hanging open in amazement. "I don't know why I'm still surprised by anything that might happen in Whimsey, but I am."

Ethan sat down across from her, "Yep, know what you mean."

Lou settled in beside her husband, "Well, it is kinda magical, I think."

"Magical." Emma said with a trace of doubt.

"Yep." Lou said firmly.

Emma sat quietly for a bit, then asked, "About the Whimsey magic. Have you ever tried to explain it to anyone from off the island?"

Lou and Ethan looked at one another, looked back at Emma and shook their heads.

"Well, the reason I'm asking is that I do have a couple of friends back in Atlanta who want to visit. How do we explain some of the stuff that happens here?"

"Stuff?" asked Ethan with one eyebrow raised.

"Oh, Ethan." Emma looked at him in exasperation, "You know - stuff!"

"I know what you mean, Emma," responded Lou. "And so does Ethan. He's just being purposely dense to aggravate you. But, honey, you don't need to worry about it, I don't think. When visitors come to the island, they just assume they imagined some of the things they see. It's rare for anyone to be perceptive enough to realize they really did see a pixie or two zipping around. Most of them will just assume it was a larger than usual bug of some kind, or the sunlight, or that third drink they had caused them to think it was more than that. The Whimsey magic is more a feeling we locals wear in our hearts. It helps us be creative. It was here on the island waiting for us and because we've respected it, it has stayed with us. It's a *way* more so than a *thing*. Does that make any sense?"

"I don't know, Lou." Emma shook her head, "When I see one of the island dogs wearing eyeglasses and reading the Wall Street Journal, it gives even me pause."

Ethan whooped loudly and slapped his hand on the table.

Lou laughed with him, "But honey, the Whimsey dogs aren't going to allow an outsider see that. You know that. You've had college friends visit when you were at school in Savannah. None of them were ever the wiser. They just found Whimsey to be charming, right? And the pixies who live here pretty much keep to themselves anyway. I think they're a whole breed of introverts, truth be told."

Emma nodded, "If you say so."

Lou reached across the table and took Emma's hands in her own, "Sweetie, magic is a hard thing to understand. Impossible to explain. Obviously, you're having some doubts and feeling conflicted. Here's what I suggest. Stop thinking about it so hard. Maybe it exists for some and not for others. Maybe it's all in our heads. I suspect after you've been home for a while, you'll know in your own heart if it exists for you. Or not."

Emma cocked her head to the side, "Lou Tatnall, you're one of the smartest women I know. Conflict and doubt are two things that have been chasing me for entirely too long. And not just when it comes to Whimsey magic. It's time for me to relax and let things just happen without me trying to force things to fit where and how and why I want them to fit. Starting right now. Thank you." She leaned over the table to give her friend a hug.

In an attempt to overcome the lump in her throat, Emma looked around the room and asked if perhaps they'd considered asking Ethan, Jr. to build on another room and turn it into a library. Books were everywhere. On every piece of furniture in every room, having outgrown the bookshelves many years past. There were stacks upon stacks on the floor. When Emma inquired if either of them had read the latest Lee Child, Lou hopped up and scurried off to another room.

"Love that Jack Reacher!" she said when he returned to the kitchen with a book in her hand, "Want to borrow this one? It's his best yet."

Emma chuckled as she accepted the book. Before putting it in her bag, she opened it and saw it had been personally inscribed to Lou and signed.

"Love Ya! Hope to see you, Ethan and the kids soon, Lee"

"I'd love to! Thanks. I'll return it in a few days."

Noticing Ethan's eyes getting heavy, Emma yawned and stretched, "It's been a long day, y'all. I think I'll turn in if that's okay with you guys." She stood and walked around the table, giving her friends each a hug and an "I love you," before moving to the big plump sofa she had slept many a night on. She kicked off her sandals, pulled the quilt off the back of the sofa and curled up under it. With a deep laugh, Ethan remarked that he guessed they could take a hint, and he and Lou said their good nights.

Before drifting off to sleep, Emma turned her head to look at the pictures of the Tatnall family lined up on the end table. She stared at the picture she remembered Ethan taking of her and Eli sitting on the dock when they were kids. They were so close back then. Inseparable. Two peas in a pod, people used to say. If she'd known how it would turn out for them, she might have pushed him off the dock and let him drown. Better yet, maybe she should have jumped off herself. After a few seconds, she turned away and closed her eyes, counting on her internal clock to wake her up in a couple hours.

Three hours later, Ethan opened his eyes and noticed a wedge of light under the bedroom door. He reached over to pat Lou awake and realized she wasn't there. Once he had padded quietly to the door and peeked out, he saw her stooped on the floor sweeping something onto the dust pan. When she felt his presence, Lou turned around and put her finger up to her pursed lips, "Shhhh. I'll be back in just a minute."

When she turned off the lights and crawled back into bed, Ethan asked, "Was that silver glitter I saw you sweeping up?"

"Um hmmm. Wonder if Emma realizes she still has that Whimsey magic. She didn't seem to notice the glitter, did she?"

"No, but it was there. Every time she moved, a little more shimmer landed on the floor. I mean, it's not a whole lot, but once you've noticed it, it's clearly and purely there. I wasn't sure you noticed."

Lou nodded. "Oh, I noticed all right. And that Emma. She pretends she doesn't notice in hopes no one else will."

"As if. I suppose it's a good thing it only happens when she's here on the island - otherwise it could be pretty tough to explain, huh?"

Lou chuckled, "I guess!"

"Is she still on the sofa?"

"No, I 'spect she's already headed over to Zoe's, probably going to walk down to the beach and enjoy the stars. It was good having her here with us tonight, wasn't it, Ethan? I couldn't help but think about how she had changed in some ways, but remained the same in so many others. Laws, that hair! Funny, isn't it, how all the Calhouns were born with that wonderfully odd head of silver hair? Remember how Emma's used to hang so wildly around her face and shoulders? Even now with her expensive big city haircut, it still seems to have a mind of its own. Who would have imagined she would grow up to be so gorgeous?"

Ethan nodded, "She's grown into a beauty, for sure. But still the same sweet, funny girl we've loved and welcomed into our lives since the day she was born. Well, I reckon she's on her way to the beach for some star gazing, like you say."

"I'm thinking she'll want to spend some time alone and then watch the sun come up. It'll be a nice way to feel like she's really come home."

"Mm hmmmm. Be fun to see the look on Eli's face, too . . . ."

"Now, Ethan . . . ."

CHAPTER ELEVEN

Emma reached over to turn up the car stereo as she sang along with Willie Nelson, her thick, shiny, wild tangle of curly silver hair blowing free around her face.

She had timed it perfectly. The pre-dawn hours were quiet and soft, just as she remembered from her days here as a child. She'd been back often to visit, but this was the first time she could remember as an adult allowing herself to just "be." To let her heart open and accept that this was home. This was where she was meant to be.

The top to her little yellow VW bug was down, and she couldn't help but throw her head back to sing the words to "Georgia," along with Wille. Emma knew full well she couldn't carry a tune, but some things just deserved music - even if it was hers, and done badly.

She preferred thinking of it as a joyful noise. A joyful noise was appropriate, she thought, as an accompaniment to beauty. And right then, she was surrounded by beauty.

She drove along roads she remembered well, recognizing the hodgepodge of sprawling white farmhouses and stately Queen Anne homes along with quirky cottages of various styles and sizes. Here and there, she'd see one of the original island homes made from a popular building material at one time called "tabby" - - part art lime, water, sand, oyster shells and ash. The tabby homes were a mystery yet to be solved. No one knew who built them or when.

When Emma's Great Aunt Elizabeth bought this island to develop in 1949, it was uninhabited. Yet, she discovered a few of these small homes built from the oyster shell mix scattered around the island, which had obviously once been occupied, but at some point, deserted. Now, all these architectural styles mixed together willy nilly were part of the charm of Whimsey Island. All given a ghostly pearly sheen by the almost full moon and bright stars.

Emma pulled off the oyster shell road and was immediately beset with the unmistakable combination of pungent earthy smells from the marsh to her left and salty smells from the ocean to her right. She felt salt in the sea breeze as it gently floated across her face. She gazed across the road, savoring the quiet. Smiling, she realized she had been unconsciously connecting long cherished memories to these familiar landmarks. She also realized some of the salt she felt on her face was actually from a few salty tears. She was home.

Smiling as she sat in her little VW, parked in front of her Aunt Zoe's house, thinking about her time shared with Ethan and Lou Tatnall, Emma reached behind her to the backseat for her thermos of coffee and the bag of delicious pastries she'd helped herself to from the plate on the Tatnall's old pine table. Emma stretched her legs out across the passenger seat to settle in for the show she was sure the sky of Whimsey would provide. She pulled a chocolate croissant out of the bag, sighed a contented sigh with the first bite, and drifted as memories washed over her. Tall enough so her toes grazed the passenger door of her much loved little yellow bug, she scrunched down in the car seat and used the open window frame as a pillow, tilted her head back and gazed into the sky.

It was still dark, and she was able to clearly see what had to be a beezillion stars dotting the skies just like she remembered. Amazing how spectacular the stars can be without interference from street lamps and people's lights and TVs shining through their windows. The only lights here were the teeny white fairy lights Aunt Zoe had woven through the trees surrounding her home, and the small shop - soon to be gallery - next to it. Their dainty twinkles made them seem a part of the sky, as if the stars reached all the way to the grassy slope of the yard and into the marsh behind the houses.

Emma wondered, not for the first time, if Whimsey might be the only town on God's green earth that had an ordinance against lights. There were no street lights, and no one turned on their outside light unless there was a problem. A light turned on after dark immediately put the neighbors on alert and the police were called to check on the residents. If there was a problem, help was on the way quickly. If there was no problem, the resident could be fined. This was the way the residents of Whimsey wanted it, this was the way it was.

Emma heard the waves gently rolling in to her right on the ocean side. She gathered up her quilt, wrapped her shawl around her shoulders, grabbed her coffee along with the bag of pastries and quietly closed the car door. She wanted to spend some time alone gazing at these stars the families of Whimsey practically worshipped. They proudly declared the Whimsey stars were brighter than any others. And that there were more of them clustered over their small town than anywhere else in the world. The Whimsey stars were doing an impressive job of living up to their reputation this night, for sure.

As she walked across the grassy edge and up the steps to the narrow boardwalk, she felt a prickle of anxiety on the back of her neck. Was there some else out here? She turned in a slow circle but didn't spot anyone. With a shake of her head, she shrugged it off.

It's the middle of the night. Who on earth would be out here, for heaven's sake? And besides. This is Whimsey, not Atlanta. It's not like I'm gonna get mugged or anything.

Continuing her walk, she felt the salt off the ocean sprinkling her face a little harder and she heard the waves - some gentle, some with a little more assertiveness - saying "Pay attention. We hold the power here." And it was true. All anyone had to do was stand on a beach in the presence of this huge ocean and they would know how very miniscule they and all their problems were in relation to Mother Nature and all her glorious wonder.

Emma thought she might explode with all the emotion she was feeling and took off running. As she ran over the dunes, she dropped her bundle and kept running till she was hip deep in the salty water with waves crashing around her. Throwing her head back and yelling a loud and rowdy rebel yell, she did what could pass, possibly, for a Happy Dance in the surf with her arms up over her head.

She then stood with her hands clasped over her heart, gazing up at the stars and murmured a quiet, "Thank you."

Walking back to where she had dropped everything, she spread her quilt on the sand, took off her wet jeans and pulled one side of the quilt up over her legs.

Dumb. Why didn't I think to take these off before I went running into the water like a four year old? Oh well, a cup of hot coffee and one more of Lou's croissants and all will be right with the world. I can lie here and watch the stars and stick around for the sunrise. The perfect way to start my new life back in Whimsey.

Was leaving here and staying gone so long the most singularly stupid thing I ever did? Or is coming back? Am I really ready to be swooped up into the arms of Whimsey again, or will I miss the freedom, independence, and anonymity of the big city?

"Are you nuts?" squeaked Madeline. "We hated it there!"

"Oh, shush, Madeline," Emma said. "I'm just thinking out loud. I'm allowed!"

Emma watched the stars with the waves crashing around her while being swept along in memories, Emma realized the real show she had driven all this way to see was about to begin.

The first pale colors of the sun began to emerge. The pearly skies were slowly starting to awaken into soft vanilla tinged by a frosty pale shell pink and luminous apricot. As she watched, it never occurred to her that she might be seeing things a bit differently than the average sunrise watcher. Where most people would be quite satisfied, perhaps even in awe, of the beauty presented to them, it would probably never dawn on them to seek out and grasp how the sky slowly changed with thin rays of clear creamy yellow turning into rich saffron streaked with soft lemon to bright canary and strong amber.

With the eyes of an artist, Emma watched as a background of delicate lavenders and pinks merged into vibrant blues and violets laced with deep lapis. In the middle of it all, as if orchestrated by an unseen conductor, a sudden burst of gold that made Emma's eyes blink, followed by a huge orb of a heartbreakingly beautiful orange that knows no name, shot with blood red and fuschia, spread its colors across the ocean, mixing with the hundred shades of blues and greens in an unlikely abstract. Much like the huge paint palate she remembered her grandmother Lillith holding as she tried, endlessly, to capture this morning ritual she so loved.

Emma wished, momentarily, for her pencils. It was not unusual for her to spend her mornings watching a sunrise with her sketch pad and colored pencils, hastily rubbing colors onto paper in hopes of, much as her grandmother Lillith had done, duplicating some of the sky's gift of color. These scribblings had been the basis for some of her best work.

She looked up at the sky and gave a little salute. Her grandparents, Benjamin and Lillith, who were more than likely sitting up there on one of those clouds tinged in gold, would be happy she had finally come home to stay. She was sure she could feel their smiling eyes on her and she smiled back. She noticed a wink of light as the sunlight bounced off the silver bracelet her grandfather had made and given her when she was sixteen. It was a piece she always wore. She touched it with a gentle caress. There was an inscription on the inside which said, "Find your crimson and hold on tight!" She had no idea what it meant, but she knew someday the meaning would be clear to her.

I hope you guys are proud of what you've done here. You and Great Aunt Elizabeth. Whimsey is one heck of a place.

CHAPTER TWELVE

Walking back to her car with all the glory of the sunrise still living in her mind, along with the stories she vaguely remembered hearing about how Great Aunt Elizabeth had helped her grandmother Lillith "find her voice" for her famous abstract paintings, she felt at peace.

I must say. I come from a long line of smart women. And strong. They always managed to figure out where they were going and how to get there. With their personal lives and with their art, and so will I. Emma laughed, and realized she was beginning to get excited about seeing everyone.

Suddenly remembering she was still just wearing a sandy T-shirt and her panties, she scampered quickly to the Volkswagen and dug around in her bag until she found a hot pink tank and a long flowy cotton skirt in pink and red flowers and stripes. Enough to make her presentable and keep her legal in case early morning beach walkers might come by. It wouldn't do to cause a scandal her first day back by being spied slipping around in her undies.

It was still awfully early, so instead of waking Aunt Zoe, she decided to have another, but just one more, cup of coffee and maybe another of Lou's croissants.

"Hmmm," Emma wondered aloud, "how many does that make already this morning?"

Looking to her left, Emma smiled as she gazed upon the two yellow houses set back from the street. One was a small yellow craftsman style home with white trim and black shutters. A big white rocking chair porch and a red door. It had been Aunt Zoe's home for many years and was Emma's second home when her parents, Zelda and Scott, were off traveling the world as they were wont to do. The small garden surrounding the front porch was a riot of color with the old fashioned flowers Zoe planted, seemed to forget, but which nonetheless still flourished. Reds, and yellows, purples and blues, oranges and greens and every shade of each, sprouted in abandon with no rhyme or reason and brought a smile to anyone's face as they walked up the steps to be greeted by a row of rocking chairs in as many riotous colors as the flowers.

It wasn't as small as it once was, though.

And it was no longer Zoe's home.

What had been known for the past few years as Zoe's Little Shop was soon to become Gallery Les étoiles, as the final details for the change from shop to gallery were almost complete.

The women Emma held in her heart as close as sisters were going to be showing their work here. Emma was extraordinarily proud of them. Would she, in time, be able to join them?

Emma looked toward Les étoiles. This is what brought them all back.

Aunt Zoe, clever soul that she is, had created what they needed to come back home. And now, a series of events had come about so that the time was right for all the women to be gathered back into the nest. Permanently.

When Aunt Zoe moved out of the large family home her Great Aunt Elizabeth built, she'd had this small house built. She wanted, needed, a place of her own to live and to work. To create. To be able to work all night if she wanted, then sleep all day. Without ever having to explain to her parents, her aunt and her sister that, "Yes, she had eaten, thank you very much. Yes, today - she had eaten today. She was sure of it."

Zoe's parents, being artists in their own right, understood. Her younger sister Zelda, Emma's mother, was getting ready to start her own life's adventure traveling raveling the world, and having Zoe move out first was just what was needed to help her convince her parents, Ben and Lillith, that the time was right. Ben and Lillith didn't really put up much of a fight. They had plans of their own for the girls' rooms, after all. Benjamin needed additional space for his jewelry making business. It was time to hire someone to help him execute his designs so he could spend more time doing the actual crafting he so loved.

Lillith had long envied her daughter Zelda's large room at the back of the house overlooking the dunes, the beach and the ocean. She was sure it would make the perfect studio where she could catch the colors of the sun rising in the mornings and perhaps finally capture them on canvas.

Aunt Elizabeth was still living with them in this grand old home, and wasn't about to give up an inch of her own space - the entire third floor. She also welcomed Zoe and Zelda's request for freedom.

While Zoe lived in her new house, it slowly evolved from being mostly a home to being mostly a studio - a happy, nurturing space which seemed to exude a creative spirit.

Zoe realized after a while, though, that she would be needing another house. One she could actually live in and not be forced into one small corner as all the studio and shop space grew, crowding her out of her living space.

Since Zelda and her husband Scott Foley were traveling the world as a team - Scott an award winning journalist and Zelda winning as many awards with her photo-journal pieces - their two children were reaching an age where they needed to be in a proper school. Traveling the world had been a grand adventure for the four of them for a few years, and had given Emma and her brother Jonathan an education not to be equaled. But the world was changing. The topics Scott and Zelda were now tackling took them to war torn countries and political hot beds. Certainly not safe for them, and less so for two young children.

The decision was made that the two children would live with their Aunt Zoe during the school year, and Scott and Zelda would travel less fraught parts of the world during the summer so Emma and Jonathan could travel with them then.

Zoe's new home was built on the lot adjacent to the small craftsman.

The small craftsman became a shop.

Zoe's mixed media collages became quite famous - as did much of the work done by the community of Whimsey. And somewhere along the way, a pixie named Earlene took up residence in the shop storeroom. And refused to leave.

The thought of Earlene made Emma shiver. Silently promising not to even acknowledge the wicked little pixie, and hoping maybe now that she was back, Earlene would simply leave. Leave and go back to wherever she came from.

"I wouldn't count on it," said Madeline. "We're going to have to contend with her for the rest of our days."

"Oh, hush, Madeline," said Emma.

Zoe had closed down the shop for several months while the plans for the gallery were drawn up and the work completed. She was keeping her plans a secret. So far, the only ones who had seen what had been accomplished were Eli and Ethan, Jr., the workmen they had hired, Zoe and Earlene. Earlene had continued living in the shop during the entire renovation.

Emma pulled herself up quickly, splashing coffee over her wrist and silver bracelet.

Earlene. Pixies. Wicked little pixies. Magic.

Shaking her head, she rolled her eyes and made her confession. *Truth telling time, girl. It's past time for you to admit to yourself it's not the Whimsey magic that's got your panties in a twist. It's not even Earlene. Well, maybe Earlene a little. It's you. It's you and your feelings of inadequacy. The rest of the Wicked Women have made huge names for themselves while you drifted along taking baby steps with your art. Wasting time trying to make a marriage work that was doomed from the beginning.*

And it was doomed from the beginning because as much as you wanted to love Hunter, you knew there would always be someone you loved more. So. Get over it!

Having Eli as a friend is better than going years without seeing him at all. Take the friendship and be happy with it. Don't make any more waves like you did when he came to see you in Atlanta. Your work is finally reaching the level it should be - for the second time. Not many get a first chance, let alone a second. No one here is judging you, so why are you being so hard on yourself. Get over yourself, learn to accept the gifts life has handed you and enjoy them.

With a smile, she looked at the heavy pottery coffee mug she was holding, her coffee still steaming. Her friend Maggie made these mugs thick and sturdy enough to keep coffee hot even longer than those tacky insulated coffee mugs you could pick up in any gas station in the world. But they were gracefully designed and molded into a shape that seemed to fit in your hand as if made especially for you. Tall and sized to fit in the cup holders in automobiles. And, unlike their insulated counter-parts, were safe to go in the microwave - Ta DA!

And darned if Maggie hadn't used the Whimsey stars to help make her pottery famous.

Every piece of pottery Maggie made was an unusual shade of red. A red that people had been trying to duplicate for a number of years. The silver sheen that would randomly shine through in certain light mystified potters worldwide, and when they contacted Maggie to inquire, her response was always the same. It was the Whimsey stars. She swore she used her usual red glaze but somehow during firing the stars would beam their stardust into the kiln. Ridiculous. But, the result was a unique warm red with an ever so slight shimmery silver lustre. Each mug, in addition to being hand signed by Maggie, had a very small silver star - maybe even one or two. The stars weren't always readily apparent, so some of the fun was looking for them. Her talent, along with brilliant marketing savvy, had made Maggie a very wealthy woman. She had been offered obscene amounts of money to sell the secret recipe for her glaze, but she stuck to her star story and swore that was the only secret, so therefore, not hers to sell. Oddly enough, none of the other potters in Whimsey ever managed to achieve that silver lustre.

Magic.

'Course the Whimsey magic also included that damned wicked little pixie, Earlene . . . .

Pushing Earlene to the back of her mind, Emma studied the two houses which were so familiar to her. Both loved and cherished.

The two yellow and white houses with their black shutters and the same red doors, were separated by a wide expanse of lawn, but were fronted with the same wild profusion of bright flowers and shrubbery. The rest of Whimsey tried, without much luck, to duplicate this abundance of flora, but marshlands are not known to be as welcoming to the varieties of plants Zoe seemed to be able to coax into such glory.

Next to Les étoiles, Zoe's home was a miniature Victorian. All the gingerbread was there, only on a slightly smaller scale than one was used to seeing in a Queen Anne structure.

The craftsman and the Victorian lived in perfect communion, complementing one another and exuding an air of happy harmony.

As Emma watched, she saw the always aristocratic Pyewackett rouse herself lazily from one of the white wicker rockers and stretch with a noisy "mrrrow,", just as Fred lifted his head from the wicker settee a gave a gentle good morning "woof" to his housemate.

There had been a long, continuous line of long-haired black cats named Pyewackett, along with chubby little Corgis named Fred for as long as Emma could remember. Zoe insisted they were the same Pyewackett and Fred she had always known, but that couldn't be. If it were true, then Fred & Pye would be in their 30's by now. Not even Whimsey pets could live that long.

And then, there was Aunt Zoe coming through the door, giving Pye and Fred their good morning scratches.

When Emma noticed the cane her aunt was using, she gave a little gasp. She knew, of course, about her aunt's broken leg. But still, it was disconcerting to see her usually exuberantly nimble aunt needing the assistance of a cane. As if hearing Emma's thoughts, Zoe turned her way, and they locked eyes.

Before Emma could even think twice, she found herself running across the street and up the steps into her aunt's outstretched arms.

"Emma! Oh my, child. Look at you! Have you gotten taller still? Just since I saw you in Atlanta? How can that be? And your shoes. You've lost your shoes again."

"Oh, Aunt Zoe, you know I haven't gotten taller. Don't be silly. I've been taller than you since I was eleven."

"Harumph. One thing I do know - you lose one more pound and you're going to be nothing but breath and britches, as my Great Auntie Belle used to say."

"Pfft! Not so!"

Neither of them made mention of the fact that Pyewackett was busy batting at fine silver shimmery dust particles which seemed to drop off Emma as she moved.

As Fred bumped against her leg, Emma glanced down, "And lookie here - here's Fred and Pyewackett dancing about to welcome me! Actually, I'm a little surprised, and maybe even a tad disappointed. I was sure you would have some big marching band prancing down Main Street."

"Don't be fresh, child. If you had been a bit more specific about your arrival, I may have been able to arrange that."

"Oh ho ho - I feel quite sure you could have. Give this gal a break, Auntie. I'm going to need to let my head clear a bit before you whip me into a social whirl, please. I knew if I told you what time to expect me, we'd start talking and carrying on just like we're doing now, and I needed some time by myself. I wanted to, I don't know, let Whimsey say 'Welcome Home, Emma.' And I wanted to hear that welcome in private. Does any of that make any sense?"

Zoe stood back, looked into Emma's eyes, and put her hands on her shoulders, "Yes, child, I understand. And I hope the welcome was all you hoped for."

"Thank you, Aunt Zoe." She hugged her aunt close and could feel her heart beat. She could smell the familiar

scent of the ocean, the marsh and Elizabeth Arden's Red
Door, the scent that was pure Zoe. "The welcome couldn't
have been more perfect. The stars outdid themselves, and
then the sunrise was purely outrageous. I swear I saw
colors no one has ever seen before."

They laughed and tossed their arms over one
another's shoulders, "Well, child, we'll expect you to find
those colors in some of your stones you have stashed away
and make us a miracle of Mother Nature's color wrapped in
silver.

Emma looked at Zoe in puzzlement, "I don't
remember having any stones stashed away."

Zoe looked at Emma with the same degree of
puzzlement, "You don't? I ran across a rather large box
when we were cleaning your apartment. Just a box. It
wasn't marked and it wasn't sealed, so I looked to see what
it was. It's full of loose stones. Probably been there forever.
I put it in your closet. We'll look at it tomorrow or the next
day. There may be things in there you'll be able to use."

"Strange I don't remember them." Emma shrugged,
"Too much going on in my mind, I guess."

Zoe nodded, "Probably so. Who knows, they may
be just what you need to help you get over this block
you've run into."

"Pfft." Emma blew through her lips, "Block. That's
a kind word for it. I am making headway, but I've had
some trouble choosing the right stones, for one thing. Who
knows, Auntie, you may be right, they could be helpful.
Let's cross our fingers and wish on a star that these stones
have some Whimsey magic attached to them and will
answer all my prayers."

Zoe laughed and squeezed Emma's hand, "Don't make fun, Emma. It could happen."

"Yes, well. We'll see." Emma yawned and stretched.

Zoe glanced at her watch, "I think you have time for a nice long nap, and then a long leisurely bubble bath. How's that sound?"

"Sounds like heaven. I think I'll go on up and do just that, but first I'll grab my bags out of the car." She started walking towards the porch steps, "But, what did you mean I'll have time? Are we expected someplace?"

"Well, the girls thought it would be nice to get together for a little brunch, you see . . . . "

"The girls - really? All of them? I can't wait to see them!"

"All of them. It should be fun."

"It will be. Brunch – yum! Cappuccino Brownies? Ice Cream? Chocolate Sauce?"

"Slow down, child! Of course, but that will be dessert if that's okay with you. I thought we'd have your favorite crab quiche before we served dessert."

"Perfect!"

Zoe laughed again, "And who knows, perhaps you'll even find your shoes by the time they arrive. Let's go bring your bags in. I know you'll fall sound asleep quickly, seeing as how you've been sitting out here all night reacquainting yourself with the magic of Whimsey, after all.

"And, of course, we'll be having a few folks over this evening for supper." Zoe said as she walked towards Emma's car.

Emma spun around, "A party! You've planned a party, haven't you?"

"Oh well, just a few folks . . ."

"Ha!" Emma rolled her eyes, "Aunt Zoe, you don't know the true meaning of 'just a few folks.' Brunch and a party – I think I will take that nap."

"I'm so happy to be back home," chirped Madeline.

"Are you, Madeline? Me too," replied Emma.

CHAPTER THIRTEEN

Awakening from her nap, Emma opened her eyes and watched the long white gauze curtains float on the ocean breeze coming through the open window.

She propped herself up with some of the pillows covering nearly every spare inch of the big white iron bed.

Zoe had asked Emma to decorate this small suite of rooms as her own when she built the house. It had, since then, undergone a few bouts of redecorating, but surprisingly few. Emma still had the room she had as a child in the big house also. But, since Jonathan and Olivia had married and had two children, Emma didn't want to intrude. Olivia needed to know it was her home now, so it was always accepted that Emma stayed with Zoe whenever she came home to Whimsey for a visit.

Emma's small apartment here embraced her, and she still loved every inch of it as much as she had when she first moved in.

This was proof of the saying about a home reflecting a person's personality. Anyone taking a peek into these rooms would believe the inhabitant to be organized in an easy-going, relaxed way. A lover of beauty. Creative and sentimental.

Emma looked around the room, smiling at the photos lining the mantle. Aunt Zoe had added a couple new ones of her niece and nephew. Max and Abby were the spitting images of their parents. Max a miniature Jonathan, and Abby a mini Olivia. Both, however, had Olivia's wild red hair.

Zoe had filled one of the red pottery bottles Maggie made many years ago with white tulips.

A funny long stocking hung from the fireplace mantle, hand-knitted by her friend Sarah Kate back when they were in high school. Who knew these ridiculously silly long red and pink striped stockings with hand-made lace inserts at the heel and the toe would be the thing to bring fame and fortune? Sarah Kate was now making them in every color of the rainbow, usually in combinations that defied human logic, but seemed to work. And at the very least, put a smile on your face. They each contained a little surprise tucked in the toe. The seller of the stocking would tuck in a lagniappe and ask a promise from the buyer not to peek until they got home. It would be a teeny hand-knitted something. Maybe a little horse, or puppy, kitten or giraffe. Maybe a bear or a hippopotamus. When Sarah Kate gave Emma hers all those years ago, it contained an itty bitty sock monkey. An exact replica of a sock monkey named Sissyfriss Sockmonkey she had kept with her since she was a toddler. Sissyfriss, Sr. and Sissyfriss, Jr. were still with her and still much loved.

A hand-woven cashmere pink cocoon with red silk ribbon trim lay sprawled across the arm of the loveseat.

Will you look at this? My colors and it is scrumptious!

She looked inside, knowing she would find the little white and silver tag - "Handmade by Alexandra Swinney, Whimsey Island." And pinned on the inside, she found a small piece of ivory stationery saying, "Welcome Home! xxoo Alex"

Oh, my. Welcome Home.

Holding the soft cashmere close, Emma continued looking around.

There was an assortment of stained glass stars made by Zoe's friend Jacob hanging in the bay window.

One of Olivia's paintings hung over the fireplace. The painting awakened the rest of them to the realization of how truly talented Olivia was. Up until then, they recognized her talent and appreciated it, but only at a certain level. This particular painting brought them up dead short. They all knew in an instant that Olivia had hit on something that unleashed previously untapped reserves of talent. They knew a brilliant future was all hers for the taking.

She copied the painting from an old photograph of all of them when they were about six years old. Emma, Olivia, Sarah Kate, Maggie and Alexandra. They had been playing dress-up in Grandmother Lillith's attic, which was full of steamer trunks and wardrobes filled with vintage dresses and hats, shoes and purses. Granny didn't seem to give a whit if the girls were dressed in Worth and Chanel. She knew that even as little girls, they had a sense of responsibility about these clothes. They adored them, seemed to recognize their preciousness, and were as careful with them as they were with all the small furry creatures that seemed drawn to them. There was a gentleness of spirit amongst them, even given the fact that they were an exuberant bunch, given to loud squeals and boundless energy. They were clearly sisters of the heart, bound together by their likenesses and their differences from the day they met. Their creativity led them into performing plays complete with set decorations right down to the most

114

minute detail, and exquisitely adorned with many costume changes provided by Lillith and Benjamin's attic.

The parents looked forward to the invitations that would arrive by mail requesting their presence at one stage play after another. To sit in the audience of these plays was a delight for each of them, enormous pride visible on their faces as they watched these magical young women. Knowing, at some base level, that each of them was capable of greatness.

The painting showed not just five little girls playing dress-up, but the depths of their joy in one another. Each making sure they were all equally visible, unable to be separated without a hand holding another's hand, a finger touching another's nose, one giving another's big picture hat a minor adjustment. The joy was infectious. The love was palpable. The quiet shades of white and sepia tones tinged with the palest pink, recognized widely as Olivia's signature palette, giving it an aura of timelessness. Emma loved this painting as much as anything in her life. It had been hanging in her condo in Atlanta, but was perfect right here.

On another wall, Emma spotted one of her Grandmother Lillith's vivid abstract sunscapes, this one reflecting those same pinks and golds she had witnessed that morning. Colors and shading ranged from pearly vanilla effervescence to such vibrant intensity it was hard to imagine them coalescing into the miracle of beauty that Lillith had captured on canvas. It was only with a patient curiosity that Emma was able to discover the mysteries hidden in the depths of her grandmother's painting, making it all the more precious.

An antique cherry dental chest with dozens of small shallow drawers, cubby holes and pigeon holes sat under

the painting. Inside was some of her Grandfather
Benjamin's jewelry. Pieces he had made especially for her,
or pieces they had made together while he was teaching her
the skills of jewelry designing and crafting. It also
contained notebooks full of his designs and notes, which
were every bit as precious to her as the jewelry. Emma
remembered sitting on the floor with her grandfather as a
girl while he showed her some of the pieces, talked with
her about them and allowed her to play with them. As she
grew older, these play sessions became a little more serious
and became the part of her life that opened a well. She
found what she needed to do. She was at her most "Emma
Self" as she sketched her ideas and designs and then
worked to find the most suitable materials to utilize in order
to create her visions. She always felt her grandfather's hand
guiding her toward the proper tool while working, the
proper stones to match with the proper metal, his soft voice
in her ear encouraging her to try new things.

Two collages hung on the wall over Emma's bed,
done specifically for her by Zoe. There was a wealth of
personal memories encased in these pieces, including an
engraved invitation to her parents' wedding, a silver
pocketwatch that had belonged to her great grandfather
Wallace, a book jacket with the author's name, Samuel Eli
Whimsey, in black script across the top of the page, much
larger than the book title. It was that name, after all, that
sold the books. And made the possibility of this island a
reality. The locals knew where to look on Zoe's collages to
find the one thing that would help them know who she was
thinking of when she was working on a particular piece.
The collages were wildly popular with the tourists who
didn't mind paying the prices Zoe Hamilton's work was
bringing, but it was with a little sadness the islanders
watched the pieces leave knowing the new owners would
never really understand exactly what they had bought.

The room made her laugh a little. How many people have this many creative people in their lives, let alone in their immediate and extended family?

"I'm so happy we're home," Madeline whispered.

"Oh, Madeline. Me too."

On the low coffee table in front of the red striped sofa were two large books containing columns written by her father, accompanied by photographs taken by her mother. The two continued to travel the world as a team freelancing as correspondents and doing it all their own way. Some of the subjects were heartbreaking pieces related to wars and the destruction it left behind. Some were love letters they composed together to those out of the way places they found and fell in love with. There were people pieces, travel pieces, even food pieces.

And next to those, were the three books - two novels, one a non-fiction best-seller adapted from his dissertation thesis - written by her brother Jonathan.

Emma heard her coffee machine click on in the small kitchen and in moments had a perfect cup of her favorite blend, milky with fresh cream and a little sugar. She sat at the open window and enjoyed the smells - the richness of the marsh mingling with the salt from the ocean across the road from the house, the waves an ever present lullaby of life force.

She wandered back into the kitchen nook to rummage through a basket of pastries she knew would be there and fished out one of Lou's chocolate croissants. Sinful. Rich. Buttery. Heavenly. If she kept this up, she'd weigh a ton in a week.

She felt the wet nose on her ankle about the same time she heard the tap tap of Fred's nails on the wooden floor.

"Good Morning, Sir Fred. Here for a little scratch on the belly, or one of Lou's little pieces of homemade sin? Better stick with the scratch. It looks like you might have had a little too much homemade sin lately with that poochy little belly of yours. Besides, chocolate isn't good for little doggies or kitties. What? Don't you grumble at me, short stuff."

As the chubby little corgi rolled over on his back and gazed at Emma adoringly, she stooped down to give him the promised scratches and scritches. While they were having their little love fest, in wandered Pyewackett - not to be ignored. Making sure her plumey black tail was complimented, her throaty purrs got louder and louder as Emma gave her scratches and scritches as well.

"Ruined. You are both spoiled rotten and ruined."

She watched with interest as Fred and Pyewackett appeared to be having a conversation, including sly looks in her direction.

"What are you two talking about? Wait. What am I talking about? Animals don't chat with one another and have conversations, right? That stuff is only in novels, right? I have finally, truly, lost my mind. But, it's a fact, this is without a doubt, the oddest island on God's green earth."

With a shake of her head, she announced to the animals she was off to take a shower. And that they were to keep out of her pastries.

Seeing the array of bath bubbles, lotions, salts and scents, Emma decided to relax in the big clawfoot tub instead of taking a shower.

After slipping Willie Nelson's *Stardust* CD into the stereo, lighting some fragrance candles, and pouring a little of one of her favorite Jo Malone scents into the warm water, she took a deep breath and slipped under the soft, frothy bubbles while sipping her coffee. Looking up, she was able to watch the leaves of the huge old live oak right outside her window that wrapped around the corner walls at the end of the bathroom. The windows were set up high where the only things visible were the tree draped with Spanish moss and the sky.

Directly overhead was a large square skylight rimmed with stained glass. Emma had soaked in this tub many a night, losing herself in the Whimsey stars. The bathroom, just like the rest of her small apartment, had been designed with comfort and pampering in mind. Zoe believed a home needed to nurture the soul, and this one did all that and more. Emma sighed deeply, luxuriating in the scented bubbles while singing along with her favorite singer ever.

"Ol' Willie's still got it, but *Stardust* will always be his best album ever. I wonder if I've been to more Willie Nelson concerts than anyone else? Bet I have."

As she looked around the room, she couldn't help but smile. Her love of decorating, along with her almost obsessive need for organization was well displayed in this small space. Everything had its place. There were nooks and crannies all around, each one home to the objects within. Everything she could ever want or need was right here, in miniature efficiency.

Emma knew the time would come that she'd have to find her own place, but she felt like she needed to be close at hand while Zoe recovered from her broken leg. She'd be limited with a lot of things until she was completely healed, and that could take a while. Although it was a bad break, the doctors assured them it would heal properly, and while Aunt Zoe was in excellent health, facts remained that life can change in an instant. And loved ones do grow older. Emma's place was here for the time being.

It was all still feeling a bit like a dream. Or, just another visit. Emma had said her good-byes to the friends she had made in Atlanta. Some she had grown close to would be coming for visits. They were all anxious to spend some time on Whimsey, having been charmed by Emma's stories of the island, her family and her friends. Her friends in Atlanta knew a lot about Emma, but they also knew there was an awful lot they did not know and probably never would. She was generous and giving, but also quite private.

The people who knew her well were the people here on Whimsey. Some had never left, some had recently returned.

The September following the Class of '96 Graduation, Emma, along with her life-long best friends Olivia, Maggie, Sarah Kate and Alexandra, left the island, determined to live away. They started their new lives at The Savannah College of Art and Design. They had spent the summer after graduation having fun with friends who would also be leaving the island - not knowing when or if they might ever reunite. They each recognized they had reached the crossroads of adulthood, and the choices they made now could set them on the road they would travel for many years, possibly the rest of their lives.

The Class of '96 was a small, close-knit group, not unlike the Whimsey classes before or after them. That was the last golden summer of their youth, and they were all determined to make the most of it and make memories they would cherish in the future. Except for one incident which seemed minor at the time, they pretty well did exactly what they set out to do.

A lot of their graduating class had chosen to stay on the island instead of going away to college. Many would step into family businesses that their parents, grandparents, and in many cases great grandparents, had started. Some as far back as 1949 when Whimsey was developed. Family history and tradition was a large and important part of this much-loved island.

The Wicked Women of Whimsey had each declared to their families that they would be the best at what they did. In order to reach that goal, they recognized they would need formal education in the fields each of them were already exceptionally well trained. They would then need additional journey-level assistantships with masters in their fields. The obvious starting point was the highly respected Savannah College of Art and Design.

SCAD filled their needs for four years, and they perfected the crafts each of them had already developed a talent for. It was, after all, impossible to grow up in a community of artists and not learn to love and appreciate it. Along with discovering where your own talents lie and the need to create.

When the time came to move on after graduation from SCAD, the girls were already on their way to lucrative careers in a field they loved.

Emma became a jewelry designer who also crafted her own pieces, Olivia a painter, Maggie a potter, Sarah Kate a knitter and lace maker, and Alexandra developed her talent as a weaver.

And now, many years later, here they were. Right back where it had all started.

Remembering that the Wicked Women were coming over for brunch got Emma moving. Excited, she hopped out of the tub, humming to herself.

Feeling a draft of air, she looked around to see Fred and Pyewackett nudging their way into the bathroom.

"Laws - you two! Is there no such thing as privacy in this house?"

Pye hopped onto the side of the tub, turned her back to Emma and proceeded to bat at the bubbles as the water drained away.

"Well, Pye, if you're going to ignore me, why bother to come in?"

Fred put his nose against the back of her calf and made her jump.

"Oh, Fred. Are you smiling at me? I missed you. Both of you."

She leaned down to give Fred a kiss on the nose. He gave her a quick little lick on her nose, then smiled up at her.

"Gotta get ready, kids. Make yourselves comfy."

They watched as she dried her thick silver hair and put on her make-up, Pyewackett taking an occasional swat at make-up brushes.

They followed her into the bedroom and hopped onto the bed as she pulled one of her long flowy skirts out of the closet.

"I can't believe this. All my bags are unpacked already. Aunt Zoe must have sneaked in here while I was sleeping and taken care of all this. Why didn't you guys wake me up so I could help?"

She grabbed the feather light cashmere cocoon that had been tossed across the loveseat.

"This is gorgeous, huh, guys? Pretty sweet of Alex to welcome me home with this, don't you think?"

It was perfect with the long abstract floral pink silk skirt.

"Now, if I can find my shoes . . . . "

Just as she found one pink and red kitten heel sandal, she heard the doorbell, followed by what sounded like a hundred squealing teenage girls.

"They're here!"

CHAPTER FOURTEEN

Emma went flying down the steps, but when she reached the landing, she stopped and gasped.

Tears sprung into her eyes when she saw her best friends gathered around Zoe.

The Wicked Women of Whimsey. All together again. And this time it would be forever. They would grow old together among the people they loved on this magical island.

Emma looked down to find Pyewackett sitting to her left, Fred sitting to her right.

"Okay, guys, let's make an entrance, what say?"

With that, she hopped on the banister and with a "Yeeeeee Haw," went sliding down backwards into the living room. Pyewackett and Fred raced along with her, Fred barking loudly to announce their arrival.

The room came to complete silence. Momentarily.

Emma slipped off the banister, hopped around to face the women, placed her hands on her hips and shouted "Ta DA! Hi, honeys, I'm home!"

Amid an eruption of shrieks, giggles and barks with an occasional loud mraow from Pyewackett, the women hugged and cried and did it all again. Voices running over one another, laughter mingling, Zoe stood off to the side wiping tears from her cheeks. Tears of happiness blurring the present till it seemed as though these beautiful women were slipping back in time to when they had been beautiful young girls, hopping and squealing and hugging now as they had all those many years ago.

Zoe tried to keep up with who was saying what, but with all the shrieking, giggling, hugging and yelling, it was impossible, and she decided it didn't matter. She leaned against a wall, crossed her arms, and let the chaos roll.

"You look smashing!"

"You do, too!"

"Are thirty-four-year-old women allowed to slide down banisters?"

"Need you even ask?"

"Oh, you're wearing the cocoon I made you. Turn around, let's see."

"Of course I am, silly! It's delicious and I love it. Thank you."

"You smell heavenly, Emmaline!"

"You do! What are you wearing?"

"Jo Malone. And don't call me Emmaline."

"In case you forgot, that IS your name."

"Is not. It's Emma. I can't abide the thought that I'm named after a restaurant!"

Aunt Zoe laughed, "Yes, but it's a very special restaurant. It's where your father proposed to your mother, you know."

"Sooooo mushy," said Emma with a grin.

"Emmaline, where are your shoes?"

"Again?"

"Woman, can't you keep your shoes on your feet?"

"I can't believe you're still losing your shoes!"

"I have not lost my shoes," Emma shot back. "Here!" She brandished a single pink and red kitten heel sandal over her head, and glared at Olivia. "Don't call me Emmaline! How many times am I going to have to remind you?"

Laughing hysterically, Olivia said, "Uh huh. Don't change the subject. Where's the other one?"

"Somewhere. It's just temporarily misplaced."

"Those shoes of yours have a mind of their own," said Olivia.

Emma moaned, "It's that Earlene, I'm just sure of it."

This got everyone's attention.

Alex asked, "Have you seen her yet?"

"No. It's been a perfect day," said Emma. "Let's keep it that way, please."

Sarah Kate said, "Oh, now, she's not that bad."

Maggie slapped her knees and said "Pfft!"

"By the way," Alex looked around at everyone, then made sure Emma was looking back at her and paying attention. "Guess who we saw earlier while we were chatting with Harry?"

"Trying to chat, you mean," Sarah Kate interrupted.

"Right. Trying to chat," Alex slid her eyes over to Maggie.

"Well, okay, so I gave him a little kiss," Maggie said. "I haven't seen him since yesterday."

To a rolling of eyes and a chorus of moans, Maggie responded by sticking her tongue out at them all.

"Wait," Emma said. "Before we get into this story, I have to say this right now. Maggie, honey, you are every bit as thin and fit as you were back when you were our star soccer player at Whimsey High. You are gorgeous!" Emma stood back looking at Maggie and her wild mane of black hair which she still wore piled messily on top of her head, even though it was now streaked with a few strands of silver. "Are you all settled back on the island now?"

"Yes! Can you believe it? I've moved in with Harry." Maggie had taken a couple years to travel, both in Asia and in the US to apprentice with a few potters of some renown.

Emma pretended to be surprised, "Really? Would that be Harry Lanier? That guy you've been in love with since we were three?"

127

Maggie playfully punched Emma on the shoulder, "Yeah, him. Did you know he's expanded his landscape design business to include a nursery and a floral shop? The shop's downtown. You can't miss it. And you will love it!"

Emma hugged Maggie, "I know I will, sweetheart. And I am so happy for you both."

Sarah Kate hopped up, put her hands on her hips and looked up from her little 5'1" self at Emma, "What about me? Aren't you happy for me? I've moved back, too, you know."

Emma looked down at her, "Have you now? Do tell!" She then hugged the petite blond blue eyed girl who knew words that would make a sailor blush. And loved using them.

"Yes, ma'am. When I resigned my full time job at Jonathan Campbell Folk School, they assured me I could come teach workshops whenever I wanted. Gray's building me a studio in back of his place for my lace and knitting work. It'll be right next to his dulcimer studio. We can work closely, but not be under one another's feet. Isn't that just the sweetest?" Sarah Kate's long-time boyfriend Gray Trammell taught music history on the mainland and had a studio behind his home where he crafted some of the finest dulcimers available. It was also where he and his friends would meet to play and sing and jam for hours on end.

Emma beamed, "Oh, Sarah Kate. I love this. You guys are adorable together. I'm glad you're finally going to be able to really be together instead of only on weekends. It must have gotten pretty old doing all that traveling."

"It did. But oh my, it was worth it, if you know what I mean." And she winked.

They all howled.

Emma said, "What a devil woman you are, Sarah Kate Storey!"

"Yes. Yes, I am."

"Well, can we get back to the subject at hand?" asked Emma. "You're making me nuts. Who did you see? Remember? You were telling me you bumped into somebody at Harry's. Who was it?"

"Reese Prescott." Maggie said.

Emma grimaced, "Aw jeeez. You know, I was kinda hoping she had moved away."

Sarah Kate shook her head, "No such luck. She's our permanent pain in our collective asses."

"Well, yes - she is that." Olivia walked over and pulled Sarah Kate's hair, "Your language gets worse the older you get, woman."

Alex and Maggie nudged one another. "Oh," said Alex, "and we were just talking about how restrained she's become."

"Quit picking on me about my language," Sarah Kate said. "I just can't seem to help it. I learned these words at my momma's knee."

Maggie shook her head, "Uh huh. Anyway. She asked about you, Emma. She said she heard you were moving back home."

"You know, I'm just not going to worry about Reese Prescott. Surely to God she's not still carrying that dumb grudge."

"Well, Emma, in case you've forgotten," said Alex, "it's not that same dumb grudge you're thinking of."

"She's right, Emma." Olivia walked over and took Emma's hand, "This isn't about Eli and the prom any longer. It's about her dating Hunter a couple of times, and still blaming you for breaking them up."

Emma looked stunned, "She dated Hunter? How did I not know that?"

She looked around at her friends, "You all knew about this, but no one told me? How could you do that?" Her bottom lip quivered, "It's bad enough knowing Eli chose her over me all those years ago and broke my heart. Now I'm learning she tried to steal the man I married? What else don't I know here?"

"What?" Olivia was stunned, "How could you not have known?"

"Oh, honey," Maggie wrapped Emma in her arms. "We all thought you knew and just didn't want to talk about it. It was only a couple dates, after all, and it didn't amount to anything."

Sarah Kate walked over and joined the hug, "That's right. Hell, honey, it was before you even dated him! And it was over before it got started. He was Writer in Residence at Jonathan's retreat that year, and he was immediately smitten with you, but you wouldn't give him the time of day. I remember we were all whining about turning 30. So what did you do - you beat the ol' turning 30 blues by getting married. But, Hunter was here for six months before you even gave him a nod. I know you remember this! Anyway. Reese tried to drop her hooks into him, and they went out a couple times. But that's all it was, a couple dates."

"Except in Reese Prescott's simple mind," added Alex, as she joined the hug also.

"She is simple minded, for sure."

"And a hateful wench."

"And a silly bitch."

"Why does she hate me so?" wailed Emma, as the other girls almost smothered her trying to hug her.

Aunt Zoe clapped her hands, "Girls. Enough. If y'all start your bawling, you know you'll never stop. Now listen to me. We are not going to bring this party down with talk about this Reese person. She's just like her mother. Two of a kind and crazy as a pair of loons. The fact of this whole matter is, Hunter's no longer living, and even Reese can't be crazy enough to continue carrying a torch for a dead man. And she certainly can't blame you for his death. You weren't even on the same continent when it happened."

She walked over and took Emma's face in her hands, kissed her on her forehead and looked at her with a tender smile, "Let's get on with our party, child. What say? Mimosas all around?"

"I love you, Auntie."

"And I love you back. Now how 'bout pouring your tired old auntie a Mimosa, please."

Olivia clapped her hands. "O-TAY, Zoe has spoken. Let's drink!"

And the girls began chattering away again, talking over one another, their own personal radar keeping them on track when no one else would have been able to.

Sarah Kate began pouring drinks, "It's been too long, that's for sure."

"It has," Maggie nodded her head in agreement. "But you know, the timing really wasn't quite right for all of us until now."

Zoe reached for her drink, "I think you're exactly right, Maggie."

"Yes," said Alex, "but now that we're all home again, we'll be back under foot, Aunt Zoe, and you'll wish us all gone again."

"Never," Zoe replied.

"Here, now. A toast," Alex lifted her glass, "To us. And to Zoe. We can't wait to see what you've done with Les étoiles!"

Zoe threw back her head and gave a laugh, "Oh, girls, I think you're going to just love it. It's heaven. I'm quite proud, if I do say so myself."

"It's always been heaven!" squealed Maggie.

Zoe stood back and took a bow, "Well, I know that, but now that we've been able to make a few changes and have all of Whimsey represented together, well - you have to admit, it's pretty special, even if it did cause me to break this leg."

Emma took her aunt's hand, "You broke your leg in Les étoiles? Whenever I've asked, you've only said you tripped. You tripped in the gallery?"

"I did. Unbelievable, huh? I think when we moved out one of the showcases we used when Les étoiles was a shop, we must have left a board loose, and I caught my toe on it. It seems to be fixed now, so no worries."

Olivia shook her head, "It's supposed to be fixed, but I think we better check with the workmen to be sure. We don't want any more broken bones in your lovely gallery."

Zoe waved one hand in the air, "Oh, pafooey. I've been in and out of that shop since before it was a shop. Remember? It used to be my home, after all, and this is the first mishap I've had. Don't fret. Truly, it'll be fine fine fine."

Zoe cocked her head to one side as she sat back down and looked at each of them wistfully, "I want to say something to you all, but this is especially for Alex. The gallery really belongs to all of us. It's grown as we've all grown, born and bred of Whimsey. It was my Aunt Elizabeth who started Whimsey, but let's not forget, Alex's great grandparents helped her. Alex, darling, we all know how very proud your family has always been of your successes and what a wonderful woman you grew up to become. I would give worlds to be able to change time around just enough so that your great grandparents could still be around to see what you've done with the talent they passed down to you."

Alex lifted her head and smiled, "Oh, Aunt Zoe, thank you. But you know, sometimes when we look up at the big house and see Elizabeth? Well, if you look closely, I think you'll see Rupert and Annie in the rocking chairs right next to hers. They haven't left us to our ownselves quite yet."

Sarah Kate stomped her foot, "And now, dammit, you've got us all boo-hooey! Let's lift our glasses to Elizabeth and Rupert and Annie, what say? And then get on with this party!"

"Hear, hear!"

"And to Aunt Zoe and Gallery Les étoiles!"

"Hear, hear!"

Zoe stood up from her chair, and stumbled just a bit as she reached for her cane, "Girls, perhaps it's time we eat."

"What're we having? Does it go with mimosas?"

"We're having crab quiche and a salad," Zoe said. "Just a light little something so we won't spoil our big supper I have planned for tonight. Britta, bless her heart, has done most of the cooking. The girl is a God send. Having a housekeeper/cook is something I should have thought of years ago - although I admit, I asked that she use my recipes for some things, such as my Crab Quiche and Cappuccino Brownies. With all she's done plus the fact everyone on Whimsey plans on bringing a little something, we should have plenty of food tonight, for sure." Zoe sat back down and put her hand on her forehead as the room began to swim a bit. "Oh, boy. Yes, I do believe I need to have a bite to eat."

They moved to the kitchen, chattering like tipsy magpies, as they pulled out chairs and clustered around the big oak trestle table in Zoe's cheerful yellow and white kitchen. The same table they had all clustered around as girls for snacks after school, or while doing their homework together. As Emma listened to her friends talk, it dawned on her that it was as if no time had passed. They all seemed to just pick up where they had left off. What she and these women had among themselves was a unique bond. One few people are lucky enough to ever experience. It was going to be heaven with all of them back together again.

After an hour of eating and drinking, Sarah Kate yawned. Then Alex. As the yawn made its way around the room, Zoe chuckled and suggested it might be time for that nap. "But first," Zoe said, "I'd like to make another toast." Everyone raised their glasses as Zoe said, "Here's to my girls – The Wicked Women of Whimsey, now Artists in Residence in Whimsey's new gallery. May we all prosper, live long and have the time of our lives."

The woman all shouted "Hear, hear!" and clicked their glasses against one another's.

Zoe continued, "Although our Emma isn't ready to join us quite yet, she will."

The other women murmured their agreement, and Emma smiled.

"Thank you, Aunt Zoe. Let's just say I hope to join you. I'm working hard. It would be untruthful to pretend I wasn't devastated in the beginning to learn you would all be a part of something this wonderful when I couldn't be. But. Being back on Whimsey and having all of you around me being so supportive, well, we'll see how it goes. I think my work is progressing. I'm feeling hopeful. In the meantime, I'm loving being a part of everything, if only from the sidelines.

Olivia took Emma's hand, "But you're only there for the time being."

"Do you have some new work you could show us?" asked Maggie.

Emma shook her head, "No, not yet."

"But soon?" asked Alex

"I hope so."

"Well, hell, yeah, woman, we hope so too!" said Sarah Kate.

Everyone laughed, including Emma.

They all helped clear the dishes away and made their way to the stairs to go up for their naps.

Emma had taken a nap earlier, but after the riotous time she's spent with the girls, along with a couple of mimosas, she was ready for another one.

CHAPTER FIFTEEN

After the girls hooted and giggled their way upstairs for naps, Zoe made her way outside and onto the pier at the back of the house. She walked down the pier slowly enjoying, as always, how it curved and meandered a good way out into the marsh. This was her spot. This was where she renewed her soul. It was also where her muses lived. Every collage she had ever done had originated in this marsh in some way. It may have come from sounds she heard as the birds shared their evening gossip with their neighbors, the turtles, frogs and fish, or from the way the wind rustled through the grasses as the sun was setting. Or the unmistakable fragrance that only someone who shared a lifelong connection with the marsh could truly love.

While many favored the ocean, Zoe was partial to the marsh and its inhabitants. She inherited this love from her great aunt Elizabeth. With her in mind, she turned to look behind her down the marsh line to the big old rambling house Olivia and Jonathan now called home. Sure enough, on the large back veranda up on the third floor, she could see Elizabeth sitting in her favorite wicker rocking chair drinking her afternoon toddie, a cigar smoldering in the ashtray. No matter that Elizabeth had been gone for two years after dying peacefully in her sleep at age 102, her spirit was always going to be around as long as that house was still standing. Things are what they are. Especially on Whimsey.

As she settled into her own chair, she looked up to see her friend Jacob walking down the pier towards her, and felt that same little shiver of pleasure she always felt when seeing him. Jacob was a fine looking man, still fit and trim, but it was his obvious pleasure in life that made him so handsome.

He leaned over and gave her a light lingering kiss. "Zoe, I brought us a fresh pitcher of tea. Let me fill your glass there, old girl."

"Jacob, if you continue calling me *old girl,* I may pour that pitcher of tea over your head. And please, not so loud. I have a tad of a headache."

"Oh, now . . . " He chuckled, "A headache? Hmmm. I'm sorry, old . . . sweetheart. So, are the little ones all tucked in for afternoon naps?"

"Yes, well deserved naps after all the mimosas and quiche they put away."

"And the energy they put out. Woman, we could hear that laughter all over this island. Made everyone smile and laugh along with them. It's been too long since we heard those voices mingling like that."

"Yes, it has, Jacob. But the chicks are all back in the nest now, and life is how it should be."

He settled into the chair beside hers, "Would that headache have anything to do with those mimosas, by any chance?"

"Got it in one, love."

They shared a smile and sat quietly drinking their tea as they watched a heron take flight.

"Ah ha!" Jacob said, "Looks like that one there left you a feather or two for your work."

"That she did. She must have known I was in need of feathers for this particular piece. And I thank her."

"Is this a commission piece, or will you put it in Les étoiles?"

"Les étoiles. It'll be fun for me to have some of my own work in there."

"It's quite a place you've put together, Zoe. You deserve to be proud."

"Oh, I am, my dear, I surely am. Whimsey deserves to have its treasures showcased, and we're ready now to share with the world, I think. Not just with the folks around the area who know about us. Having all the girls' work here will put us on the map. I only hope it doesn't prove to be too much for the island."

"I think that matter is well in hand thanks to the foresight of Elizabeth who made this a private island back in the very beginning. Keeping it in the hands of the families of the original settlers was smart thinking. That and not allowing any tourist vehicles. We could have ended up in sad shape like some of the other barrier islands have."

Zoe gave a little shudder. "Horrors. Condos and outlet malls built on marsh land. Who would have thought we'd live long enough to see the day?"

"Elizabeth must have had a bit of The Sight. You think?"

"I do think." Zoe nodded, "Let's toast the grand old dame, what say?"

They both turned toward the big imposing house and raised their glasses. Neither was surprised when Elizabeth raised hers in return with a nod and a wave.

"Whoa! Jacob? Is Elizabeth alone?"

Jacob looked again and shook his head, "Well, I'll be. No, no she's not. Who are those two people up there with her? Have you ever seen them before?"

"A long, long time ago. It's Rupert and Annie Jackson. Alex's grandparents."

"You're kidding. When do I get to hear this story?"

"Sometime, sugar, but not now. I do believe I'm getting a little bit of a hangover. I think I'll join the girls for a nap before everyone arrives this evening for a late supper. Everyone's expected about nine. See you around eight, Jacob?"

Jacob leaned over and gave Zoe another kiss, "Why sure, love, you know I'll be here. Hope that headache passes," he said with a little chuckle.

"No need to be a smart-ass, love."

CHAPTER SIXTEEN

By the time the girls giggled and bumped into one another through the mass confusion of sharing just two bathrooms amongst the five of them, most of the guests had arrived. When they finally made their collective entrance onto the front lawn. they were greeted with applause and cheers.

"About time, girls!"

"Did you forget you had guests out here waiting for you?"

"What are y'all trying to do, make an entrance or something?"

"Welcome Home!"

Laughing, each of them took a bow or a curtsey and ran to give and receive hugs from their family and friends.

The lawn looked as though the fairies had descended. The white twinkle lights Zoe loved were draped over every tree and shrub. There were small tables scattered everywhere, each covered with a white linen table cloth and topped with small vases of fresh flowers and candles. And off to one side was a long table covered with Lowcountry food the area was famous for.

"Holy Kittens!" squealed Madeline.

"I'll say!" said Emma.

There were huge pots of she-crab soup, gumbo and brunswick stew. Lowcountry boil, shrimp and grits, country captain and rice. Mounds and mounds of steamed shrimp, and oysters cooling on ice. A couple of big hams, and platters of fried chicken. Biscuits and yeast rolls. Pitchers of sweet tea. And another table full of desserts, tall coconut cakes, chocolate cakes, even a red velvet Smith Island Cake a friend had shipped down from Maryland. Pound cakes of all shapes and sizes. Chocolate meringue pie, Lemon meringue pie, Key Lime pie and fruit pies of every assortment. At the end of the mile long table were big buckets of ice holding sodas, water and beer. And a passel of kids churning out homemade ice cream.

Emma made her way over to a corner of the yard and stood under an old magnolia tree where she could watch everyone and not be noticed while she soaked it all in.

She spied Jacob giving Aunt Zoe a little kiss every time he passed close, and Zoe all aglow in having everyone she loved gathered here at her home. Almost everyone. It looked like her parents, Zelda and Scott, weren't going to make it after all. Getting to Whimsey from the other side of the world was no easy feat.

She watched Olivia lick her finger and wipe a smudge of chocolate ice cream off Max's chin as Abby curled up on the grass beside her, intent on pulling a resistant Pyewackett into a hug. Apparently, Abby thought it was time for all God's creatures to be asleep.

And there were the guys, pulling out guitars, banjos, harmonicas, fiddles, an old set of drums and a saxophone. And an old guy she didn't recognize with spoons. *I guess we're going to have some entertainment. Oh, boy!*

And there, acting like 18-year-old groupies were Maggie, Sarah Kate and Alex, shouting out their song requests. No surprise that beach music was getting the most requests. What did this crowd have against country music anyhow? Truth be told, the crowd would be entertained with a wide assortment of music from the oldest musicians in the crowd right down to the youngest.

She wondered if Eli would make it to the party, hoping he would. The band would be counting on him to sing, and Emma always enjoyed standing back watching Eli sing.

Since Eli was an integral member of Aunt Zoe's team in the renovation process, they would be bumping into one another regularly. She'd just have to act real casual about it all.

And casual is how it's going to stay, Emma said to herself.

"You always did like hiding under this big ol' tree."

Emma jumped a foot and spun around, "Eli. Hey!"

"Hey, yourself. Sorry I'm late."

Before Emma could respond, they heard a loud voice from the stage, "Hey, Tatnall, you gonna stand around with the ladies all night, or are you gonna get up here and make some music with us? I wouldn't bother you, but nobody else up here can sing 'cept you."

"I'm coming! God help us one of you guys might start singing. Aunt Zoe's not gonna like you running everybody off with all this food still here." He turned to look at Emma, "See you later?"

"You bet. See you later."

And with that, he ran off to join his friends in their make-shift band.

And Emma ran over to join her gal pals and act like an 18-year-old groupie right along with them. As she was shouting out her song requests - "On The Road Again" for starters - she heard the voice she remembered as the very first voice she ever heard.

"Scott, don't you think we raised that girl better than that?"

"Why yes, honey, I surely do. And look at her standing there shouting at those boys like she's got no pride."

"Mama! Daddy!" Emma threw herself at them both and the three of them rocked in a hug, laughing and crying a little.

She stepped back to get a better look at her parents. Zelda, with her short cap of spiked silver hair, possessed an air of constant movement and electricity about her, even when standing still. She had grey eyes which would change with her moods, just like her sister Zoe's. Right now, they were sparkling, full of laughter and excitement.

Scott's blue eyes were sparkling also. He was still the most handsome man Emma had ever seen. Tall, at 6'3", she had to reach up to hug him. She tugged on his hair which was, as usual, in need of a trim.

"I was just sure you were held up in some airport in some unpronounceable place on the other side of the world."

"Well, darlin', we were," said Scott, "But, once your mother gets her mind set on something, it's a foolish person who tries to keep it from happening."

"And that's the truth!" said Zelda, laughing, "So, my lovely daughter, here we are to welcome you home. And happier I have never been!"

"Oh, Mama."

Scott Foley watched as the two most beautiful, much cherished, women in his life hugged one another. Their heads close and their silver hair mingling into one luxurious mane, reflecting the full moon and the Whimsey stars. He didn't think he'd seen a lovelier sight ever.

Next thing he knew, there were people all around them, hugging, laughing, and pounding him on his back. God, it was good to be home among friends and family. There was no place like it. And after having been around the world more than once, he felt he could say that with pretty good authority.

Suddenly a total hush came over the crowd. After what seemed like an awfully long time, it was broken by a loud guitar riff and a very familiar voice singing the words

"Whiskey river . . ."

At the same time, he heard a loud "EEK!" from Emma. When he turned his head to look at her, she had her hands over her mouth, but her eyes were as wide as saucers. "What on earth?" Then he looked at the band. "Could that be . . . .? Naaaah . . . ."

But the man he was now pretty sure was really Willie Nelson reached his hand out, grasped Emma's hand, and pulled her next to him, "Darlin', I believe I've seen you at almost every concert I've played the last few years. I'm betting you know the words to this song. Want to sing along with us?"

Emma stared at him, her hands still over her mouth. Her eyes, if possible, getting bigger and wider.

"Uh oh, honey, looks like you've lost your shoes," said Willie.

With that, the crowd roared with laughter. Emma included. She punched Willie on his arm and threw her head back to sing along. The crowd went crazy, and next thing Scott knew, they were all dancing and singing along, including himself, "Huh. I didn't even know I knew the words to this song."

Hours later, after having said their good-nights to everyone, including Willie Nelson and his friend Mickey Raphael, the legendary harmonica player, Emma sat on Aunt Zoe's front porch steps with Olivia, Maggie, Sarah Kate and Alex. They had shooed Aunt Zoe to bed and cleaned up what had been left behind after the caterers cleared out, finding a few assorted pieces of clothing in some odd out of the way places. Including a bright red strappy sandal belonging to, not surprisingly, Emma, who was left wondering where the other one might be.

Emma hadn't seen Eli again after he left to sing with the band. After a couple hours, she wandered around looking for him. Casually, of course. After all, they were only casual friends now, nothing more. She ran across

Ethan, Jr. and asked – casually – if he'd seen his brother. Ethan said Eli had been up since four a.m. working on the gallery and was so tired, he fell asleep in a chair. Ethan said he took Eli home and put him in bed. Emma told him that was good. Eli needed the rest.

Still, it would have been nice if he'd come over to say good night.

"Wow. What a party, huh?" Sarah Kate said.

"Did you know Willie Nelson was going to be here?" asked Olivia

"Are you kidding?" Emma said, "I wouldn't have been able to take that nap this afternoon if I'd known that!"

"Wow," whispered Maggie, "Willie Nelson."

"Only on Whimsey," said Alex as she turned around to finger Maggie's earrings, "These are scrumptious earbobs you're wearing, girl."

"Thanks," Maggie said, "One of my best gal pals made them for me." She nodded in Emma's direction.

Emma leaned forward and kissed Magie's cheek, "And this gal pal is happy you like them. Happy Belated Birthday."

"I want a pair, too."

"Harumph. Me, too."

"And me, too, pretty please."

Emma laughed, "Well, my pretty little greedies, it just so happens there's a pair for each of you in my bag upstairs. I meant to give them to you today, but well - we've been a little busy, haven't we?"

That little understatement was met with laughter, followed by a few yawns.

"We're all tired," Emma said, "Let's save them till tomorrow, okay?"

Maggie looked up from the book she was reading, one that had been left on the porch by a guest the evening before, "When is Aunt Zoe giving us the grand tour of the new Gallery Les étoiles?"

"Not for a few days yet, she said," Emma replied. "She said she wants to sleep late tomorrow - actually, that would be today, wouldn't it? She says she has a few last minute things to finish up before she'll let us see. The grand opening is still a few weeks away. Surely she'll let us in before that!"

Maggie snorted, "Pfft. She's never slept late a day in her life."

"True enough," said Olivia. "She's just saying that so we can all sleep in without feeling guilty. Don't you adore Aunt Zoe?"

Alex turned toward Emma with a devious grin, "Oh, golly, yes. But you know Emma here takes after her aunt. She'll be up at the crack of dawn taking that morning run of hers. Right, Emma?"

Emma chuckled and raised her hands in surrender, "Yep. Busted."

"And where might you be running to so bright and early, m'dear?" asked Olivia with one eyebrow arched higher than the other.

Sarah Kate stared at Olivia and began scrunching her face in odd shapes trying to raise one eyebrow, "How do you do that thing with your eyebrow, Olivia? I've been trying to copy that for about a hundred years."

"Quit doing that, Sarah Kate," said Maggie. "You're scaring me with those faces!"

"Yes, Emma dear, where will you be running to tomorrow?" asked Alex.

"Why do you think I'm running anywhere in particular?"

The women all shared a look.

"Well, you know," Olivia said, "we couldn't help but notice how happy you and Eli seemed to be to see one another this evening."

"Well, you old silly," said Emma, "Of course we were happy to see one another. We've always been happy to see one another. You know that. We're friends. We're both happy to be friends again, but that's all."

"Um hmmmm."

"He's an early riser, too, as I recall."

"Um hmmmmm."

"Yep," said Emma, "I seem to recall the same thing, but me getting up early and running tomorrow morning doesn't have a thing to do with Eli Tatnall." She shook her head, "Tacky women."

"Pfft!"

"Tacky!"

"Oh, ho, ho."

"I wouldn't be tossing the word *tacky* around so freely if I were you," said Alex, pointedly looking at Emma's bare feet. "You're the one whose shoes keep showing up under bushes, in gutters and oh Lordy, look - there's one up on the roof!"

All heads turned to look up on Zoe's roof and sure enough, there sat one lonely looking strappy red sandal.

"How the . . . . "

They all collapsed into one another's arms laughing, agreeing to leave the shoe there till later. Somebody, maybe Jonathan or one of the guys, would bring out a ladder and get it down.

Saying their good nights, the women went their separate ways to walk home and get some well-earned sleep.

Olivia stopped and hollered back, "Don't forget, Emma, your folks and Jonathan and the kids are expecting you tomorrow for lunch. Come on over whenever you want though, okay?"

"Will do. See you then. Love you, Olivia!"

"Love you back, Emma."

CHAPTER SEVENTEEN

Even after only a couple hours of sleep, Emma was wide awake at five a.m and feeling happy with her lot in life. Pulling on shorts, a Tshirt and her tennis shoes, she looked forward to a run on the beach.

"Hey, you guys want to join me for my run this morning?"

Pyewackett peeked over the covers, put her head down and went right back to sleep. Fred growled and rolled over.

Clearly dismissed, Emma chuckled as she made her way down the stairs and out the front door.

Before heading toward the beach, Emma circled the house, stepped up on the pier and walked to the end. Just as she thought, she found Aunt Zoe there with a book and a cup of coffee.

"Good morning, Auntie mine," she said as she leaned over to give Zoe a kiss on the cheek.

"Emma! Good morning, dear. Going for your morning run, I see."

"Yes, this early morning thing runs in the family, you know."

"It surely does," She turned to wave to Great Aunt Elizabeth up on the third floor of the big house.

Emma waved too, "Can everybody on Whimsey see her, or just family?"

"Well, now, I'm not sure. I'm guessing, though, she allows the whole world to see her. Elizabeth was never one to keep her light under a basket. Why would she start now just because she up and died?"

They shared a laugh but quickly stopped as Elizabeth raised her voice to yell across the marsh, "I can hear you, you know. My hearing's better than it ever was."

Chastised, they both mumbled "Sorry, Auntie" under their breath and pretended none of that had just happened.

"Coffee, m'dear?"

"No, I'm going to run along. Maybe I'll get some in town at the bakery."

"Sounds perfect. Tell Ellie I said "Hey," and bring home a few of her croissants if there's any left when you get there. Enjoy your run."

"Bye, Auntie. See you later."

"Later, love."

Emma ran her familiar route across the island, waving to other early risers along the way. She ran across the street, over the boardwalk, across the dunes and down the beach to the shoreline.

As she ran, her thoughts meandered, and she gave herself over to the rhythm of the surf as it gently caressed the sand.

After a long hard run, she dropped her speed for a while to cool down and then dropped her bottom onto the beach for a rest. She leaned back on her hands and stared out over the ocean, not thinking a thing, just enjoying this moment of being.

"I'm so glad to be back home," whispered Madeline.

"Oh, Madeline. Me too."

After a while of sitting, a shadow passed over her, and she looked up to see Eli standing over her, "Mornin', Eli."

"Mornin', Darlin', as Ol' Willie would say."

"Wow. Willie Nelson. Can you believe it? Did you know he was going to be here?" asked Emma, smiling widely.

"Ha! You give me a little more credit than I deserve if you think I travel in those kinds of circles. The story I hear is that Willie's been doing some writing, and he and your brother Jonathan have crossed paths a few times. Jonathan mentioned, more than once, I understand, how many concerts of Willie's you've been to, and the man was dying to meet you. And, of course, you charmed him just like you have every other man who has had the pleasure of meeting you.

"Oh, you."

Eli laughed, "I'm going to finish my run. Care to join me?"

"I don't know. I'm just getting back into this running thing, and I don't want to overdo."

Eli nodded, "Smart girl. Well, how about coffee at my place?"

Emma shook her head, "No, thanks. I think I'd better be getting back."

"Scared?" Eli asked.

"Scared? Of what?" Emma asked in a huff.

"Oh, I don't know, you tell me," Eli said as he turned and started running.

Emma started running, passed him, left him in her tracks and shouted, "Meet you at your place!"

It didn't take her long to reach Eli's and as she approached, she saw him sitting on the front porch of his tabby cottage. It was one of the original Whimsey cottages, and had belonged to his great grandfather. Eli's brother Ethan lived here before he and Bay got married, when Eli took it over. The two brothers spent a lot of time restoring the cottage and bringing it up to date, and Emma was curious to see what it now looked like.

She stopped and put her hands on her hips, "How did you get here before me?"

"I know a shortcut. Nanana boo boo," And Eli stuck his tongue out at her.

"Pfft! Nice. Real nice. Now how 'bout acting like a grown-up and let me have that cup of coffee you promised, please."

"At your service, darlin'."

Eli handed her a hot cup of coffee, already fixed exactly as she liked it, in one of Maggie's red pottery mugs, "Let me know how it is."

"Delicious! Do I taste honey?"

"You do. Eli Tatnall Honey, one of the things I've recently gotten into. I have some hives scattered around the island."

"You are full of surprises, Eli." Emma held up the mug and examined it, "Aren't these mugs something? I'm in love with them."

"They are. I'm pretty over the moon about them myself. They just fit my hand, and they keep my coffee hot forever. And, of course, they're not bad looking either, I might add."

"Not bad looking? They're gorgeous!"

When she saw he was laughing, she realized he was teasing her - yet again.

"Oh, you."

"Sit, Emma. Let's let you rest from your run and enjoy the morning while it's still quiet and peaceful. I expect you have another busy day ahead of you."

"Lovely idea. This really is my favorite time of day. Look at that sky. Whenever I get to watch a sunrise, I know there has to be someone up there I need to thank. Can beauty like this just happen?"

"Oh, Emma. You're asking some pretty hard questions early this morning. You always have had a soft spot for sunrises. For all of Mother Nature's glory, really."

"I think I've about decided I'm a Pantheist."

"Is that right?"

"Are you making fun of me again?"

"Never!"

They shared a laugh and watched the sky as it changed colors, and the sun came up out of the ocean.

"What a view you have here, Eli. I could sit on this porch forever."

"My great grandfather pretty much had his pick of spots to build back then. I'm guessing he was a big a fan of watching a sunrise as you are."

"He must have been a lovely man."

"Like all us Tatnall men."

"For real."

"Emma, you know one of the things – one of the many, I might add - that had ol' Willie charmed last night?"

"How did we get back to him? He's not a Tatnall, is he?"

"Not that I'm aware of, no. But he was very curious about the silver glitter you scattered about while you were singing along with him. Congratulations, by the way, for not missing a single word. That was pretty impressive."

"Thank you again, Eli. You're just full of nice compliments this morning. I do not, however, wish to talk about this imagined silver glitter you speak of."

"Emma, you crack me up."

"That damned Earlene. She's the one who's done this to me. She thinks it's funny that I shed silver glitter everywhere I go. I try to pretend I don't notice even though I know everyone else does. I want to kill her. Actually, I think I will kill her. Maybe even today. Ha! Yep. That's what I'll do. It's good to have a plan."

"You are not going to kill Earlene. You know you don't really want to do that."

"Don't be so sure, Bucko."

"Well, your Aunt Zoe is not going to allow you to do that."

Emma slumped down in her chair, "You're right. I'll have to figure out a way to hide it from her."

Eli spit coffee through his nose and got choked.

Emma got tickled and they both fell into gales of laughter.

After a while, Eli wiped his eyes. "Emma, seriously. Tell me, please, what it is between you and Earlene. She's perfectly nice to the rest of us - well, as nice as a wicked little old pixie can be, I reckon. But she really does know how to push your buttons. I don't understand. Never have."

"Oh, Eli, I wish I knew. Do you know the very first time I ever met her I was so excited. I mean, a pixie! A real live pixie living in Aunt Zoe's house. How cool was that? I was just a little girl, and there she was with that outrageous bright red hair of hers piled up in a teeny little beehive on her teeny little head. She was sitting in a teeny little leopard skin chair watching a teeny little TV. And she was wearing silver high heels and a bikini. Purple. With polka dots."

"You're making this up."

"Swear to God. I am not making it up. Ask Aunt Zoe, she was there. So I looked at this crazy little pixie and said 'are you TinkerBelle?' It made her mad as all get-out. She looked at me and said 'TinkerBelle?! Hell no, honey, I'm Earlene. Don't you forget it.' And she's been mad at me ever since. She makes my shoes disappear. She makes me sprinkle glitter wherever I go. What's next?! I am just going to have to kill her. Simple as that." She slumped even further down in her chair.

"Oh, now, let's think on this. I'll bet we can come up with another solution before we do anything as drastic as all that. What say? Can we think on it?"

"All right. If you come up with anything, let me know. But it better be pretty soon. In the meantime, can I see what you've done to the cottage?"

"I thought you'd never ask! C'mon," Eli took Emma by the hand and walked her to the front door. "Wait. I have a question I really need to ask you."

Emma turned slowly. "You sound serious, Eli. What is it?"

"Where do you think Earlene shops? I mean, is there a little bitty pixie department store that sells all that itty bitty stuff, or what?"

Emma wagged her head back and forth. "Eli, you are crazy. Certifiably crazy."

"Well, okay, so you don't know either. Let me show you the house where everything is, I guarantee, regular size for regular size people. After you, darlin'."

Emma stopped short as soon as she entered.

"Oh, Eli."

Morning light filled the small cottage through old eight-over-eight windows with wavy glass panes, and the newer stained glass windows which had been added in a pattern around the room, but appeared at first look to be placed randomly.

"Who did the stained glass?"

"Jacob, mostly. A couple of the old pieces he had stored away which I was able to talk him out of for a price."

"I love how he's integrated so much etching and beveling."

"It takes him a long time to get a piece finished, but worth the wait."

Emma walked slowly around the room and realized there was nothing random about anything in this jewel box of a home Eli had created.

"Everything is perfect! How did you do all this? I'm overwhelmed."

"It's been a learning experience, but I picked up Jay Shafer's THE SMALL HOUSE BOOK, and one of the first things I read was a quote by someone about not having anything in your home that isn't useful, or that you believe to be beautiful. It's harder to do than you realize, but once I put my mind to it, I was able to cull out a lot of unnecessary things, or things that just really didn't add to the feeling I wanted."

"But you've managed to find the perfect spots for pieces done by your artist friends from Whimsey."

"Of course. They're beautiful, and in their own unique way, useful. They create the environment I feel at peace in."

Emma dropped into an overstuffed butter soft leather chair and propped her feet up on the ottoman, "Wow. I'm in love with this place."

She admired the handwoven rugs scattered across the pine plank floor, knowing them to be Alex's work. She recognized small paintings on the linen cream walls done by Aunt Zoe and Olivia, and two black and white photos done by her mother. The pottery lamp to her left was most definitely a piece done by Maggie, the shade covered with a piece of ecru lace made by Sarah Kate.

Her eyes kept going back to one small photo hanging inside the bookshelves. As she made her way over, trying to place where she recognized the scene from, it suddenly came to her. That was her tree. The very tree she had unconsciously gravitated to last night and where Eli had found her. The photograph had been shot at dusk when the sky was streaked with a little bit of lavender turning a deep plum, with the tree's shadow looking lacy across the pale green grassy area outside Zoe's home. A wicker loveseat sat under the tree with a pair of bright pink flip-flops tossed carelessly in front of it and a book face down on the seat next to a big straw hat.

"That's my hat."

"It sure is. Do you still have it?"

"I do. It's pretty beat up, but I love that hat." She turned to look at Eli and asked, "Did you take this?"

Eli reached up and scratched his head self-consciously, "I did. I had been with your mom all day taking a photography lesson. She dragged me all over this island trying to teach me to be more aware when it came to composition. She was getting pretty aggravated with me 'cause I wasn't seeing what she was seeing. But when we were in the process of doing the developing, she was fairly impressed with this one. Said she just knew I had that certain something I needed to be a good photographer if I would just let it come to me, and that this shot proved it. Do you like it?"

"I do. Very much."

She turned to look at him and the look they shared seemed to shift something in them both.

Flustered, she turned away, "So. What other treasures do we have here?" She fingered the books, not surprised at how eclectic the collection was, and picked up several random doodads scattered amongst the books, including a few old shells and seaglass."

"It's lovely, Eli. You deserve to be quite proud."

"Why thank you, darlin' - it means a lot to hear you say that. It's been a fun and rewarding project. But I still have one more thing to show you. It's upstairs in the loft where the bedroom is."

The climbed the stairs and Emma gasped as she saw the sloped roof was one big skylight. "Whoa. Talk about being able to enjoy the Whimsey stars!"

Eli grinned, "Yeah, I couldn't resist doing this when it was time to replace the roof. Why pass up an opportunity like that?"

"Gorgeous quilt," Emma said as she fingered the old quilt hanging on the wall behind the headboard of the old white iron bed.

"Mama says her mother made that," Eli said softly, "and gave it to her and my dad as a wedding gift. She's loaned it to me. I couldn't bring myself to take it when she tried to give it to me, so it's here on loan." Eli shook his head as he chuckled, "My mom. Always gonna have her way, you know."

Emma moved towards the window, "And, oh my, Jacob outdid himself with this piece. It's exquisite!"

"That's what I wanted to show you. Look closely. At the center."

Emma moved closer and looked at the red bull's eye center of the large piece of stained glass, "Is that what I think it is?! Is that one of my pieces? I think I made that brooch for your mom when I was just a kid!"

Eli nodded, "You were sixteen, I think, and gave it to her for Christmas. The pin broke on the back and she never wanted to tell you she had been that careless, so she kept it in a dish on her dresser where she could look at it often. I begged it off her when I was working with Jacob on the colors for this piece. We kinda worked around that brooch. Turned out to be the piece Jacob is the proudest of."

Emma stood back so she could see the whole piece and take it in. It was like one of Aunt Zoe's collages, only done in glass. Jacob had captured the essence of Whimsey, including a heron, the marsh, the dunes and the stars. And the light. The light that seemed to set the island apart in a world all its own. And there in the center was one of the first pieces of jewelry she had done all on her own with no help from her granddad, "Wow. I don't know what to say. I feel like I've walked into Alice's Wonderland here. What did you put in my coffee anyway?"

They laughed and Eli said, "Must be the magic honey."

After a biscuit with homemade honey and a second cup of coffee on the front porch, Eli filled her in on what had been happening on Whimsey and some harmless local gossip.

A short while later, Emma turned to Eli, "Well, this has been lovely, Eli. Thank you."

"Sure. We'll do it again," Eli said, "I need to take some hives over to the mainland this afternoon. Care to join me?"

Emma wanted so badly to say yes, but decided she shouldn't. She had to keep it casual.

Laws, she was starting to hate that word.

"Oh, golly, I'd love to, but better not. Not today."

"Another day then," He got up and walked toward the kitchen door. "I'll get a couple jars of honey for you to take home with you."

As Emma was waiting she was attacked by a large, heavy furry animal with rings around its tail jumping up onto her lap.

Eli came running out to the porch when he heard her scream and arrived to see her with her hands over her face yelling loudly something that sounded like "Raccoon! Raccoon! Get it off! Get it off!"

He scooped up the animal and let it curl around the back of his neck like a fur stole, then pulled Emma's hands away from her face, but noticed she kept her eyes closed.

"Shhh, shhh. Emma, honey, it's all right. It's only Bertha."

After a long silence, she said, "You have a raccoon named Bertha?"

Eli chuckled, "No. No raccoons. Bertha is my Maine Coon cat."

Emma finally opened her eyes and they grew huge when she saw Bertha around Eli's neck, "Good Lord! That's a cat? How much does she weigh?

Eli nodded, "She is indeed a cat, and a beauty, isn't she? She weighs about twenty pounds, I think, but probably looks heavier 'cause of all this long hair. Bertha here's my baby." And with that, Bertha gave a loud yowl.

Emma laughed, "What a clown she is, and yes, she is beautiful." She reached her hand out for Bertha to sniff. Bertha sniffed, then stared unblinking at Emma for a very long time. She then hopped off Eli's shoulder back onto Emma's lap. She rubbed against Emma while purring loudly.

"Friends, you think?" Emma asked.

Eli nodded, "Looks like."

"Whew. That's good, huh? I think if Bertha here decided she wanted me out of the picture, darned if she couldn't find a way to make sure it happened."

Bertha leaped from Emma's lap onto the porch rail. She was grooming her huge fluffy tail when Fred and Pyewackett strolled up on the porch. Pyewackett joined Bertha on the rail, and Fred hopped up on the glider, both acting as though they belonged here.

Emma looked at Eli, "Do they visit often?" she asked with her head cocked to one side.

Eli shook his head, "No. Not unless they visit with Bertha while I'm not at home. That's possible, I suppose."

They looked at one another and started laughing.

"Oh, God, I love this place." Emma said.

"Welcome home, darlin'."

"Speaking of home, I need to get on my way,"
Emma accepted a basket filled with several jars of honey,
and started her walk back to Aunt Zoe's.

CHAPTER EIGHTEEN

It was a gorgeous day and still early. She was expected at Olivia's for lunch, but her parents would enjoy some alone time with Jonathan, Olivia and the children until she got there, so she decided to take a detour to the downtown square.

Emma couldn't get Eli's cottage out of her mind. She was stunned at the simple beauty of the place Eli had turned into his home, and impressed that he had done it all himself. He had quite an eye for putting things together.

"Wow," said Madeline.

"You said it."

Emma realized she was smiling. It had been a nice morning. She and Eli had fallen easily into their casual banter they had had as children and later as close friends. Maybe it was possible they could be close friends again, nothing more than that, and forget all the serious and bad stuff that happened between them. It would appear that it hadn't been too hard for Eli to move on without her in his life, so settling for friends would have to suffice. That was fine with her. Suit her to a T, it would.

In the short time she'd been back, it was becoming more clear to her that as much as things were still the same on the island, a lot had changed. Of course it had. Had she expected time to stand still waiting for her to wise up, grow up, and move back home? Actually, she realized, that's exactly what she expected. But the truth was beginning to settle in. They had all grown. Not just in years, but in depth and all the ways that were more important than counting the years.

They had all been shaped and molded by their past into who they now were, how they were living their lives, and planning their futures. Emma was brought up a little short realizing she was included in this group. She had a future and plans and it felt lovely.

I wonder if I'm now suffering from cottage envy after seeing Eli's place? Emma giggled to herself.

Finding a place to live on Whimsey was no small task where the building restrictions were so tough. Necessarily so, in order to keep Whimsey the paradise it was instead of allowing it to become just another commercialized piece of tackiness where the original beauty that had lured people there in the first place was completely demolished and paved over.

The storefronts never seemed to change, but were always brightly painted and well cared for. This was comforting for the slightly melancholy state of mind she was in. It made her smile to see the large wooden barrels of fresh flowers on the sidewalk in front of all the shops and the flower beds circling the white gazebo which had sat in the center of the square for as long as Emma could remember.

The first shop she came to was Ellie's Bakery. Peeking in the window, she spotted Ellie putting a tray of freshly baked baquettes in the display case. Ellie looked exactly the same today as Emma remembered her looking when she would visit here as a little girl. A short, softly round woman of about sixty, with whispy white fly-away hair. She sang out "Woo hoo," as she opened the door and watched Ellie's face break into a big smile. As always, there was flour in Ellie Hampton's hair, along with a spot of it on her nose.

"Honey, come on in here and give me a hug!"

After a short visit, during which Ellie added to Emma's growing repertoire of local gossip, Emma hugged Ellie and left with a bag of baquettes to take to Olivia's.

Just as Emma heard the bell tinkle over the door as it closed behind her, she heard a familiar voice.

"Well, well, if it isn't Miss Emmaline Hamilton Foley."

Emma felt the hair stand up on the back of her neck when she heard that whiney voice.

She turned and faced Reese Prescott. Not for the first time, Emma was struck by just how very odd looking Reese was. She seemed to go out of her way to make herself stand out, but it always seemed to go badly. Her latest attempt was, apparently, Goth. Emma's thoughts were that Reese might be a little old to be making this statement, especially since she was making it so strongly. Her hair was cut to a gelled and spiked quarter-inch and was dyed flat black. Her make-up was deathly white with the expected black eye make-up and vampire red lipstick. She had earrings going from top to bottom of both ears and a too-large diamond stud in her nose. Reese was layered in black, including a long duster which hit the tops of her black boots. At least the duster is silk, Emma thought to herself.

Determined to be pleasant, Emma smiled, "Why, hello, Reese, how lovely to see you. You're looking well"

"Uh huh. Lovely to see you, too."

After an awkward silence, Emma said, "Well, hate to run, but Olivia's expecting me. I sure don't want this bread to get cold before I get there. Ta Ta!"

"Ta Ta? Is that what they say in Atlanta? Ta Ta? Don't tell me you're going to play the big city girl card and put on airs now that you're back on Whimsey. That would be pretty hard to take coming from you."

"No. No indeedy. No airs from this country mouse. See you later, Reese," And she tried to step around Reese to continue on her way.

But Reese stepped in front of her, "I see where your parents are back on Whimsey also. I know you must be happy to see them. Bless your heart, you saw them so seldom when we were all children. My mother always talked about what a shame it was they were never around and basically abandoned you and Jonathan for Zoe to raise. I expect they're making every effort they can, now that Jonathan has become somewhat famous, to get back into the fold, so to speak. And who knows, I suppose they're thinking you might make a little bit of a name for yourself with the little trinkets you're making. It just wouldn't do, after all, for them to be left out of the spotlight now, would it?"

And with a sly smile, a nod of her head, a wave tossed over her shoulder and a murmured "Ta Ta," Reese turned slowly around and started walking away. She stopped and turned around to look at Emma, "You better believe you'll see me later, Emma Foley. You just better believe it."

Emma was chilled to her very core, not only by the words, but by the cold meanness she'd seen in Reese's eyes. Speechless, she suddenly just wanted to be away from Reese Prescott and craved the warmth of a friend. As Emma went flying down the street she heard another familiar voice calling after her, "Where's that fire, girl?"

She spun around to see Harry Lanier hanging his head out the door of his floral shop.

"Harry! Oh, hey! Am I glad to see you," She ran over and gave him a long hard hug.

"Well, sweetie, good to see you too! Come on in for a minute."

Emma walked into the small flower shop holding Harry's hand. Harry was all of six feet, six inches tall a foot taller than Maggie. He was quiet, and seemed somewhat aloof until you realized he was observing everyone and everything around him before allowing himself entry into a group or conversation. He and Maggie, whose personalities were as different as night and day, complemented one another. Few people knew about the many causes they were quietly dedicated to, helping with both their time and their money.

"Great party last night," Harry said, "But you look like you're distressed about something. What's going on?"

"Harry, I do have a little something worrying me. I bumped into that odd Reese Prescott and all her weirdness on my way over here," Emma gave a little shudder. "The girl always did give me the creeps."

"Gives me the creeps, too. You know, sometimes I start feeling sorry for her, and I swear I'm going to try to be nicer, then she lets some nasty comment fall out of her mouth, you know how she does, and then I realize she is one dangerous piece of work. She's always had it out for you, and now that you're back, I'd advise watching your back."

"Oh, Harry, she's just weird is all. And sneaky. And a proven liar. But, you know, she's not dangerous. I have to admit though, she does seem to get creepier and creepier."

Harry nodded, "I've been watching her, Emma. I'm not so sure you're right about her being weird, but harmless. She might be more dangerous than any of us are giving her credit for."

Emma shivered, "Oh, we're both being silly. You've been reading too many books. We'll talk about this again though, okay?"

"You bet. A quiet night for dinner with you, me and Maggie. You and Maggie pick a day and let me know." Harry handed her a bouquet he had been holding. "I can't let you leave without a little something. Welcome Home."

Emma gave him another hug and a kiss on the cheek. "Oh, Harry, thank you. These are incredible."

Harry smiled as he watched Emma bury her face in the bouquet of lavender hydrangeas and white tulips. "Enjoy, and tell Aunt Zoe I'll be by to see her soon."

She thought about what Harry had said as she walked. Surely, he was being overly imaginative about Reese, but the look in her eyes when she first spotted

Emma had been enough to startle her. "I'll need to talk to the girls about this and see what they think."

Emma arrived home to an empty house. She felt a little restless and wanted to gather her wits after her confrontation with Reese. After pouring a tall glass of iced latte, she walked to the end of the marsh pier and sat in one of the old adirondack chairs that had been there as long as the house. The marsh sounds were hushed but busy, and Emma imagined hundreds of creatures up and down the food chain exchanging opinions and taunts. She was able to catch ripples in the water out of the corner of her eye, wondering if it might be a fish or something else that might have just caught a fish for lunch. Emma inhaled deeply and smelled the salty water mixed with the plants decomposing which brought forth a fragrance like no other. Not altogether pleasant for someone unfamiliar with coastal wetlands, but a whole lot more pleasant to Emma than the air she'd been breathing more recently in Atlanta – and the nastiness she'd just endured from Reese Prescott. She needed this dose of Whimsey cleanliness to wipe all that out of her mind.

Her thoughts were interrupted by shouts of, "Aunt Emma, Aunt Emma," accompanied by childish giggles, and she spun around to catch Max as he launched himself into her arms.

"Whoa, big boy, you'll have us swimming in the muck if you're not careful!"

As she squatted to set him back on the pier with one arm around his waist, she reached with her other arm to pull her niece Abby into a hug, "Oh, you guys! You are both more beautiful every single time I see you! Let me squeeze the goodness right out of you both!"

Abby squealed and giggled and flung her arms around her aunt's neck, "Welcome home, Aunt Emma. I love you."

"And I love you back, little miss. Has your hair gotten redder?! You and Max look like your heads are on fire with all that gorgeous red hair!"

"Mama says it's good we got her hair 'cause if we had Daddy's hair we would look like itty bitty little old people," said Max with a great deal of sincerity and seriousness.

Abby could be heard to say a soft, "Oh," as she put a hand up to cover her mouth.

"Oh, she did, did she? Does that mean she thinks your daddy and I both look old just 'cause we have silver hair? Harumph. We'll just see about that when she and I chat, won't we?"

"Aunt Emma, don't pay any attention to Max. You know how boys are. He just got that all mixed up."

"Did not!"

"Did!"

"Sweeties, it's okay. I promise. Your mom and I have had this chat before. Not to worry. She just likes to tease us. And where is she anyway?"

Max pointed to their house down the marsh shoreline, "She's at home. She sent us down here to get you."

"She's fixing us lunch," said Abby," and she didn't want you to miss out 'cause she says she knows how much you like shrimp salad."

"Shrimp salad! My favorite! Yum, let's go, shall we?"

The three of them walked along the marsh holding hands as they approached the big house.

Emma looked up and realized she had always taken this grand old house for granted. She had heard it referred to as imposing, but never really thought of it that way until now. It was indeed a stately old place, and some of Elizabeth's somewhat regal nature must have rubbed off on it during the years she was its matriarch.

The house was built in 1949, but designed to look much older. Elizabeth loved the grand old rice plantation homes of the Lowcountry, and had this one built to somewhat copy one she especially loved, Grove Plantation on the Edisto River.

Elizabeth's house was a perfect example of late Federal style architecture, three stories tall, in a raised cottage design. The front of the house rested on pillars of brick, and on arches at the rear of the house - a feature indigenous to the region known as a "raised basement." Raised in order to take advantage of the cross currents coming off the ocean and the marshlands. The basement in Elizabeth's house plan was a modernized version with the first floor being a living level. Bedrooms along with art studios for both Ben and Lillith were on the second floor.

The third floor was also altered from the original to be Elizabeth's apartment with everything she would need to be completely self-sufficient, including a piazza across the back overlooking the marsh she so loved.

Over time, a guest bungalow was built on the property which now housed Jonathan Foley's writer's retreat. Downstairs was a comfortable common room, individual suites for paying retreat clients, a lecture studio, and a small, well stocked eat-in kitchen with a fulltime chef. The bungalow included an upstairs apartment set up for the Writer in Residence, which changed each year

When Emma opened the front door, the laughter of her family wrapped itself around her like a hug. Max and Abby ran across the foyer and disappeared into the great room where, from the sounds of it, the family was gathered. Emma was anxious to join them, but needed a moment to herself first

The excitement of seeing Max and Abby had worn off, and her encounter with Reese Prescott flooded over her again. She leaned back against the door, closed her eyes, and the memory of the hateful words Reese had thrown at her came rushing back. She had never felt abandoned as a child, but somehow, the zinger had found its mark and pierced her heart.

"Emma? Sugar? Are you all right, my darling?"

Emma opened her eyes and saw the concerned face of her mother. Startled by her own emotional reaction to seeing this face she loved so very much and feeling her arms around her, Emma hiccupped and hugged her mother close, "Oh, Mama, I've missed you so much." And the tears poured, unbidden and unnoticed, down both their faces as they hugged wordlessly.

Zelda moved back, placed her hands on Emma's shoulders gently, and looked deep into her daughter's eyes, "Tell me."

And it all poured out. Emma started talking and seemed unable to stop. She told her mother about all the many times Reese had hurt her over the years and how she had just learned during the luncheon with the girls at Zoe's that she had also dated Hunter. She ended with the words Reese had thrown in her face earlier to ruin what had started as a perfect day. Emma admitted to being ashamed of the fact that Reese could still hurt her after all these years.

"No, Emma, you have nothing to be ashamed of. If you were hardened to her words, that would be the saddest thing of all because it would mean you had become as unfeeling as she is, and I know, love, that is never going to happen. Honey, that's why she dislikes you so much, because she knows in her heart of hearts that you are the better person. A person she can never be."

"Oh, Mama."

Giving her daughter a light kiss, along with another hug, she took her hand, "Go wash your face and let's join the others. What say?"

Emma nodded. "You bet."

"And Emmaline? You do know that all those things that witch said are simply not true, don't you? Your father and I love you and your brother above life itself. And always will."

"I do know that. I've never felt abandoned or unloved. Not for one minute. It's just . . . . I don't know how to explain it. I just feel out-maneuvered by her, and frankly, I'm a little scared of her."

"Oh Pafooey! You? Scared? Of some little guttersnipe of a girl? You can't be serious. And if you are, well, we're going to work real hard on getting you over that bit of trivialness, okay?"

With a mock salute and a giggle, Emma nodded her head, "Yes, ma'am!" And left to find a quiet spot to compose herself and wash her face.

CHAPTER NINETEEN

A few minutes later, Emma stopped outside the kitchen and leaned against the wall, smiling and listening to the sound of her family's voices mingling, interrupting one another and going about the business of getting lunch on the table with two puppies racing around underfoot.

"Tell me again whose idea it was to bring these monster dogs into the house?" Jonathan called out as he tripped over one dog while trying not to step on the other.

"Daddy, noooooooo - you'll hurt their feelings if you call them monster dogs," said Abby with a look of horror on her sweet face.

Olivia chuckled, "If I remember correctly, Jonathan, we sat down and had a family conference. At your request."

Max was hopping up and down in his chair, "Where's Aunt Emma? I'm hungry. Can we eat without her?"

"Here, here, I'm here," Emma walked around the kitchen giving everyone a hug before she sat down.

She looked around the room. Her mother and aunt were bent over a cookbook, oohing and ahhing over some recipe. Her father, with his reading glasses down on the end of his nose, was reading the newspaper, but still they each seemed fully engaged with the ongoing conversations happening around the table.

Jonathan handed a fat little pooch to Emma, "Here, Sis, hold Katy. She needs a smooch."

"Well, hello, Katy. What a doll you are."

"Oh, hell," Jonathan said, "Now you have to hold Hubbell, too. He cries if Katy gets too far away." And handed her the second puppy.

Emma laughed as both puppies squirmed around in her lap, yipping at one another and hopping up to lick her face, "They are too much! Are they Fred's children? Or grandchildren, cousins or what exactly? How many corgis are there on Whimsey anyway?"

Jonathan laughed, "More than in Buckingham Palace, by a long shot."

"The Queen would be proud," said Emma.

"Y'all," wailed Max, "I'm hungry! You said we were going to eat." He looked as though he might burst into tears any minute.

"Coming, coming - on the way," Olivia put a shrimp salad sandwich down in front of her son, and gave him a kiss on his head, "And here's your milk, and here's a basket of those kettle chips you love for you to pass around, please. Abby? Here's yours, sweetie. And will you pass the pickle tray around after you've helped yourself, please?"

Olivia plopped into the chair next to Emma, "Everyone else, you're on your own. Dig in!"

Emma leaned over and gave Olivia a kiss on her cheek, "Thanks, honeybun. Everything looks delish."

"And thank you, Emmaline, for bringing some of Ellie's bread. It is purely sinful, and I love it."

"Olivia, how many years have I been asking you not to call me Emmaline? Emma is my name."

She scrunched her face and stuck out her tongue at Olivia. Olivia returned the same gesture, and they giggled and hugged.

Then Emma got very quiet as she lifted Katy and Hubbell out of her lap and back onto the floor.

Abby, who was sitting on the other side of her, looked at her aunt's lap and said, "Uh oh, those puppies pee-peed on Aunt Emma's shorts."

The room broke up into laughter as Olivia led Emma away to have a quick wash up and a change of clothes.

Once things had settled down and everyone was comfortably seated around the table enjoying their lunch, Aunt Zoe tried to explain the pups' relationship to Fred. Scott piped up with, "Oh, Zoe, you may as well just not even try. There's no explaining southern bloodlines, and that includes southern dogs."

Emma had been staring at the wall, "Speaking of animals, is that a big mouse face I'm kinda sorta seeing on that wall? What IS that?"

Jonathan dropped his head, and she noticed his face was turning red. Everyone was looking in his direction, but he never looked up.

Olivia rolled her eyes, "Um hmmmm. Look closely. You'll see Mickey Mouse, Minnie, Donald Duck, Pluto, Dumbo and who knows who else. Aunt Zoe and I took the kids to Savannah one day a few weeks back, and Jonathan was in charge of painting this room, which hadn't been done in more years than any of us can recall. Well, you know how this place is - people in and out all day, every day. Eli dropped by, and then Jack. Then Gray and Harry. And they all offered to help paint so they could go out on Jack's boat. No one will confess to how the first Disney character found its face on our wall, but when we got home, that's what we found. Disney characters grinning at us from all around the room. We're fairly certain adult beverages were involved."

"And it was beautiful!" squealed Abby.

"VERY cool!" agreed Max.

"Well," said Olivia, "I seemed to have been the only one who didn't particularly care for the look. We painted over the faces, but as you can see, when the sun shines through those windows just right, there they are."

After a short stunned silence, the room erupted into laughter.

Emma and Zoe spent the rest of the afternoon at Olivia and Jonathan's with the family. They all had news and loads of things to catch up on and stories to share.

Later, while stretched out on one of the sofas in the living room, Emma looked over at Olivia, who was stretched out on the sofa with her, their heads at either end so they could face one another, "Olivia, you have done an amazing job. I'm quite proud of you. You've managed to continue keeping this house the same as it's always been, comfortable and homey, for all its formality."

Olivia nodded, "Thank you, sweetie. Elizabeth knew what she wanted, and she wanted a big plantation house. And the original one, Grove Plantation, that she adapted this house from was, indeed, quite formal. So we have the octagonal rooms, the molding and wainscoting and sweeping stairway, tall ceilings and chandeliers. Rooms that are huge. Windows that are forty-four beezillion times bigger than the average window, and ancient wood plank floors that are so thick nobody on God's green earth could or would even want to spend the money for these days. All that. But. What Elizabeth knew was it could be brought into, plain and simply - a home, by the spirit brought into the house by its inhabitants. It's a home meant for living. Not for show. Never just for show. The big rooms are big to hold lots of people comfortably. The windows are huge so all those people can enjoy the views of the beach, the dunes and ocean on one side, and the glory of the marshes on the other. Far be it for anyone in this huge extended family of ours to allow a mere building intimidate them into anything less than who we are. And who we are tends to be boisterous at the best of times, damned ungovernable and unseemly at the worst."

"So you mean, the house just feels lived in."

"Exactly."

And they cracked up.

"It's good to have you home, Emma."

"It's good to be home."

"Are you going to be happy now, you think."

Emma looked at her friend for a long time, then nodded, "Yes. I do."

"I think so, too. You're where you need to be now."

"Leave it to you, sister of my heart, to know that. I needed to leave Whimsey for a while, but I probably stayed gone too long. And probably for all the wrong reasons."

"I've missed you, Emma. I love my life. Never doubt it for a second. But without you here, it all seemed to fall just a hair short of perfect. Now, I know none of us should expect perfection in our lives, but dammit - why not? And with you back home, it feels perfect."

"Oh, Olivia, you're going to make me cry. I have cried more in the past two days than my entire lifetime. My emotions are just sitting right there at the very edge. I love having my family close. I want to watch your Max and Abby grow up. What wonderful little people they are already. You're a wonderful wife, and you have turned out to be a mother any kid would be lucky to have. I'm very proud of you. And, I have to say - having the rest of the Wicked Women here will be the icing on our cake, don't you think?"

"Thank you for that. I was scared to death about the whole mommy thing, but it turns out to be the most fun I've ever had. Those two little munchkins surprise me every day. Jonathan is a great daddy and watching the three of them interact is like watching a miracle happen right in front of my eyes. And I get to watch it over and over again. It is a lovely thing. And yep, I agree. Having Maggie, Sarah Kate and Alexandra all home, well, who knows what miracles we'll all get to witness."

"And fun! Don't forget how much fun it'll be!"

"Boy Howdy, will it be fun!"

They laughed, sat up and exchanged a high five, fluffed their pillows and settled back into their nests they had made for themselves on Olivia's big slouchy over-stuffed sofa.

Olivia cut her eyes at Emma, and with a sly little grin, asked, "Sooooo, what else is going to make you happy here, sweet pea?"

"What do you mean, devil girl?"

"HA! Okay, make me spell it out. Eli. How are you and Eli getting along?"

"Oh, Olivia. I don't really think Eli and I were ever meant to be more than we are right now. Friends. We'll always have a special connection that comes from having so much history between us. We've known one another since we were crawling around in diapers. In this house, as a matter of fact. And every other house on Whimsey, I guess. Me, Eli, you and all of us. But I don't think it's meant to ever be any more than that. And you know, I'm okay with that."

"Emma, we both know that the connection you're talking about has a bit more to it when it comes to you and Eli."

Emma lifted her coffee and took a sip as she gazed out the window. "I have never stopped loving Eli. Not for a minute. Not my entire life. Even when I married Hunter. Isn't that the saddest thing ever? Hunter deserved better." When she looked back at Olivia, the tears were standing in her eyes, "I'd never say this to another living soul, Olivia, but I deserved better too."

"Oh, Emma."

Olivia got up and took Emma in her arms and rocked her.

"Emma, sweetie, don't you think it's time to talk about all this? I know there are things you haven't told me, or probably anyone. Am I right?"

Emma stayed very still for several seconds, then nodded.

"Want to talk about it?"

Emma shook her head, "Not yet, Olivia."

Olivia stroked Emma's hair, "It's okay. I'll be here when you're ready. Okay?"

Emma nodded.

"It's gonna be all right. Everything is gonna be all right."

Emma had gotten up and washed her face and she and Olivia were chatting quietly when Zoe and Zelda walked into the living room holding hands and laughing.

"And what are you two pretties up to?" asked Zelda.

"Just chatting and catching up, you know how it is," answered Olivia.

"Well, this old gal is ready to head home," Zoe said. "Want to walk with me, Emma, or are you going to stay awhile longer?"

"I'm ready, Aunt Zoe. You know, I'm not used to all this activity and socializing. I don't see this many people in Atlanta during a whole week. I think I'll go to my apartment and curl up with a book. And I think I'll just plan on staying home tomorrow. I need to get back to the business of designing if I ever hope to be able to contribute to Les étoiles."

"Speaking of which," said Zelda, "Zoe, when do we get our sneak peek?"

"Right," added Scott, as he and Jonathan entered the room. "We're dying to see what you've done."

"You've got a whole group of very interested folks here, Zoe," agreed Jonathan. He gave Zoe a hug.

"Funny you should ask," said Zoe. "I called Ethan, Jr. right after we had lunch, and he tells me he and his crew are officially finished. He had them bring all the art in from the storage facility, and Eli is planning on having the same crew spend the next week helping him do the gallery staging. How about we have our own private showing a week from today, if that works for Eli."

"Hooray and Yippee Skippy!" shouted Emma.

"Yeah, what she said!" agreed Olivia.

CHAPTER TWENTY

Emma and Zoe walked home together, talking quietly about how nice it was for the family to be able to spend that time together. And how smart, funny and beautiful Abby and Max were. Both agreed they could do with a nap, but when they got closer, they saw Eli sitting in a rocker on the porch.

"Why, hello there, Eli," Zoe said. "I was going to bring out a pitcher of tea. How lovely to have you here to share it with us."

"I'd love that, Zoe. Thank you."

"Well, hey you," Emma said. "What's up?"

"Emma, we need to talk."

"Oh, God. Don't you know those are the worst words imaginable to say to anyone?"

Eli nodded.

Zoe appeared with a pitcher of tea which she placed on a table. "If y'all will excuse me, my leg's been bothering me a bit today. I've been trying to get around without my cane, and I can see it's too soon." She walked over and hugged Eli, then Emma, "But you two sit a spell and enjoy this breeze, I'll see you both a little later."

Emma and Eli were still looking at one another when Zoe went back inside the house.

Emma stood up to leave, "Whatever this is, I don't want to talk about it."

Eli stood also, "When I saw you in Atlanta that last time, you had a question you wanted to ask me. Why don't you ask it?"

"No," Emma tried to get around him, "It was nothing."

"Emma?"

"All right!" She shouted. "Yes. A question. I want you to tell me why you took up with Reese Prescott while I was away at college, and why you couldn't be up front about it and tell me."

"I thought it was something like this. And, Emma, I have tried to talk to you about this. I tried to talk to you about this back when you just broke it off with me without being up front your own self. Pretty hypocritical of you to be casting stones, I'd say."

Emma's eyes got huge, "WHAT? Hypocritical? How dare you! My heart was broken. But because of how stubborn I am, I couldn't tell anyone, so I carried it all on my own for ages and ages. I trusted you, Eli. I had trusted you since we were playing in our cribs together. I loved you. And you betrayed me."

Emma stopped talking because her voice was beginning to shake, and her lips were quivering.

Eli shoved his hands deep into his pockets and stared down. After a moment, he said quietly, "You should have, Emma."

"Should have what?"

"Told someone."

"Why? My heart would have still been broken."

"No. It wouldn't have because what you're saying never happened."

"Eli,I saw you. I came home from Savannah one weekend without telling anyone. When I arrived on the island, I went straight downtown looking for you. I thought you might be at the dock helping your dad. You were at the dock all right, but you were in your truck. And Reese was with you. She had her head on your shoulder, and you had your arm around her. Looked pretty cozy to me. And then I knew that all the things she had been taunting me with were true. You were seeing each other while I was gone. You were playing me for a fool, or just dangling me along so as not to hurt my feelings until you could think of a way to break it to me and break it off between us. So, I just thought I'd skirt all the drama and make it easy for you."

When Eli lifted his eyes to Emma's, she was startled to see there were tears in them.

Eli wiped a hand across his face and spoke softly, "I've been thinking about what you said that last time we saw one another in Atlanta. I didn't have a clue until that moment what had happened between us. All I knew back then was one week you were there and we were happy. The next week, you told me it was over and it was time to move on. Move on. Hell, Emma, I didn't have a clue where to go from there. Not without you. And I didn't want to try to figure it out. I was just lost."

Eli stopped and cleared his throat before he continued.

"When I left your place, I went back to my hotel room, and I sat down determined to figure out what the hell you were talking about and how Reese Prescott might have been involved. I was still puzzling it out when I got back here. It took a long time and a lot of piecing things together, but I think I finally figured it out. And I have to say this here and now, Emma. You were a fool."

Emma pushed him, "I want you to leave."

Eli shook his head, "No, ma'am. I'm not going anywhere until you hear me out this time. You can either sit back down or you can stand there with your arms crossed, but you're going to hear what I say."

Emma turned her back on him.

"If you'd told anyone on Whimsey what you'd seen, you would have gotten an explanation about why you saw Reese Prescott with me that afternoon. Reese didn't have many friends. I know, I know, she didn't really deserve them because she treated people badly. No excuses, but the girl was probably the loneliest little girl on Whimsey. None of us knew how sad her life really was. We only knew she lived with her mother and that her father was dead. Adele Prescott was a hateful shrew of a woman, not fit to be a mother. And she proved how hateful that day. That was the day she and Reese had a big fight and Adele told her - her only child - that it was her fault her father wasn't around. He wasn't dead, he was just gone. According to Adele, he said Reese was so needy and whiny he couldn't stand it, and he left. Never to be heard from again."

Emma sat down. She put her face in her hands.

"Can you imagine, Emma? Your own mother telling you that your father found you too whiny and needy? As a baby? Jesus." Eli raked his hand through his hair.

Emma couldn't quit shaking her head. This was just too much to take in. "So, Reese came to you? To tell you about the fight with her mother?"

"She did. Reese and I never had the relationship she tried to make you believe we had, but we were friends. I knew she was an unhappy person, and I just tried to treat her decently. The way I'd hope to be treated."

"All those years wasted."

"All of them."

"And now?"

"I don't know, Emma. I just don't know."

As they sat across the table from one another looking into one another's eyes, their hands found one another's and they just sat. Holding hands. There were no words to reach across all the years that had passed and all the years of what might have been.

After a very long time, Eli got up and slowly walked down the steps.

Neither of them said a word as he walked away.

Emma went inside and upstairs to her apartment, slipped out of her shoes and stretched out on her bed. She nudged Fred and Pyewackett aside so she could have enough of the bed to comfortably snuggle under the light throw. She fluffed up her pillows and picked up her book, pretending everything was fine. She could hear her aunt quietly singing as she roamed about the house. Emma smiled a wavery smile at the animals, and could have sworn they both smiled sad smiles back.

She sat up in the bed, stared out the window in the quiet and slowly sorted through the evening and the things she had just learned about Reese.

It seemed impossible that everything had gone as wrong as it had between her and Eli based on misinformation.

What Eli didn't know, and could never know, was none of it mattered any more.

It was too late.

CHAPTER TWENTY-ONE

Emma woke up groggy and disoriented. It was dark outside. Finally able to focus on the bedside clock, she couldn't believe it was 9:30 at night. Falling asleep late in the afternoon was unusual for her, and now she remembered why she didn't do it very often - at least, not on purpose.

The house felt too quiet, and that was disorienting also. She couldn't get Eli's visit, or his story, out of her mind.

She left her apartment and walked downstairs to the kitchen where she found a note from Aunt Zoe letting her know she had gone to Jacob's and for Emma not to wait up. And a PS to let her know Britta had made some of her yummy ceviche.

The note elicited a "hmmmmm" regarding the not waiting up part, and a "yum" regarding the ceviche, which she loved. Perfect.

Emma fixed herself a tray with a big pottery bowl filled with the cold seafood soup, a baguette and a glass of white wine. She left it in the kitchen to browse through a stack of books she'd spied next to Aunt Zoe's favorite chair, snagged a couple of the latest mystery novels and added those to her tray. Maybe a good mystery would help her forget what a mess she had made of her life. Maybe she'd even find a clue as to how to fix it.

When she got back upstairs, she spotted Fred and Pyewackett curled up together in one of her big red overstuffed chairs, both making little wiffle noises while they slept. "Aren't we the laziest bunch on God's green earth today?"

Emma pulled out a TV table and placed her tray on top, settled in the other red chair with her books.

Sated after her dinner, depressed and restless, and unable to concentrate on reading, she decided some soft music and a bubble bath might be just the thing to help her relax and think things through rationally.

Leaning back in the tub with her eyes closed, humming softly along with Diana Krall, a noise startled her. When she opened her eyes, she saw a shadow cross the skylight over her head and continue past the window. At the same time, Fred and Pyewackett came running into the bathroom. Pyewackett's hair was ruffled up along her back and Fred growled deep in his throat. "What the hell was that?" Emma jumped out the tub. threw on her robe, and ran down the steps to the front door. She had her hand on the doorknob when she realized she was about to do something stupid. Opening the door not knowing who was out there would be beyond dumb. Opening the door wearing nothing but a robe would make her too stupid to live.

She moved away from the door, pulled back the curtains, looked out the front window and tried to listen for someone running. She heard nothing but the sound of the waves and it was too dark to see anything. For a moment, she thought perhaps it was all her imagination, but only for a moment. Remembering how the animals reacted, she knew someone had been on the roof and had looked down at her through the skylight as she was bathing. She flipped the switch turning on the front porch light. She was shaking all over as she walked into the kitchen to use the phone, but her hands trembled so badly she dropped it. After she dropped it a second time, she slammed the receiver into the cradle in frustration and walked to the back door to flip on the outside light. By ignoring the "No Lights" ordinance, she knew what would happen, and the phone rang almost immediately. She was happy to answer it and happier still to hear Charlie Ostwalt's voice on the other end.

"Emma? Everything there okay? I've gotten a couple of calls about you and Zoe having your outside lights on. You're not gonna make me fine you for that, are you?"

Emma felt herself sliding down the wall until she was sitting on the floor. "Oh, Charlie, I'm glad it's you. Are you working by yourself tonight?"

"No, Harrison's here. I'll be right there."

Within what seemed like only seconds, Emma heard a knock at the door, and the familiar deep voice of Charlie Ostwalt announcing his arrival.

When she opened the door, the Chief came in, wrapped one arm around her shoulders, and walked her to a sofa in the living room. "Here, sugar, you sit and let me get you a glass of water. I'll turn off the outside lights, too. We don't want the whole island showing up here."

After a few minutes, he returned with her water, sat next to her, patted her hand and said, "Tell me."

By the time Emma had told her story, she had stopped being frightened, and moved to the stage of being angry.

"What pervert would crawl up on our roof like that? This is Whimsey, for God's sake! No one here is like that! Not unless you've had a sudden rash of Peeping Tom events that I haven't heard about yet. Have you?"

"Well, no. No. Of course not."

"Why do you say 'of course not!' It just happened, didn't it! You don't think I made this up?"

"Well, no. No. Of course not."

"Charlie! You're repeating yourself!"

"Listen, Emma. We're going to investigate this, but I gotta tell ya. This just beats all I've ever heard, and that's the truth."

Emma sighed and fell back against the couch, "I know, Charlie. I agree. So. What? Is it that proverbial 'wandering hobo' who just happened to be on my roof? A stranger that not one person on this island has noticed? I don't think so. Do you?"

"Well, no . . . ."

Emma cut him a look and he had the grace to look abashed.

"Emma, let's quit dancing around this, okay? Who on this island dislikes you and would like to scare you? I know you've been gone for a long time, but we both know if there was someone on your roof . . . yes, yes, okay . . . we both know the someone on your roof had to have been someone who knows you. Someone you know. So you need to be honest with me and tell me who's on that list of possibilities. Or, on the other hand, who on this island *likes* you - in his own perverted way - enough to want to catch a peek of you without you knowing?"

Emma looked appalled at either option, "Nobody!"

Chief Ostwalt just looked at her and continued looking.

She shook her head, "No. That makes no sense. No sense whatsoever."

"Tell me."

Emma stood up, "Chief, this could take a while. I'm going to fix some coffee for us, okay?"

He looked at his watch, shook his head, sighed, and said, "Okay, what the heck. I'm not going to get any sleep tonight anyway. Coffee sounds good."

They were sitting at the kitchen table when Aunt Zoe and Jacob came in the back door.

"What on earth? What's wrong? Charlie, why are you here? Is someone hurt? Why didn't you call me?"

Emma jumped up and hugged her aunt, "No, no, Aunt Zoe, everything's fine! Please calm down. Here, sit. Jacob ,you, too. Sit down. No one's hurt. If you'll just sit and calm down, we'll explain it all. I've got coffee brewing. It may be a long night."

After she'd told Zoe and Jacob about her harrowing evening, Emma said, "I know it doesn't make any sense that Reese Prescott would be up on our roof peeking at me through the sky light. It's ludicrous. The most ridiculous thing ever. And it's almost laughable. Almost. But, Chief, I swear to you, she's the only person on this island I know of who fits either of the scenarios you mentioned."

Chief Ostwalt looked at Zoe, "What do you think, Zoe? Can you think of anyone this could be? It doesn't necessarily have to be Emma who's the peek-ee. It could be you."

"Peek-EE?" Zoe exclaimed. "Charlie Ostwalt, you fool. Is that even a word?"

"Now, Zoe, no need to get like that. And Jacob, I see you trying to hold back that laugh. Go ahead, laugh, damn you. But, remember, there *was* somebody up on the roof of this house. And I can guaran-damn-tee you, there is no reason whatsoever that could possibly be a good one."

The realization that what he said was true brought a sobriety and somberness back to the room.

Zoe shook her head, "No, Chief, no one I can think of. Truthfully, the craziest person I know on this island is, unfortunately, Reese Prescott. And Reese does have a thing about Emma. And I'd have to say that hate is not too strong a word for it."

Charlie Ostwalt lowered his head, rubbed his hand across his short gray hair and sighed deeply. "Aye. She is one very odd bird, and that's the God's truth."

They all sat quietly around the table, each drinking their coffee and lost in their own thoughts about the odd bird named Reese Prescott.

Emma looked up, "I have an idea. "Whoever it was will come back. Isn't that right? The criminal always returns to the scene of the crime? Well, I can take my sleeping bag out on the roof and sleep there, and when she comes back . . . " She looked around the table and saw three faces looking at her as though she had lost her mind.

Her smile faded. She let her head drop to the table with a loud thump and groaned, "I have totally lost my mind."

Aunt Zoe reached out to touch her shoulder, "Now, Emma . . . . "

Chief Ostwalt nodded his head and agreed with Emma, "Yes, yes, I believe you have."

Emma lifted her head and sputtered, "Now wait just a minute. "

The Chief raised his hand, "Look, Emma, of course I don't think you've lost your mind. But you're not thinking clearly. And that's understandable after what you've experienced. But listen to me. If it was Reese on the roof, that means she's capable of more than just pranks. She could be dangerous and feeling cornered by you playing Nancy Drew. Setting up some elaborate trap you dreamed up on the spot could be just the thing to set her off. You stay out of this now, okay? We'll handle it. We may be a small force in a small town, but that doesn't mean we're complete idiots. I promise you, Emma, we'll get to the bottom of this. Now I need to get on back to the station. And the three of you need to get some sleep."

Jacob got up, too, "I'll walk out with you, Charlie, but then I'm coming back. No arguments, you two. I'll be sleeping here tonight."

Zoe smiled at Jacob and gave him a little pat on his face, "No arguments, Jacob. It'll be a comfort having you here."

Chief Ostwalt gave a tired wave, "We'll talk tomorrow. Night all."

After the Chief left, Zoe, Jacob and Emma stayed up only long enough to say their own good nights after making sure Fred and Pyewackett were safely inside and that the doors were locked.

CHAPTER TWENTY-TWO

When Emma opened her eyes the next morning, she turned towards the big bay window looking out over the beach and thought what a gorgeous day it was.

In the distance, the sky and the ocean melded into one huge expanse of shades of blue, calming and peaceful.

In just a few minutes though, she remembered last night and realized she was trembling. First with fear, then with the returning anger she had felt before falling asleep. When she sat up, she startled Fred and Pyewackett who both made noises of disgruntlement for being woken so early and so rudely.

"Oops, sorry, you two. I forget what lay-abouts you are. Whoa! Was that a dirty look I saw? I'm just playing. Don't get all grumpy on me, okay? Truth be told, I'm grumpy enough for the three of us."

"Four!" piped Madeline.

"For the four of us," said Emma.

Fred and Pyewackett snuggled up to Emma a little closer. They adored her and they knew she had been badly frightened last night. No way could they stay angry with her.

Emma enjoyed a few more minutes of quiet time, gazing out the window and gently stroking her little fur buddies.

"All right, guys. Time for coffee and a walk on the beach. Who's going to join me?"

They both ignored her invitation by closing their eyes and going back to sleep.

"Just me and Madeline, huh? Okeey doke - your loss. I'll catch you two a little later."

Emma got ready as the coffee was brewing, slipped into shorts and a Tshirt, poured herself a to-go cup, grabbed her tennis shoes and headed to the beach.

Determined to put the incident from the night before out of her mind, she started thinking about the designs she had dancing around in her head for a collection she wanted to present to Zoe. She had put some of the ideas down on paper, but many were still in the thinking stage. She had gotten a lot done, but still had an awful lot to do.

She felt close to making a breakthrough, but she was still missing a piece of the puzzle. It was right at the edge of her mind, trying to get through.

Maybe if she quit thinking about it so hard, just allowed it to drift around in her head, it would come to her. After her run she started her walk back home along the quiet beach where she was alone with her thoughts and with the sounds of the surf lapping around her feet.

When she returned home, she could tell by how quiet it was that no one was home. There was a note on the kitchen table from Aunt Zoe to let her know she was at Jacob's, but would be home for supper. That worked out perfectly and would give Emma a few hours in which she could quietly get some work done.

She fixed herself a sandwich and took it to her studio.

Emma glanced up at the clock hanging over her worktable and was surprised to see how late it was. She had worked right through their usual dinner hour. Wondering where Zoe might be and hearing her stomach growl had her getting up, stretching and walking downstairs.

Zoe had apparently been home while she was working as there was another note in Zoe's sprawling backhand on the kitchen table.

"Dropped in to see if you wanted to join us for dinner, but you looked so engrossed and so happy about it, you didn't even notice. I decided to leave you to it. I did put a shrimp and artichoke casserole in the fridge for you to heat up when you're hungry. Jacob made it. He's been taking cooking lessons and we're having the best time sampling all his efforts! There's also salad made to go with. Enjoy!

xxoo

Auntie Z"

Emma smiled at the thoughts of Jacob and Zoe having so much fun with one another and trying so many new things. They both enjoyed life to the fullest and were a delight to be around.

She also smiled at the thought of a shrimp and artichoke casserole. Yum.

As she closed the oven door after sliding in the casserole, she heard the doorbell ring.

Peeking out through the front window on her way to the door, she saw Eli and stopped to watch him for a few seconds. His head was down, and he was pacing with his hands in his pockets.

Uh oh, Emma thought. *This is a man with some things on his mind.*

She opened the door and leaned against it, "Hi."

Eli smiled at her, "Hi. Um. I thought you might want to go grab a burger. Or something. Are you hungry?"

Emma thought for a few minutes, opened the door wider and invited him in, "Actually, I'm heating up a casserole. Care to join me?"

"Did you make it?" Eli asked tentatively.

Emma blew a "Pffft" out of lips, "No, of course not. Have you lost your mind? I haven't changed that much."

They both laughed lightly.

"Well, okay," Eli said. "I guess. Thanks."

Eli followed her back to the kitchen. Emma could feel the tension bouncing off the walls, so she blabbered and rambled non-stop about the casserole, Jacob's cooking lessons, how he and Zoe were so cute together and anything else that randomly popped into her head and directly out of her mouth.

As she started putting some dishes on the table, Eli moved to help her.

"Emma, how 'bout this. Tell me what you think. I've been thinking. And, uh. . ." Eli laughed and shook his head. "This isn't coming out well, is it?"

Emma looked over at him, "Tell me. What is it you've been thinking?" Her heart pounded.

"We're certainly, neither of us, ready to just try to pick up where we parted, and it would be ridiculous to think we could. Both of us were hurt, and the hurt isn't going to just disappear because we now know what happened. We're going to have to deal with the fact that neither of us trusted one another back then enough to push and push hard to find out what was happening to break us up."

When Emma made a sound as if to protest, Eli stopped her.

"No. As hard as it is to face that fact, it's a fact, Emma. Neither one of us fought for *us*. For what we had. So, maybe, just maybe - we would have broken up anyway. Who knows? That's just it. We do not know what we might have been. We can't spend the next several years mulling it over, and we can't live the rest of our lives thinking what if. It's pointless because we just don't know. It's happened. It's over. What I do know, though, is that we've been given another opportunity. Maybe as older and wiser people, we can try this again."

Emma gave a little snort.

"What? You don't believe I'm older and wiser?"

Emma said, "Actually, I think we're both fools of the grandest sort."

"Maybe so. So. . .um. . .how 'bout we go out to dinner? And, how 'bout we call it a date? I'd like to take you someplace nice, Emma. Someplace we can go that warrants you getting dressed in something fine and pretty and sexy. What say? Would you like to have dinner with me?"

"So, are you saying maybe we start dating?"

"Well, I'm saying I'm asking you out for a date. But who knows? It may not work out, and we may decide not to date any more at all. Ever. You might slurp your soup too loudly, or I might dribble food down the front of my shirt. We just don't know now, do we?

"Oh, Eli, I don't know . . . ."

Eli looked at his feet and shuffled them, "Well, what have you got to lose? At least you know I'm not a serial killer."

Emma rolled her eyes, "Well, yes, there is that to be thankful for, I guess."

"So. Tomorrow night?"

"Um. Eli, I'm sorry. I don't think so," Emma looked away.

"Emma?"

She shook her head, still not looking at him.

"Would you at least look at me, please?"

Slowly, Emma turned back around to face him.

"Look," he said, "I guess you've made it clear you don't want to date me. Okay. Okay. I'll learn to live with that."

Emma nodded.

"But," he said, "here's the deal. Things are really uncomfortable between us even after I felt like we had overcome a lot of that. Does the friendship we had for all those years not mean enough to at least be able to do friend type stuff together?"

"Oh, no, Eli Tatnall, you're not playing fair," Emma put her hands on her hips. "You just said you wanted to take me out on a date. Which is it?"

"Truth?" Eli looked at her sheepishly, "A date. But, I'll settle for a dinner between friends. What say? Or are you scared?"

"Pfft. I'm not scared of much, Eli, and that includes you."

"Okay then?"

"Okay," she replied.

"Tommorow night? Eight o'clock?"

Emma nodded, "Okay."

Eli grinned, "Cool! Put on something pretty, and we'll go to Bacchanalia. How's that sound?"

"Wow," Emma cocked her head to one side, "There's a Bacchanalia in Atlanta. Is the Whimsey Bacchanalia run by the same people?"

"It is. The owners, Angelica and Joseph Frazier, discovered Whimsey a few years back, and it's been their dream to open a place here. And they've opened a little bed & breakfast next door. Eight rooms. So. Eight o'clock tomorrow. Cool."

Once that was settled, the two spent a casual evening enjoying Jacob's casserole while Eli tried to bring Emma up to date on his family and their Whimsey friends. They moved to the front porch for coffee, and that's where they were when Jacob and Zoe arrived.

The four of them rocked on the porch and chatted until Jacob announced it was time for him to carry his tired old bones home, and Eli said he would walk with him.

After the two men left, Zoe looked over at Emma who shrugged her shoulders and shook her head. "Aunt Zoe, I swear, I have no idea what's going on, so don't even ask."

They both giggled and continued rocking and enjoying their coffee, listening to the sounds of the sea.

After Zoe went upstairs to bed, Emma stayed on the porch rocking, listening to the sea and thinking about Eli's visit.

The fact that Eli thought they were being given a second chance seemed pretty preposterous. Like something in a novel, not something anyone could expect in the real world of stark reality. But. There it was. Maybe they were being given a second chance. Except for the fact that Emma knew no good could come of it.

Of course they still had feelings for one another. Any relationship ending as abruptly as theirs had without being given a chance to thrive on its own or die of natural causes would naturally leave residual feelings needing to be sorted. Questions and answers blowing and bouncing around begging to be heard and resolved.

Eli was right about one thing. Her being back on the island would be throwing them in one another's paths often if not daily. He deserved to know where they were going and if they would be going there together, or going there separately.

And sometimes one date was all it took to know.

Sometimes.

Sometimes, it was simply hopeless with or without that date.

"Maybe not," muttered Madeline.

"Oh, Madeline. Hush up, honey."

CHAPTER TWENTY-THREE

The following evening, when it came time to get ready, Emma was a wreck. Determined not to go out and buy a new outfit, she had pulled every single piece of clothing out of her closets. They were scattered everywhere -- in piles on top of her bed, on top of the chair in her bedroom and even on the sofa in the living room where the light might be better to see if the black bolero jacket went with the little black dress or if the blacks were off.

This was insane. She had no idea, really, where they were going. How could she possibly know what to wear?

Yes, Eli had said he was taking her to Bacchanalia, but he was known to be a bit of a joker. Suppose she put on those delicious Louboutins, and he took her bowling? No, no, no. He wouldn't do that. He wouldn't dare. Surely he's grown up some since he'd last done that. Besides, he was trying awfully hard to get back into her good graces. He would not dare pull a stunt like that.

And she really wanted to wear the Louboutins. What a deal she had gotten on those. Wow. Olivia would be beyond jealous. They were killer.

She finally decided the little bolero jacket wasn't right, but she did find the perfect black silk boucle shawl to wear with the little black dress. She could decide later whether to keep it on with one end tossed casually over her shoulders or to remove it and show how the demure looking dress was actually cut down to the waist in the back.

She was just putting on her lipstick when she heard Eli knock on the door and Aunt Zoe letting him in. She had a quick memory of this exact same scene many many years ago. She sat on the bed, shaken.

I can't do this. Emma dropped her head into her hands. *I just can't. My heart is not strong enough to take being broken again.*

She tiptoed over to the stairwell and listened to Eli and Zoe's voices mingling with laugher as they teased one another. Easy and comfortable with one another. Like she and Eli had once been.

She leaned over the banister so she could see him. My God, the man was gorgeous. Sexy as all hell and really had no idea how handsome he was, which only added to the attractiveness.

As if he felt her eyes on him, he turned around and looked up into her face.

She saw his eyes travel from the top of her head right down to her peep toe shoes as she walked down the stairs.

"Emma, you are a vision. But, honey, can you bowl in that outfit?"

Eyes wide, she punched him in the arm.

"Eli! I am not going bowling with you tonight!"

He laughed, "Okay, no bowling. Not tonight."

She looked him up and down in return, "Besides, you're not dressed for bowling. You're looking pretty

212

spiffy yourself, Mr. Tatnall." And he *was,* in his dark charcoal pinstripe suit with a black silk Tshirt.

"I was just telling him how handsome he looked," said Zoe. "And, child, you have outdone yourself, I must say. Spin around and let me take a look at you."

"Oh, Auntie . . . ."

Zoe chucked and gave them both a kiss, "Run along. Have fun. Tell the Fraziers I hope to see them soon."

Eli reached his arm out for her to take, "Then come along, Ms. Foley. Let's go trip the light fantastic, shall we?"

"Wait. No. I'm not going. I only came downstairs to tell you I'm not feeling well."

Eli looked at her. Zoe looked at her. Zoe shook her head and left the room.

"Emma?" Eli asked, "Have you changed your mind?"

"No. Yes. No. I just don't feel well."

Eli put a finger under her chin and tilted her face up to his, "I don't believe you. But, if you don't want to go, I understand. Maybe another night." He turned to leave.

"No." Emma reached out and took his hand, "I'm sorry, Eli. I'm scared. And that's the God's truth. Scared to death."

"Honey, you ain't scared of nothing," He looked at her and grinned, "And if you are scared, well, I know you.

You'll do whatever it takes to stop being scared. That's what you've always done. You were the bravest little girl I knew, and I suspect, you still are. You've just forgotten how brave, how strong, you are. Time to remember, don't you think?"

Emma looked up at him, saw a gentle smile on his face and the love in his eyes. She knew she was a goner. She knew he still loved her every bit as much as she loved him. Would it be enough?

Emma sighed and slipped her arm through his as they walked out the door and down the steps.

"How's Bacchanalia sound?" Eli asked.

"Lovely! And I'm starving. Good thing they serve those really decadent five course meals. Yum!"

Eli laughed, "I was wondering if you still had that truck driver's appetite. One of these days, it'll catch up with you, you know, and you'll have to start counting calories like the rest of us mortals."

"Hush your mouth."

Eli looked at her feet. "Can you walk in those things?"

"Of course I can walk in these things, silly."

Emma fell in love with Bacchanalia the moment they walked up the steps onto the wide covered porch. Rocking chairs had been pulled into random conversation areas, but seemed to be merging into one large party where everyone, all Whimsey residents, knew one another. Emma and Eli stopped for a chat before going inside, graciously accepting some of the teasing tossed their way.

Inside was utterly charming. The old home turned restaurant retained many of the original features. Any renovations the Fraziers had done were handled with the architectural integrity of the building kept in mind and truthfully tended to. The wide plank oak floors were gleaming, as were the eight-over-eight windows, which were open to the soft sea breezes, allowing the sound of the surf to gently caress the diners. Gauzy white curtains rippled on the breeze. The tables were covered in crisp heavy white linen tablecloths which fell to the floor, topped with soft pink linen squares falling half way down. Each table had a crystal vase of fresh flowers sitting on a small silver tray. Dinnerware was mismatched pink and white china. The stemware and silverware mismatched also, with everything working together beautifully for an ambience of quiet, comfortable, easy elegance. There were old fashioned chandeliers casting soft light through the rooms and Lowcountry scenes done in pastels hanging on the walls.

Emma turned to Eli, her eyes glowing, "This is just enchanting, Eli. Thank you for bringing me."

Eli smilled, "I hoped you would think so. I'm pleased you like it."

Angelica Frazier approached and gave Eli a hug. She surprised Emma with a hug, "I've been hearing all about you, Emma, and happy to finally meet you. Come have a seat and enjoy your evening. Our chef, who happens to be my handsome husband Joseph, will be out to say hello shortly."

Eli had been wise in his choice of restaurant. Not only was it lovely, but it takes a while to eat five courses, especially timed as impeccably as the professionals at Bacchanalia did things. It was a chance to relax and talk, but still have something to keep them occupied should awkward silences overtake them if they weren't able to find anything to talk about.

There were no awkward silences. The silences that did occur were pleasant and comfortable. They were easy with one another.

When they sat back with their after dinner coffee, laughingly comparing notes on who had made the best choices - Emma's lamb versus Eli's prime rib - and teasing one another about who had eaten the most, they shared a slice of chocolate ganache cake with homemade vanilla ice cream and agreed it was a nice first date.

They walked back to Zoe's holding hands. Emma admitted her feet were killing her, so she slipped out of her shoes and carried them.

Eli escorted Emma to her door, gave her a short sweet peck of a kiss, and said good night, promising to talk with her soon.

And so it went.

Neither had any idea how things would play out in the future - not the long term or the short term. And they didn't discuss it. Both willing, for tonight at least, to let things go their own natural course.

Emma looked up at the Whimsey stars, "Can this really be?"

She heard a little voice whisper, "Oh, Emma, hush up," said Madeline the imaginary evil twin.

The following week was uneventful in the drama department, which was a welcome relief to Emma and Zoe.

"Thank God," said Madeline, "For a few days there, I was worried we had somehow slipped into some sleazy soap opera."

"Madeline, do hush," said Emma.

Not a peep was heard out of Reese Prescott. No one appeared to be scampering around on the roof. Life went on.

The Wicked Women were staying busy. Zoe, confident in the sales they were going to see, had requested they all try to maintain a sizeable inventory, which meant a great deal of work. Happy work. This was their dream come true.

Zoe had corralled most of the Whimsey men into helping Eli and Ethan, Jr. with finish work and running errands to keep the grand opening on schedule.

Although Emma's work would not be included in the "Sneak Peek," everyone had stopped being concerned. She was working and assured them she was pleased with how things were coming along. Not ecstatic, but hopeful. She would shake her head and mutter things about missing that final piece to the puzzle so often they were able to repeat it along with her.

And finally, it was time.

CHAPTER TWENTY-FOUR

Emma stood up and stretched. She had been totally and happily immersed in her designs most of the day, but had stopped working and spent the last hour getting cleaned up and dressed. The day has finally come. It was time to scoot over to Les étoiles for their sneak peek.

When she turned off her work lamps to leave, she heard the front door open and a "Whoo Hooo, Emma. Time to go, girl!" and she had to laugh.

She leaned over the stairwell and shouted, "Down in a minute."

"Don't make us come up there to get you, girl."

"Shake a tail feather, honey."

"Yeah, what they said."

True to her word, Emma was down the stairs quickly, dressed in a short cotton tie dyed dress in shades of pinks and reds with a bright yellow shawl tossed over her shoulders, and yellow high heeled sandals.

"Wow, aren't we bright this afternoon?" said Sarah Kate. Maggie and Alex stood beside her.

Emma looked at her three friends, and they all started laughing.

Sarah Kate wore a little bright sapphire blue dress with a lime green shawl and sandals, Maggie was in purple and lavender with a red shawl and sandals, and Alex was in a fuchsia dress with an orange shawl and sandals.

Maggie wiped her eyes, "Um hmm, quiet and retiring. That would be us."

"Oh, Laws, what do you suppose Olivia will be wearing?" asked Emma.

"Well, let's just hope she doesn't cause us all to clash," said Alex as she rolled her eyes.

"As if," said Sarah Kate.

Olivia stood looking down on them from the front porch of Les étoiles with her hands on her hips, "Well, it's about time! I thought I was going to have to come in there and get y'all." In fire engine red stilettos, a short black sleeveless voile dress with a huge red poppy embroidered on the hip, and a red ombre silk voile shawl tossed over one shoulder, she, of course, fit right in with the rest of them.

"Wow," said Aunt Zoe from just inside the door. "Aren't we all glad this is just a little impromptu sneak peek at the gallery and not the real thing.

As the girls turned to answer, they were struck by the beauty of the two women standing in the doorway. Zoe was dressed in a blue turquoise silk caftan, with her thick silver hair down and glowing as it flowed over her shoulders. Standing next to her, their arms linked, was Zelda, dressed in a matching caftan the color of malachite. They presented a stunning picture. Both beautiful women, alike in their confidence and zest in life.

Emma said, "You're gorgeous!"

Zelda curtsied and laughed, "Yes, yes, we are. Wait till you see the gallery. Zoe has done some serious magic in here, believe me."

Zoe pushed open the door and they could see the men, not nearly so sharply attired, already taking a tour. She smiled, gave her own little curtsey, and ushered them inside with a, "Ladies, after you."

Entering Les étoiles was not unlike entering a church.

The windows along each side were stained glass. Vibrant colors blending into abstracts and sea scenes, along with renderings of some much loved old landmarks around the island, including Aunt Elizabeth's stately old home. The colors danced throughout the gallery as the sun beamed in.

The floor was wide random planks of light honey oak with the textured walls painted a soft shade of creamy vanilla.

Narrow honey oak beams extended up from the floor, meeting in the center of the high cathedral ceiling, giving the space a wide open feeling.

There were nooks and crannies and tables and shelves and pedestals. Enough so each piece of displayed artwork was holding a solitary place of honor. None were crowded or infringed upon by another.

And enough gallery wall space to equally honor each painting, drawing, collage or photograph.

The lighting was pure genius. Soft enough to create a pleasant ambience, but bright enough to highlight the surrounding beauty. Each piece was skillfully displayed.

Each artist was showcased in their own area, seemingly built with them and their art in mind. There was enough of their work on display to allow customers a pleasant variety to choose from, but just enough to have them wanting more. The colors were arranged in a manner to blend and complement and not fight amongst themselves - not unlike Zoe's large collages, one of which held a place of honor on the back wall of the gallery. The feeling was relaxing and calming and very conducive to tempting the customers into taking home the treasures in an attempt to duplicate the gentle elegant ambience of Les étoiles.

After a stunned and reverent silence, the girls burst into shouts of glee, hugging Aunt Zoe, Zelda, one another and each of the men. Eli was given special attention and praise for all the work he had done, which he graciously accepted with smiles and bows while always passing the praise along to Zoe with words about it all being her vision. "I'm just the guy she hired to help make it real with a hammer and a saw," he told them.

Emma wandered away from the crowd, drawn to a jewelry display. It was beautiful, and she felt a bit of resentment building that it was here in her aunt's gallery while hers wasn't.

Eli walked up beside her, "Hey."

"Hey, yourself."

He took her hand, "You okay?"

Emma nodded, "I guess. This is turning out to be a little harder than I thought."

"I was afraid it might," Eli said. "Do you promise not to punch me if I say something?"

"Oh, I don't think so," Emma said with a laugh edged with a little bitterness.

"Well," he said, "I guess I'll just have to take a chance." He put a finger under her chin and tilted her head so she was looking into his eyes. "Emma, yours is a special gift that's taken a shot for some reason. But I've been watching you. I know you're getting it back. You'll be here. And you'll be a star. And, I think, in your heart you know it. Am I right?"

"I wish I was as sure of that as you are. I'm trying and some days are better than others, but some days I feel like I'm wasting my time and should just give up."

Eli lifted his eyebrows and his lips moved into a goofy grin, "You won't give up and you'll make it. I've had lots of practice when it comes to reading you, Emma. I've only been wrong once, and I intend to spend a lot of years making up for it. If you'll let me, that is."

Emma looked down at her toes, "Oh, my." She didn't want to think about any of that today. She was too excited about the gallery.

Flustered, Emma did a little spin. After gazing around and taking things in, she looked up at Eli, "It's perfect, Eli. You have a great deal to do with the fact that it is. It's been a labor of love for you, hasn't it?"

"You're right, it has. I fell in love with the idea and the next thing I knew, I was spending nights sitting across the kitchen table from Zoe as we bounced ideas off one another. It stopped being a job and became much more. I'm proud of it and very proud to be a part of it."

Emma smiled at him and realized it had become deathly quiet.

Eli took her hand and nodded towards her friends, "Let's go see what's happening over here. It's gotta be something big to get them all this quiet."

When they reached the girls, Emma gasped at what she saw. They were gazing up at the wall at one of Olivia's paintings. At first, she thought it was the painting of them as girls, but she knew that painting was hanging in her apartment. When she looked again, she realized it was a takeoff on that painting, but here they were all grown up. They were grouped much the same way, and they still appeared to be playing "dress-up," but most outstanding was that Olivia had managed to capture the same playful expressions on their grown-up faces as she had on their little girl faces all those many years ago. That same feeling of shared love was still there, every bit as strong as in the first painting. The joy with one another was so alive, you could almost hear the laughter coming right off the canvas. But somehow, there was now an added dimension. She could actually feel the self-confidence of these women emanating from the painting. She looked around at Olivia who was looking a little shy and a little nervous.

"Do you like it?" Olivia asked.

"Olivia, I'm not sure I have the words to tell you how very much I love it. It's exquisite. You continue to amaze. How can you just keep getting so much better? It's as though you're seeing things differently, deeper maybe. And you're so amazingly able to transfer that onto canvas - not just what you see but what you, along with your subjects, are feeling."

"Oh, Emma, it's true. I do think I'm beginning to *feel* the work more. I think it's because I'm a mother now. Does that make sense? It's as though all my senses are on high alert. Because they have to be in order to keep my children safe, but at the same time not smother them, I have to find something to do with those feelings, and they become a part of my paintings. I leave my studio now feeling so much more satisfied with my work, but drained. As though I've opened my veins and bled onto the canvases. I'm always a little shocked when I look and they're still the same soft palette I always use, without even knowing I'm doing it. Oh, I give up - there's no way to explain it. It just happens." And she shrugged.

The girls were still discussing the painting, all in awe of the beauty of Olivia's work, when Olivia bounced up on her toes and said, "Enough, enough! I'm dying to see what else is here, but do we want to talk about that close encounter we all witnessed, Emma?"

"I say we discuss that later," said Sarah Kate with a grin. "Over drinks."

"And some snackies?" asked Maggie.

Alex laughed and slapped her knee, "Liquor and food. Sounds like a plan. What say, Emma?"

Emma lifted her chin, "What encounter?"

Eli chuckled and shook his head, "Time for me to move along. Emma? Ladies? I trust I'll see you all later? Possibly over snackies and drinks?"

They all laughed, and Emma nodded her head and said, "Yes, yes, snackies and drinks it is. But not till we've seen everything here. "

And an odd little voice which seemed to come from Emma's shoulder said, "Oh boy. Drinks! I could use a cold beer."

Emma gasped, "Noooo . . . ", she whispered.

"Why, yes, honey, it's me," said Earlene the wicked little pixie.

Emma turned around to look at the little pixie sitting on her shoulder, not surprised to see her dressed in a teeny little tight form-fitting gold lame low-cut strapless dress sprinkled with red rhinestones. And teeny little peep toe gold stilettos. Wait - Louboutins? It couldn't be! Her teeny little toe nails were painted the same bright red as her lips. Her red hair was piled on top of her head in a teeny little beehive, and she was wearing gold cat's eye glasses with red rhinestones on the corners.

Emma looked down. Sure enough, silver glitter sparkled on the floor all around her.

"Earlene, why do you do that? It's embarrassing."

Earlene grinned and shrugged, "I don't know what you're talking about."

"Yes you do. It's not just the silver glitter. You also make my shoes disappear. I want to know why."

The little pixie rose off Emma's shoulder and flew in a circle around her head. "Oh, you're such a bright girl, Emma. You should be able to figure it out." With that, Earlene fluttered away.

Olivia, Sarah Kate, Maggie and Alex had been standing close by listening to every word. As they walked over, Olivia said, "Well, I see you two are still at it."

Alex said, "Sure looks like nothing has changed in the Earlene department."

"Yeah, but," said Maggie, "let's not let that ruin this wonderful day. This is all too exciting."

The other girls danced around Emma, laughing and sharing high fives and hip bumps.

Zoe and Zelda watched from across the room. They, too, shared a high five and a hip bump, "What a glorious day this is, Zoe."

Zoe hugged Zelda and answered, "Yes, it is. And having you here makes it even more special, love. Thanks for being here."

"I would not have missed this for the world, my dear sister. Love you."

"And I love you back."

"EEK!"

"Maggie!" Sarah Kate shouted with one hand over her heart. "Quit! You scared the hell out of us!"

Maggie ran a few steps, stopped and stared at her display. When she turned around, her eyes were wide, "Look. Look what Zoe has done. I'm speechless."

On a silver pedestal sat one of Maggie's large red pottery pitchers. The pitcher had five small silver stars in a small cluster on the inside rim. Sitting on antique silver trays were displays of her red pottery mugs and glasses in a multitude of shapes and sizes. Hanging above the display were silver and glass stars, turning and gently swaying. Behind the display was an old silvered mirror the girls remembered from the attic during their days of playing dress-up.

"It's wonderful," breathed Olivia.

As they were hugging and congratulating Maggie, she pointed across the room, grinning from ear to ear. She looked at Sarah Kate, who let out a squeal and went running to her display.

Eli had built an oak mantel, one with cabinets on either side. The cabinet doors were open and on each shelf were pieces of Sarah Kate's work. A mix of her lace and of her knitting. Wonderful hand knitted sweaters and hats and scarves and shawls, each trimmed in delicate lace. And hanging across the mantel on antique iron hooks of different shapes were her long skinny whimsical stockings in a mix of stripes and patterns of vibrant colors, with heels and toes of lace. Some of the stockings had tiny hand knitted animals peeking out of them. In some, the tiny animals were snuggled inside, hiding, waiting to be discovered at a later time. And across the top of the mantel sprawled a large fat smiling cat, covered in a merry assortment of stripes and patterns in bright colors. Next to the cat was a giraffe, a grinning hippopotamus and a dog, all knitted in colors never seen in true life.

"That cat! I have got to have the cat."

"When did you start doing these? They're heavenly."

"I've been working on them for a while, but wanted to keep them a secret till Les étoiles opened. Do you really like them?"

"Oh my God! Love them! All of them!"

"Good. I've done one for each of you."

"Me too?" asked Earlene, who suddenly reappeared above Emma's head.

"Yes, darling," Sarah Kate said, "but yours isn't quite so big. I made it *your* big. Is that okay?"

"Perfect." Earlene flew over and planted a little kiss on Sarah Kate's cheek. "Thank you."

Emma looked down. Yup. More silver glitter. *Why is she so mean to me and so nice to everyone else?* she wondered. She reached up, thinking she would grab the evil pixie and throttle her, but too late. Earlene was gone again.

"This is fun!" giggled Maggie, as she glanced at Alex.

Alex was staring over her shoulder, and as the others looked to see what held Alex's attention, they all became very quiet.

Alex walked slowly over to her display.

An old loom sat to one side, dressed for weaving with a weft of boucle silk in shades of greens and blues.

Alex reached her hand out to touch the loom, "This was my great grandmother's. It looks like it belongs here, doesn't it?" She looked around at her friends, who were all holding hands. She reached out for Emma's hand on one side and Olivia's on the other so they were forming a circle. "Annie and Rupert would be so proud to see me now, wouldn't they?"

By now they were all crying quietly.

Alex chucked softly, lifted her head and whispered, "Thank you, Elizabeth."

Emma wiped her eyes, "The colors on the loom look like the ocean, don't they?"

"And oh, my, look at this!" said Olivia as she picked up a large throw woven in stripes of gold, yellow and amber.

"Want," said Maggie as she cuddled herself in a shawl of soft green silk.

"Mine," said Sarah Kate. She stretched out on the woven rug on the floor of the display.

Alex laughed and pulled on Sarah Kate's arm, "Get up, fool. Here we are all dressed up and you're going to lounge around on the floor? Get up."

Instead of getting up, Sarah Kate giggled and pulled Alex down on the rug beside her.

When Zoe and Zelda made their way over to where they were, all five girls were sitting on the floor, leaning back against the display, laughing and talking.

Earlene flew over and placed a kiss on Zelda's cheek, flew over to Zoe, gave her a little kiss, and settled on her shoulder, "I'm having a ball. I'm gonna enjoy having these gals back home, I do believe."

Zoe looked at her little friend, nodded her head and smiled, "Even Emma? Are you ever going to forgive her for thinking you were Tinker Belle?"

"Well, you know, she shouldn't have just assumed I was Tinker Belle. Tinker Belle, sweet as she is, ain't the only pixie in the world. She just lucked onto one hell of a publicity guy, is all."

Emma, who had heard their conversation, walked over to them, "Earlene, I sincerely apologize. But, you know, I was just a little kid. Tinker Belle was all I knew about the pixie world back then."

"Aw, I forgave you for that a long, long time ago."

Emma gave her a shaky smile, "Well, Earlene. There's just one more little thing." She drew in a deep breath, "I have fretted and fretted and worried over this meeting for an awfully long time. Now, while I'm glad you're forgiven me, couldn't you have let me know that a few years ago? And if you've really forgiven me, I mean really really, couldn't you quit with the silver glitter? And don't act like you don't know what I'm talking about. I told you already, it's embarrassing, and I'm asking you one more time – why are you doing this?"

Earlene hovered in front of Emma like a bright little hummingbird. Eyes snapping. "I said I'd forgiven you for the Tinker Belle thing."

Emma looked puzzled. "Well, Lord A Mercy, Earlene, why else were you mad at me?"

"I'll tell you why, Emma. You were the most beautiful and talented child ever born on Whimsey. But what did you do? You ruined everything with Eli because of some stupid mistake about him and Reese. Then you ran off and married that idiot Hunter. After that fell apart, you holed up in that stupid condo in Atlanta, feeling sorry for yourself, and letting all your talent and potential fly out the window. The silver glitter is to remind you of all the years you wasted and how you screwed up what should have been a beautiful life."

"But," Emma replied, "I'm back on Whimsey now, and I'm trying to get everything together. Can't you believe me and cut me some slack?"

Earlene pursed her lips, "Maybe. We'll see how it goes." She gave Emma a wink and flew off.

Emma put both hands over her face and muttered, "Ay yi yi."

"Yeah, that's what I say," muttered Madeline, "Ay yi yi."

Emma groaned and shook her head, her hands still covering her face. "And why, dear God, have I been blessed with Madeline AND Earlene? What have I done to deserve both of them?"

Emma felt a swish of air that ruffled her hair. Peeping through her fingers she saw Earlene, wings fluttering madly, hovering in front of her.

"Now wait just a darned second, girly. Madeline's imaginary. I, however, am the real deal and don't you forget it." And off she flew, tossing a loud "harrumph" over her shoulder on the way.

Emma gave herself a shake from head to toe and turned to her friends.

"Well, what do you think? Did that go well?"

They were all standing there wide-eyed. "I'm not sure," said Maggie.

Emma sighed, "Me either." She turned to look at her aunt.

Zoe's eyes were glittering with suppressed laughter.

"Aunt Zoe, let's forget all about that little bit of drama." She did a slow spin with her arms outstretched. "This is all totally and perfectly perfect. We've spent most of our time looking at the girls' displays, but now I'm anxious to see the rest of it. Care to join us?"

"No, honey, you girls go ahead. Your mother and I are going to go to the house and start putting together a little something for supper. I'm sure I overheard one of you mention food a little earlier."

"Oh, goodie," said Sarah Kate. "Supper!"

"That's even better than snackies, huh?" chimed in Maggie.

They all agreed they would meet back at the house a little later.

Scott came over to give each of the women a hug, offering congratulations on what they had achieved, "I knew you would all rise to the top of your games. Les étoiles is amazing, and it warms my heart to know so many of the artists represented here, especially each of you. I'm very proud of you. Now, we guys are all going to go back to the house with Zelda and Zoe and see what we can do to help, mainly by staying out of the kitchen. We'll see all of you in a little while." He gave Emma one last hug, whispered "I love you" in her ear, and winked at her as he turned to leave.

The guys each waved their good-byes as they filed out the door.

The girls wandered about the gallery, calling to one another to come see one display or another.

CHAPTER TWENTY-FIVE

After their tour, the girls walked over to Zoe's and made themselves comfortable on the porch, still excited about Les étoiles, all it contained and all it would come to mean to each of them.

Emma looked around, "Y'all, can you believe Les étoiles? Do you think it's the most dreamy, the most perfect gallery ever? And I'm just in awe with all the local talent. I knew what we were all about here on Whimsey, but new artists have popped up while I've been gone."

Olivia shook her head, "Actually, not really. A lot of the work you saw for the first time today has been done by people you've known all your life. They've grown up, like we have. You remember them as kids, is all. Those gorgeous leather bound journals? Tommy makes those."

"Tommy?! Nuh uh. You are kidding. The guy who sat behind me in class and pulled my hair all the time?"

"Yep. That's him. Isn't his work gorgeous? I always use one of his larger journals for each of my paintings as I'm doing my sketches and making notes."

Alex walked over and poured a glass of iced tea from the pitcher which seemed ever-present on this particular porch, "You know, I knew I was excited about the gallery, but it never dawned on me that I might not be prepared for the emotional slam. Wow. That was really something, you know? Seeing my work along with my grandmother's loom in that gorgeous setting, surrounded by such immense talent. Well, 'wow' is about the best I can come up with. I wonder if Zoe is completely aware of what she's built? Les étoiles is going to be a huge force in the art world."

"I think you're right, Alex," Maggie dropped into a chair next to her and nodded her head toward the front door. "But remember, this is Aunt Zoe we're talking about. Is there a better businesswoman anywhere? She's determined to keep Les étoiles exactly what her dream has always been and that's to showcase the talent of Whimsey. She believes, just as Elizabeth did, in keeping it amongst those who were here from the beginning. Those were the talents and the hearts that made this island possible. Those are the talents and the hearts that will keep it as it is and as it should be. Of course, knowing of its exclusivity, as others will see it, will only add to its allure. And profits. For everyone involved. She is a very shrewd woman, in addition to being the most giving soul most of us will ever have the privilege of knowing."

"You know, SCAD was good for us all," Olivia said. "I learned a lot while I was there, I admit. But the most valuable lessons I learned, I learned right here on Whimsey. From Zoe. You're right, she is indeed a loving and generous soul. I don't think I would be the painter, or the person, I am today without her guidance."

Emma nodded, "I agree with every word. You know I do. But right now, while she's busy inside, I want to ask you guys if you paid close attention to that huge wonderful piece she has hanging on the back wall in the gallery? If that's not her best piece yet, I'll eat somebody's hat."

"Amen!" shouted Sarah Kate, "It is divine."

"And tells a very long story," added Maggie.

"And it is full of mysteries," Alex agreed.

"Yep, " Emma said, "Some I was able to figure out, but some not. I was only getting a feeling for it when we left. I want to spend some time with that piece."

Sarah Kate stood and stretched, "You'll have to buy it then. And I'll bet this one is going to fetch a very pretty penny."

Olivia shook her head, "Nope. It's staying at Les étoiles. She was going to sell it, but the more she looked at it after she finished it, she decided it needed to *live* right here."

Emma's eyes widened, "Really? It's unusual for Zoe to be that attached to her work. Now I really do need to spend more time with it."

Alex walked over and stood next to Emma's chair, "How you doing, sweetness?"

Emma smiled up at her and reached out to take her hand, "I'm good."

"And the work?"

"It's coming," Emma shook her head, "But you know . . . ."

And she heard four voices in imperfect harmony say "there's a final piece to the puzzle . . . ."

She joined in their laugher but suddenly stopped, "Wait a minute. Wait just a darn minute . . . ."

"What?" squealed Sarah Kate.

But Emma was gone and half way up the stairs.

The girls followed her up to her room and found her with her head stuck in her closet.

They could hear her muttering, "I know she said she put it in here."

She stood up, turned to face them and put her hands on her hips, "I know Aunt Zoe said she found a box of stones and put them in this closet. Where are they?"

They all exchanged looks, shook their heads and shrugged their shoulders, "You can ask her later," Olivia said. "Right now, I'm starving, and I smell wonderful things happening down in the kitchen. Let's go eat."

The girls followed Olivia down the steps into the kitchen.

"Wow," said Olivia and the others all nodded in disbelief.

A couple of leaves had been added to the old table so they could all gather around it together.

The men all had their heads together in an argument over the latest news about the Atlanta Braves. The only thing they agreed on was the fact that there were too many players being paid way too much money. Zelda had donned a long chef's apron over her silk caftan and was stirring a huge pan of scrambled eggs while feeding bread to the toaster four slices at a time.

"Y'all come butter this toast while it's hot, please. We thought a big ol' southern breakfast would be just the thing for supper. What do you think?"

On the counter sat a platter of biscuits, in case anyone preferred a biscuit to toast, and an even larger platter stacked with bacon, sausage patties and country ham. There were bowls of fresh fruit. Two gravy boats - one with red-eye gravy for the ham, and one with white milk gravy for the sausage. A still-warm-from-the-oven pound cake to spoon fresh fruit and homemade whipped cream over. And an egg and cheese breakfast strata. Not to be forgotten, pitchers of milk, fresh orange juice, a couple bottles of champagne and a pitcher of Bloody Marys.

"Anyone want waffles?" asked Zelda. She looked confused when the question was greeted with a stunned silence followed by loud laughter. When she looked at the counter top, it seemed to dawn on her that there was a gracious plenty and she joined in the laughter.

"Scratch the waffles," she said, as she stirred shredded cheese into the eggs.

A minute later, brandishing her long wooden spoon, she turned from the stove, smiled her big Zelda smile and shouted, "Voilà! Breakfast is served."

Scott put his arm around Emma's shoulders and gave her a squeeze, "Your mother misses cooking these big breakfasts for a crowd, so whenever the opportunity presents itself, she's in hog heaven. Look at her."

Emma nodded, amused at the understatement, "So it would seem. She does look happy. And I'm happy, too. I'm so glad you're here, Daddy."

"Me, too, honey. Me, too."

And breakfast for supper commenced around the big oak table in Zoe's country kitchen amidst a great deal of laughing and teasing and reminiscing.

With no one wise to the eyes peeping through a window. Eyes filled with hatred at what they watched going on inside a happy home.

Sated and a bit sleepy after their meal, everyone settled into rocking chairs on the porch, unconsciously rocking to the rhythm of the surf. Eyes began getting heavy and yawns grew more frequent.

Even Pyewackett and Fred were snoring cuddled together on their big floor pillow.

Jonathan and Olivia were the first to say good night.

Everyone else got up to follow along as a chorus of good nights volleyed back and forth, along with hugs and promises to talk tomorrow before everyone finally got on their way.

"I forget how long it takes southerners to say good night," murmured Scott with his head leaned back on the rocker and his eyes closed.

Zelda took his hand, "And I forget just how lovely that is."

"Me, too, sweetness. Me, too."

"How 'bout we call it a night ourselves, Sweet Pea?" asked Scott.

"Yes, please," Zelda answered.

Emma, Zoe and Jacob wished the couple good night and watched them walk hand-in-hand toward the big house, Zelda swinging her shoes in her other hand, still wearing the long chef's apron over her silk caftan.

Emma gave Zoe and Jacob a kiss and climbed the stairs to bed with one eye open, changed into her long cotton nightgown, washed her face and was asleep before her head hit the pillow.

And the Whimsey stars shone brightly through the skylight over her bed.

CHAPTER TWENTY-SIX

When Emma woke up the next morning, she took her usual early morning run and when she got back home, was surprised to find she was the only one up. The house had the feel of sleepiness, as if it, too, were still in slumber.

Tip-toeing back up to her apartment so as not to wake Aunt Zoe and possibly Jacob, Emma decided today would be a perfect day to just stay in, read a good book and enjoy some quiet time.

As she ground beans for coffee, she spotted Fred and Pyewackett curled up together in her big red overstuffed chair. "Oh, well, you guys have taken over that chair all for your very own, I see. I'll just curl up on my bed, not to worry. You guys must be tired, too. Yesterday and last night were so full of emotional highs, I guess we're all tuckered out. I'll just relax with the newest Lee Child book. Some time in bed with Reacher, that's the ticket."

Placing her coffee, yogurt and Lee Child novel she'd borrowed from Lou on a tray, she moved back to her bed and fluffed up her mound of pillows to settle in for a long, relaxing, much needed day of quiet time. Along with a promise to herself to start eating a little more healthy and not give in to every scrumptious morsel that kept presenting itself to her. Otherwise, she'd have to double her morning run and buy new clothes to boot.

Okay, Reacher . . . show me your stuff, sweetheart.

And she was in the same spot several hours later when Aunt Zoe knocked and poked her head in the door.

"How's the book?"

"Scrumptious! It might be his best yet."

Zoe nodded, "Uh huh, and how did I know you would say that?"

Emma laughed, "Well, what can I say? He just gets better and better."

"Did you finish it?"

"Just did. I probably would have finished it sooner if I had been able to shut my mind off. But, you know how that goes. As it was, I kept hopping up to do other things. I sketched out a few designs that have been wiggling around in my mind, then I checked on the stones I have on hand to see what I need when I order some other supplies."

"I hope you took time out for lunch."

"Oh, I did. Then I took a little nap and worked on my designs some more. By then, Reacher was calling my name, so I settled down and read till I finished. It was terrific. Want to borrow it before I return it to Lou?"

"Yes, please! I'd love to. Thanks!" Zoe grinned from ear to ear, "That Reacher is my kinda guy."

Emma grinned back, "Honey, don't I know it!"

"Before I forget why I'm here, your mom and dad are downstairs. They felt like they wanted to get out of

Jonathan and Olivia's way for a while so they could enjoy some family time alone with the kids."

"You mean without the grandparents stepping in to spoil them rotten by giving in to their every whim?"

"Uh huh, that's exactly what I mean. Plus, I think your parents forget how much energy two little ones carry with them."

Emma laughed, "They do wear a body out, and that's the livin' truth!"

"Sure is. Anyway, it's time for dinner, and we're trying to decide if we want to go out or just hang around here and eat in. We'd love to have you join us if you'd like, and if so, we're open to suggestions."

"I'd love it! How 'bout we order pizza?"

"Now why didn't I think of that? Great idea! The usual?"

"Sounds perfect! Let me freshen up, and I'll be down in a bit."

"No hurry."

The family spent the rest of the evening over pizza, catching up with personal news, and exchanging details about their latest projects.

Scott and Zelda would be leaving soon after the grand opening in a couple weeks to work on a series of articles focusing on the burgeoning international sex trade. Appalled at what had apparently become a big money making business which they felt the U. S. media was ignoring, they had decided to do what they could to bring the subject to the forefront. Scott admitted it could be dangerous, but they had spent the past several months gathering and meeting contacts, building a relationship of trust on all sides. The project would have them traveling for several months, but they planned on a long, relaxing visit once it was complete. They had agreed that more time at home as they were getting older was sounding pretty enticing.

After many yawns and much stretching, everyone said their good nights.

Scott and Zelda decided a walk on the beach was what they needed before heading home.

Zoe went off to bed with Reacher, and Emma retired to her apartment with her sketch pad and colored pencils to see if she could capture the final designs she was having a little trouble with.

Pyewackett and Fred followed Scott and Zelda down the beach. They knew they could enter through their pet door upon returning home a little later. Life on this quiet island was paradise for pets, who were as cherished and well cared for as were the children of the island.

It suddenly dawned on Emma she had totally forgotten the box of stones again. She tossed aside her pencil and raced down to Zoe's room and knocked on the door.

"Come in, dear."

"Aunt Zoe, remember the box of stones you were telling me about?"

"Why, yes. Funny, I forgot all about them!"

"Me, too, but I looked for them last night and couldn't find them in the closet."

"Really? I'm sure that's where I put them. Let's look again."

They hurried to Emma's room, both feeling excited, but not sure why.

Zoe opened the closet door and there sat the box. She looked at Emma, whose mouth was hanging open.

"That box was not in that closet last night," Emma said. "We all looked. It wasn't there."

"This is odd," said Zoe.

"Yep."

"Let's open it. Want to?"

"Yep," Emma said, but she hesitated for a second or two before picking it up and placing it on the bed. "Why do I feel so nervous about this?" She looked at Zoe and saw she was nervous also. "We're being silly."

"Of course we are," said Zoe. "So. Open it already."

Emma took a deep breath and opened the box.

Both women gasped.

It was full of the most gorgeous turquoise and amber stones imaginable.

The turquoise stones were all shades of blues and greens. The fossilized amber stones were deep, true golden amber tones, each flicked with inclusions caused by animal and plant material contained inside.

Zoe and Emma were speechless as they ran their hands through the stones, picking out an occasional piece to exclaim over.

"Where did these come from?" whispered Emma.

"I think I might know," said Zoe.

They looked at one another and Emma raised her eyebrows in question. "Aunt Elizabeth?"

Zoe nodded.

"But how . . . ."

"Amazing," Zoe said. "Never underestimate the powers of Elizabeth Calhoun.

Emma ran a hand through her hair, "I've been looking and working and switching stones in some of my silver pieces for months. I knew I was looking for something special, but I couldn't quite grasp what it was. This is it. Aunt Zoe, these are the stones I need. The yellow amber will represent the sun, the turquoise in all its varying shades of blues and greens will represent the sea."

She looked up at her aunt.

Zoe was nodding, "Yes." She locked eyes with Emma. "Large, bold, impressive pieces. Perfect."

Emma squealed, hopped up and did a little happy dance around the room.

Zoe fell back on the bed laughing.

Pyewackett and Fred jumped on the bed, kissed Zoe, jumped off again and danced with Emma. And repeated their act of joy again.

"I have to get to work," Emma said, "Right now. Oh, wow. Aunt Zoe, do you think . . . . "

"I do," Zoe nodded, "And yes, you'll have a lot of work to do if you want your work there in time for the grand opening."

They hugged again, laughter bubbling between them.

Emma stepped back, "I'm getting ahead of myself." She took a deep breath. "I need to check something. Right now. Oh, Aunt Zoe, help me. Will you look through this bag and see if you can find a heavy sterling neckwire, please? I've kept it separate from my other work for some reason, although I'm not sure why. This might be the reason."

Emma handed Zoe a totebag and started looking through a second one herself.

After a few minutes, Zoe pulled out a heavy gleaming wide band of silver. "This?"

"Yes! Now, if I'm right about this, there should be two stones in this box that will fit right into those bezels."

Emma dumped the stones onto the bed. She and Zoe spent several minutes searching until they did indeed find two stones that fit perfectly. After Emma had worked them into the bezels, they sat back and gazed at the piece in wonder.

She had taken a large piece of oval turquoise and placed it against and slightly beneath a larger piece of randomly shaped yellow amber. The amber was spotted internally with pieces of plant matter and one tiny intact insect. The stones were set in silver bezels attached to a wide silver collar. Simple, but bold.

"It's what kept trying to come to me as we watched the sunrise from your suite in Atlanta. When Olivia mentioned remembering how much I loved sitting on the beach at Whimsey, this just came to me in a flash, but was gone just as quickly. Then it kept coming back, but only to dance around the edges of my mind. I was moving to this point, and it took the two of you to help me get here. Well, you and Great Aunt Elizabeth. She dropped by a few times, both in Atlanta and in Ellijay. I thought it was just to say 'Hey.' You know how she does."

Zoe shook her head and chuckled, "She is a scamp! Aunt Elizabeth isn't about to miss out on anything this big. She wants to be a part of things, which is entirely understandable. And she wanted to help you." The two women jumped when they heard a crash as a vase on the other side of the room fell onto the floor and broke. "And we want you to be a part of things, of course! Need for you to be, truth be told," said Zoe, looking toward the broken vase - which was an old one she remembered Elizabeth not being terribly fond of.

"When she came while I was in Ellijay, it was to leave me a red crayon," Emma said. "You know, I have always loved red crayons."

Zoe nodded, "I do remember. And you were very particular about who you would share them with."

"It took coming back to Whimsey for the walls to fall away and let me see what I needed to see. Now I know why Aunt Elizabeth has been showing up more often than usual. She tried to tell me it wouldn't be easy. She tried to tell me a lot of things. I just wasn't hearing what she was really saying. She was telling me I had to find my crimson, but I didn't get the message."

"And now you know. But she wanted you back home before she would let you know her plan. This, Emmaline Hamilton Foley, is beyond spectacular. This is going to make your name known in the world of artisan jewelry."

Emma sank onto the bed, and placed her hands on either side of her face. "Yes," she whispered.

"No one can do this quite like you," Zoe continued, "and you're the only person on God's green earth who seems not to realize it. Your work is magnificent, Emma, truly. We all knew it early - you had a special gift. It's true, you lost it for a while." Zoe shrugged her shoulders and put out her hands, palms up, "But, darling? It's back. It is truly back."

"I think I'm finally beginning to believe that, Aunt Zoe. And you know what? Elizabeth must have put a bit of a spell on me because all the silver settings I have work off this neckwire. You were right when you used the word 'bold.' But, I may be going too far. I'd like it if you'd spend a little time looking at what I've drawn up and tell me what you think, please. A truthful critique."

"I'm honored you'd ask, Emma, and, of course, we'll take a look. And quite soon. I'm going to need a great deal of your work for Les étoiles. Based on what I'm seeing here, it will be magnificent and sell quickly."

"Not to worry. I've been busy as a Whimsey bee and have a lot of settings made up." Emma pointed to the stones scattered across the bed. "I have a feeling every one of them has a matching stone right here. We'll have an extensive line of the amber and turquoise pieces."

"Wonderful!" Zoe said as she picked up the collar. "Each piece will perfectly convey the feeling of the sun rising out of the ocean. They're going to be a huge hit. Brilliant, imposing and impressive."

Suddenly, Fred gave a little yip, and Pyewackett made her chipper noises. A light shimmered in the doorway of Emma's room.

"Aunt Elizabeth?" asked Zoe.

Emma turned to face the door, "Aunt Elizabeth? Oh, my. Thank you. I don't know what to say."

The light in the doorway dimmed and the tall, regal figure of Elizabeth Calhoun appeared in its place. "It certainly took long enough for you get yourself back home, Emmaline. Those stones have been here waiting for you. I know you'll make us proud, child. Welcome home." And Great Aunt Elizabeth disappeared.

"Wow," said Emma

"Yes, indeed," agreed Zoe. "Wow."

"I'll say," said Madeline.

CHAPTER TWENTY-SEVEN

A couple hours later, Emma looked up from her work and rolled her shoulders.

Time for a break.

Even though it was well past midnight, she knew she couldn't sleep. She was too wired and making surprising headway in matching stones to pieces she had earlier crafted.

She moved around some to loosen up and looked through her CDs to find something to keep her company while she continued working and chose an Adele CD. *Wonder if Willie Nelson ever listens to Adele? I'm betting yes. Probably even sang together at some party or something. Wow. Now that would be a great duet!*

Emma suddenly stopped talking to herself and stiffened. Did she hear someone downstairs? It could be Fred and Pyewackett. It could be Aunt Zoe, or even Jacob looking for a late night snack.

No.

She wouldn't have this scared sick feeling in the pit of her stomach. She knew this house and its occupants. She knew there was someone in this house who did not belong.

She put her coffee cup down and moved toward the door of her apartment which was open, as it normally was. She spotted Pye and Fred sitting at the top of the staircase, looking down. Both were making odd sounds down deep in their throats, and the hair stood up on the backs of their necks.

She tip-toed back into her apartment and picked up the phone, dialing 911 as she continued tip-toeing down the hall to Aunt Zoe's room. She knocked gently and opened the door quietly before Zoe could answer, keeping her eyes closed in case Jacob was in Zoe's bed. There were some things she just did not want to see. Just as she heard Zoe say her name, the 911 dispatcher, Chief Ostwalt's wife Violet, answered the phone. She whispered "There's someone in our house." After a moment's silence, she said, "Emma, stay where you are, honey. Harrison's on his way, and Charlie won't be far behind him."

She sat on the edge of the bed and as Zoe stirred awake, Emma mouthed a silent, "Shhh," with one finger over her lips.

She whispered, "Is Jacob here?"

Zoe shook her head no.

"So, he's not downstairs?"

"No. Emma, you're scaring me, what is it?"

Emma quietly told Zoe about the noises she'd heard downstairs and that she'd called the police. The two women sat on the bed holding hands. After only a couple minutes, they heard the sound of vehicles pulling up outside.

They heard car doors slamming and within seconds, someone beating on the front as well as the back door. "Police! Open Up!"

Zoe put her head out the bedroom window and whispered loudly, "Harrison! Shush that noise, you'll wake the whole island. The door's open, just come on in just like you've always done your entire life."

She turned to Emma. "The whole damned world has gone completely crazy. Let's go downstairs. I guess I can find out what's going on the same time Harrison does."

When they got downstairs they found Officers Harrison Pruitt and Becky Goolesby in the kitchen, both looking serious. Becky was talking quietly into her phone and turned away from Emma and Zoe as they walked into the room.

Harrison Pruitt was an old family friend who had graduated from high school with Jonathan. His time in the service before he came home to Whimsey and joined the police force had changed the once skinny boy into a handsome, confident man.

Becky Goolesby was a petite, fit blond woman who had served with Harrison and moved to Whimsey to be with him. She was only a half time employee, basically in training to take Harrison's place when Harrison replaced Chief Ostwalt upon his upcoming retirement.

"What's going on, Harrison?" Zoe said in an abrupt tone.

"Zoe, did you go to bed and leave the kitchen this way?"

Emma giggled nervously, "Are you going to scold my aunt for leaving dirty dishes on her table, Harrison?" She looked at the table, and then at her aunt, whose face had paled.

A dish with scraps of the evening's pizza crust sat on the table along with an empty glass and a crumpled paper napkin.

"No, Harrison. When I went to bed, this table was clear."

He nodded, "I figured. Emma, you didn't come down and have pizza for a snack this evening, did you?"

Emma slowly shook her head side to side and sat down in one of the kitchen chairs.

"I knew I heard someone down here. Someone came into our home and ate our leftover pizza?"

"I'm afraid it's a little more than that," said Harrison. He pointed toward the kitchen cabinets.

Written across the front was the message, "Go back to Atlanta. You're not wanted here, you loser." It was written in lipstick, in a shade Emma recalled thinking of as "vampire red" when she saw Reese Prescott wearing it the day she bumped into her down town.

Zoe pulled out a chair and sat, "I'm telling you, the world has gone nuts."

Becky sat, "I think you ladies need to move down to the big house with the rest of the family. The Chief is not happy about this and wants you out of here until we get this figured out."

"And you women have got to start locking these damned doors!" boomed Chief Ostwalt. He came barreling through the house and into the kitchen.

Zoe popped up out of her chair, chin raised defiantly, "Don't you dare raise your voice at us, Charlie Ostwalt, and most certainly not in my own damned house!"

Emma jumped a couple inches, surprised by the tone of her aunt's voice.

"We are not used to locking our doors on this island, as you well know," Zoe continued. We all know who this was. It was Reese Prescott. She's as nutty as a fruitcake, and she's now trying to drive *us* nuts. I will not have it. Do you hear me? I will not have it! Arrest the silly bitch and let's all get back to the job of living our lives."

A stunned silence fell over the room. Officers Pruitt and Goolesby stood quietly, looking at their feet. Chief Ostwalt stared at Zoe with his mouth open and his cheeks flaming red. Emma was undecided as to whether she wanted the floor to suddenly open and swallow her whole, or to throw her arms in the air and cheer loudly for her aunt. So she sat quietly.

"Now," said Zoe. "Do we want to discuss this quietly and rationally over a cup of coffee? If so, you're all more than welcome to have a seat while I start the pot." She looked around the room at everyone, nodded her head, and moved to the coffee pot.

Chief Ostwalt dropped into a chair and ran his hand over his face and head, "Zoe, I can't just go to Reese Prescott's house and knock on the door, put handcuffs on her and drag her skinny self to the hoosegow. You know this."

"Why not?" Zoe asked, her eyes blazing. "Is it not illegal to go into someone's home uninvited to raid their refrigerator and write hateful messages on their kitchen cabinets while everyone's sleeping?" She banged coffee mugs onto the kitchen counter.

"Zoe! Get a grip. For God's sake, woman, we don't know for sure it was Reese Prescott who came in here."

"Yes, by God, we do!"

"Whoa!" Emma stood and put her hands on her aunt's shoulders. "Maybe I should make the coffee. Why don't you sit down, Aunt Zoe?" Zoe and Emma looked at one another, smiled gently and hugged.

"You're right, Emma. Thank you. You make the coffee, I'll get donuts."

There was a collective sigh around the room as Zoe went to the pantry for donuts.

"Now, what do we do next?" asked Emma, looking at Charlie.

"I'll go see Reese tomorrow. Have a little chat and lay down the law without coming right out and accusing her. After I've done that, I'll have a better feeling for how best to handle all this. Harrison, Becky. I'm going to be interested in hearing your thoughts about all this. I want you both to go with me tomorrow. Reese has known me for a long time, and like most around Whimsey, tends to think of me as a harmless old uncle. With the three of us showing up together, I'm hoping the gravity of what she's doing will sink in. Along with what the consequences might be."

The discussion of Reese, along with official statements being given and recorded on Officer Goolesby's laptop, proceeded along with the consumption of donuts and coffee. It continued into a conversation about the upcoming gallery opening and how the excitement was obvious all over the island. Everyone, it seemed, had at least one family member who would be represented by the new gallery. The opening was going to be a big Whimsey party. Everyone on the island had been invited. Most would be there. There was speculation around the table about whether Reese Prescott would attend.

"Oh," said Zoe, "I'm quite sure she will. And possibly her mother, as well. Her mother is, of course, already represented by a big time, well known gallery in New York, so won't be showing her sculptures here, but she's been supportive. Both in actions and financially. She RSVP'd to the gallery opening invite early on. For herself and for Reese. I don't turn people's financial support away even when I'm sure they're looney tunes crazy."

Chief Ostwalt shook his head and the officers both tried to hide smiles, "Great. Let's just invite the foxes into the hen house, why don't we?" he said.

"Um, Chief," said Officer Goolesby "it could work out to our benefit, couldn't it? If we stick kind of close, we might hear Ms. Prescott say something that could help us prove she's been behind these incidents. Don't you think?"

"Yes, Becky, I do. But I'm never going to pass up an opportunity to rib Ms. Hamilton a little" He grinned at Zoe. "But, yes, we're going to make use of the opportunity presented. You betcha. And we're going to get out of here now. Let the ladies get some much needed sleep. Zoe? Emma? I'll drop by or call tomorrow and let you know how our conversation with Reese went. That okay by you both? Fine, fine. Goodnight now."

After their "company" had left, Emma and Zoe settled in the living room, Pyewackett in Zoe's lap and Fred sprawled across Emma's.

"Aunt Zoe, I don't think I knew the whole island was invited to the grand opening. It makes sense, of course. And it's not as though it'll even be that huge a crowd seeing as how Whimsey's not all that big, but still. That's a lot of folks for Les étoiles to handle."

"It is, I agree, sugar. But there's no way I'm going to have a grand opening and leave some of these people out of it. This is for them. It's always been about and for the people who have made this island what it is. I've given the opening a lot of thought. Let me tell you what I've finally come up with and you tell me what you think.

"I know most grand openings are very glittery and very exclusive. That sort of thing won't fly here on Whimsey. But. Those whose work is being represented deserve some glitz and glitter and even those who are not used to that sort of thing will be flattered and are deserving of it. At the same time, it would embarrass some and make them feel uneasy. I want everyone who has a piece of art at Les étoiles to feel great pride in their work, in their gallery, and to enjoy the opening. It's a party for them and their families. So I'm making it a party in the truest sense of the word. The inside of the gallery will have tables of prissy little finger food, along with some of our Lowcountry foods we're all so fond of. We'll have a few tuxedoed waiters carrying silver trays of champagne along with some of our locals dressed in jeans and white shirts serving bottles of beer from silver trays. There will be the requisite soft music playing inside, and a local band playing a mix of whatever people request outside in the side yard. I want the opening to encompass the outdoors, too. That way, the gallery won't ever have to get too crowded. And maybe everyone still stay and party all evening. Also, to help with the crowd problem, we're starting early in the day. It'll be a drop in anytime kind of affair. Some of our old-timers will want to come see what all the hoopla is about and get home early enough to share gossip about it with their neighbors before it's time for them to turn in. And, of course, we'll have a huge cake and lots of ice cream set up outside for the kids. There's plenty of space out there for them to run wild after they've gorged themselves and are running on a sugar high.

What do you think?"

"Aunt Zoe, I think you are an amazing woman. I want to be you when I grow up. Truly. This is all just brilliant. You've thought of everything. Actually, I should say, you've thought of everyone. Every single person on this island. I shouldn't be the least bit surprised because you always have. It'll be lovely. I am so proud of you and so proud to be a part of your dream."

"Our dream, Emma. Especially you and the girls. I wanted all the young people who had left Whimsey for greener pastures to come home. There are no pastures greener than these."

Emma reached over and took her aunt's hands and nodded, "It just took some of us an awfully long time to figure out what you've always known. I'm awfully happy to be back home."

Zoe reached over and wiped a single tear off Emma's cheek, "Me, too, punkin."

They both stood at the same time, "Now, let's go to bed before we sit here getting all maudlin, what say?" said Zoe.

"I think I'll go sit on the porch for a while," Emma said. "I just want to clear my head and try to wish Reese Prescott off the face of the earth. Or at least off the island of Whimsey."

Zoe walked up the stairs with Pyewackett and Fred following.

Emma sat for a few moments more. First, there was the confrontation with Reese on the street downtown, then the business on the roof. Now this. Each time more blatant than the last. And more scary.

Finally, Emma made her weary way upstairs to her bedroom, wondering what Reese would do next. And wondering if she'd be able to sleep at all.

CHAPTER TWENTY-EIGHT

Chief Ostwalt dropped by the next morning to report that their "chat" with Reese yielded only obviously phoney wide-eyed shock and repeated comments to the tune of, "Well, bless Emma's heart. I surely do hope all this gets worked out for that poor girl. I surely do."

Emma and Zoe exploded, talking over one another excitedly, with their story about the night before.

Chief Ostwalt asked if they wanted to file charges, but Emma and Zoe agreed they just wanted it, and Reese, to go away. Far, far away.

Over the next two weeks, life returned to normal.

The sounds of scurrying on the roof had come to a stop, and no more food was found missing during odd midnight raids on Zoe's refrigerator. Reese became a minor annoyance in the back of Emma's mind.

The days went by quietly with a structure and routine settling.

Emma spent her days working, and most evenings at home. Zoe teased her that things hadn't changed a bit - her friends were still in and out at all hours. Sometimes Emma and Zoe would come home to find several of The Wicked Women along with Zelda and several of Zoe's friends gathered on the porch enjoying a gab fest.

Emma caught glimpses of Eli coming and going from the gallery, but he was usually too busy to stop and talk. When his hands weren't full of tools, pieces of wood, or boxes of who-knows-what, he would wave at her.

Her design sketches, along with crafted pieces, were now accumulating at a good rate. No "little girl" pieces in this line. These pieces were for the woman who possessed a great deal of self-confidence. Anyone else would be outdone by the jewelry and diminished by it.

Her routine still included a morning run most every day, but now also included a late afternoon workout at the gym. She had an exercise routine focusing on the areas she wanted to work on, was sticking to it religiously, and feeling virtuous about it all. Besides, she was beginning to see the results, which was exactly the inspiration she needed to stick with it.

She was still coming up missing the occasional shoe, but not as often. She was also still adrift in glitter, but since everyone on Whimsey had been witnessing this since her childhood and, therefore, were not the least bit surprised by it, she pretty much stopped fretting about it. What was, was. What more could a girl do? It could be worse, after all.

As time for the opening grew closer, she saw the Wicked Women less often. They were all busy with their own work and with life. The intensity of their get-togethers had settled into more relaxed, less frenzied times.

And – as is so apt to happen - when things are going well and one becomes complacent, the proverbial other shoe will drop.

After spending a busy day working, one that had gone long into the night, Emma was unwinding in a porch rocker before turning in.

A shadow fell over her and when Emma looked up, she couldn't help but jump a bit. There stood Reese Prescott on Aunt Zoe's porch looking down on her. It felt as though she had conjured her up somehow.

"Hello, Reese. Is my aunt expecting you?"

"No."

Emma made a move to get up and Reese leaned in, placing her hands on the rocking chair arms so Emma was unable to get up without pushing Reese away. She thought about it for about half a second, and all the anger she had felt at Reese for all the past years and for all the lies erupted.

Emma stood up quickly and pushed Reese out of her way. Reese staggered backwards but managed to stay on her feet.

"So," Reese said through clenched teeth, "you've finally gotten yourself a little bit of backbone, have you, Miss Priss?"

"What do you want, Reese?"

"Just being neighborly, Emma. That's all. And I wanted to tell you Eli and I have worked things out. We had a bit of a rough patch, but we're good now, so don't get your hopes up about seeing him anymore, okay?" And she smirked.

When Reese turned to walk back down the steps, Emma reached out and grabbed her arm and spun her around, "It's over, Reese. There is no 'you and Eli.' It's all in your mind. I'm back and I'm staying. And if Eli and I want to continue seeing one another, or not, it has nothing to do with you."

Emma could see by the flash in Reese's eyes that she had gone too far. Before she knew it, Reese pushed her backwards until Emma was against the house. Reese tightly wound a hand in Emma's hair and pulled hard. Emma shrieked with pain and reached up to grab Reese's hand, but she noticed something strange.

A garden hose rose up behind Reese and moved toward her. Suddenly, a hard stream of water from the hose hit Reese in the back, giving her a good hard dousing causing her to lose her grip on Emma and fall down. When she got up and saw the hose aiming her way again, she ran down the steps and up the street.

Emma shook her head, "What on earth? What just happened?"

Then she saw Earlene's little pixie face peeking around from behind the hose.

"Earlene, how did you do that?"

"Well, I had a little help from my friends," Earlene nodded her head towards the hose and Emma saw a hundred more pixies appear.

"Well, I'll be darned," Emma said, grinning at Earlene and her band of pixies. She gave a little bow. "Thank you, ladies. You are the best."

Earlene was flying and buzzing around Emma's head looking concerned.

"What is it, Earlene?" Emma asked as she reached up to touch her head. It was then she realized some of her hair was missing. "Noooooo. Do I have a bald spot?"

Earlene nodded, "But just a little one. You can't really notice it unless you're looking closely."

Emma covered her face with her hands, "I cannot believe this. A bald spot! Good Lord A Mercy." And she shook her head as she started hiccupping.

She heard the front door open, but couldn't bring herself to look up.

"Emma? Earlene?" Zoe said, clearly puzzled, "What's going on out here? Why's the porch all wet? Emma, you're a little wet too."

Emma's shoulders were shaking. Zoe walked over and put her arms around her. "Child, are you all right?"

When Emma pulled her head back, Zoe saw she was laughing and so was Earlene. Then she realized the little tinkling she heard wasn't distant church bells, but a hundred little pixies buzzing around her porch having a giggle fit.

"Oh, Aunt Zoe," Emma said as she sat down in one of the rockers. "You should have been here."

Emma and Earlene both fell into an explosion loud giggles.

When they finally had themselves under control, they shared the story of Reese's attack, Earlene's arrival with the pixies, and their heroics with the water hose.

Emma pointed to her head, "And the witch left with some of my hair!"

"Ow," muttered Madeline.

"What on earth was Reese Prescott doing here?" Zoe asked.

Emma put her hands on her hips, "She wanted to tell me to stay away from Eli."

"And I'm guessing you said no?" Zoe reached up to gently touch the very small bald spot on Emma's head.

Zoe looked at Emma and shook her head, "You know, I used to worry about you being in danger of a mugging or some such while you were living in Atlanta. It never dawned on me you might have something like this happen here on Whimsey. And on MY front porch. I find this unacceptable. I think Reese has some mental issues."

Emma burst out laughing again. "Mental issues. You think? How 'bout crazy as a bedbug?"

Zoe put her hand to her mouth, but couldn't help it. She, too, laughed out loud.

Emma stopped laughing and looked up at Earlene, "So tell me something, Earlene. Since you're still mad at me, why did you save me just now?"

The little pixie tilted her chin and struck a pose with her arms crossed, "Let me put it this way. If anybody's going to hassle you, it'll be me, not that idiot Reese Prescott."

With that, Earlene flew away, followed by a hundred other pixies, high-fiving as they went.

CHAPTER TWENTY-NINE

A few days later, Emma sat in the porch swing, nestled in with pillows, with a pitcher of iced latte on a table close by.

She was taking a break from her jewelry designing to clear her mind with a good book. While she was having a virtual glass of sweet tea with the fictional residents of Colleton County in Margaret Maron's latest novel, a loud thump brought her back to Whimsey with a splash of her latte onto Pyewackett's head. That in turn startled Pyewackett into jumping up on the swing with a screech, causing Fred to run in circles, barking madly in an attempt to chase away whatever was messing with his family.

"Excuse me, you guys," Eli said. "I was only stopping by to say hey. I didn't mean to upset the entire Hamilton household here!"

"Eli! You scared the beejesus out of all of us," Emma attempted to wipe cold latte off her and off Pyewackett, while at the same time calming the cat and the dog with gentle shushes.

"Scared the beejesus out of me, too," Eli grinned at Emma and moved his heavy camera equipment bag with his foot. "Sorry about the noise, but this bag is heavier than it looks."

"How was your photo shoot in Charleston?"

"It was a good one. The magazine editor who hired me is always on top of his game and knows what he wants before bringing everyone else in, so things go smoothly. Should be a good article, and hopefully do some good for the citizens he's profiling. They've done their homework on the development that's causing erosion to the wetlands, and they've got government backing for their efforts. I learned a lot. And, got some pretty amazing shots, some of which will be hard for people to look at, but in this case, that's the point of it all. Let people see the beauty that greed is destroying. Beauty that won't regenerate itself and once gone, is gone forever."

"It breaks my heart to think of the beauty of the marshes that we grew up with being destroyed. I'm glad you're able to help."

"Me, too. Now, what's a guy got to do to get a glass of whatever you're drinking there?"

"Iced Latte."

"Oh, yeah. Sounds perfect."

Emma turned to pour him a glass and was jolted with another loud thump.

"What WAS that?" she shouted as she jumped back. She peered around Eli's shoulder to see Sara Kate and Maggie grinning at her, their gym bags dropped onto the porch next to Eli's camera bag.

Once again, efforts were needed in shushing Fred and calming Pyewackett.

"You guys!" Emma said. "Did you come here with the specific intent of terrorizing the pets, or what?"

Maggie chuckled, "No, Emma, we're not here to terrorize dear Pye or Fred, but we couldn't just pass on by quietly when there might be the beginnings of a party here."

"Got any snackies?" asked Sarah Kate.

"Oh Lordy, just come on up here and have some of my famous iced latte. I'll go see what I can find in the kitchen."

Maggie put her hands on her hips, "I don't know about famous, but it truly is delicious. I'd love some."

Sarah Kate chimed in, "I think it's damned addictive, truth be told. I'll have some too, pretty please."

After everyone was settled around the table with a glass of latte , and Pyewackett and Fred were calm again, Sarah Kate looked from Eli to Emma and back again. "So. Not to be too forward or anything, but are you guys a couple now?"

Emma blew her latte through her nose.

Eli laughed loudly and slapped his knee, "Well, let's just say I'm working on it, but so far I haven't made much headway."

Sarah Kate opened her eyes wide in a mock look of innocence, "The working on it part could be a lot of fun. Don't you think, Maggie?"

"Mm hmm, could be," Maggie said, "indeed."

Emma put her hands on her hips and struck an indignant pose, "Y'all. You are evil women. Not only intent on terrorizing our pets, but embarrassing your so-called girlfriend here to boot. You are both just too much!"

"You are absolutely right, Emma. They are too too much. We, on the other hand, are your only true girlfriends."

Emma looked around to see Alex and Olivia on the steps with their arms tossed around each other's shoulders.

"Hey, you two! Come on up here!" shouted Emma. She hopped up to hug the two newcomers.

"Are we having a party?" asked Olivia.

Emma looked around and nodded, "It would seem so. We've all been working hard for too long. Time to chill out and let loose, don't you think?"

A chorus of hoorays and yays were shouted and before they knew it, the pitcher of latte had been replaced with bottles of ice cold beer and Zoe and Jacob showed up with a mess of steamed shrimp.

Zoe tapped Eli on the shoulder, "Before I forget, sugar, I wanted to tell you thank you for moving things around so Emma's display fit in so perfectly."

When everyone suddenly became quiet, Emma remembered. "Oh! Yes! I'm in, I'm in! Aunt Zoe and I wanted to wait until we were all here together to break the news!

Emma jumped up. "Stay right here. I'll be right back!"

And she was back in the blink of an eye.

272

"Honeys, Mama's got her mojo working. Sit, sit and feast your eyes on this."

Emma bowed toward Zoe as she handed her a deep blue velvet jewelry wrap. Zoe bowed back and accepted it.

She turned towards one of the tables and said, "Drum roll, please!"

As Jacob and Eli did pretend drum rolls, Zoe gently placed the wrap on the table and unrolled it, revealing the wide silver collar Emma had put together the night they opened the box of stones.

Sunshine hitting the porch glinted off the stones making the amber glisten as though alive.

Emma heard the woman gasp.

They all looked up at Emma as Maggie said, "Oh. My. God."

Then they all jumped up and the hugging, squealing and dancing began.

Emma turned to Olivia who opened her arms wide. When Emma stepped into them for a hug, Olivia whispered, "Oh, Emma. You've done it, honey. You've worked your magic. I hope now you know you're every bit as brilliant as we've been telling you."

Emma nodded, "Keep telling me, okay? I won't ever believe it unless you keep telling me." And then she grinned, "But that neck piece is hot, huh?"

They sat around exchanging stories about what they had each been up to, and the conversation eventually drifted around to Les étoiles and the grand opening.

Zoe assured them everything was on schedule. All needed tweaks had been tweaked. All arrangements still needing attention would be easily taken care of before Saturday rolled around.

"I hope you haven't changed things too much since we were all there," said Alex. "I thought it was perfect."

Zoe nodded, "I thought it was, too. Even more perfect now that we have Emma's work included. But there was one suggestion from Zelda that I agreed was needed. And it turned out brilliantly, wouldn't you say, Eli?"

Eli looked down at the porch floor and his face reddened, "I'm not as sure as you about that, Zoe."

Emma looked at Eli, but he continued looking at the floor, bouncing one foot nervously.

"But you do take credit for the other . . .," said Zoe, head tilted.

Eli grinned, "Yeah, I'll take *some* of the credit for that. It'll be a pretty cool addition, I think."

Zoe grinned along with him.

"And all RSVPs returned?" asked Olivia.

"We are planning on a larger than expected turn-out," said Zoe.

Emma asked, "And the food - all handled?"

Zoe laughed, "But of course, young'un!"

"And liquor - all handled?" asked Sarah Kate

Zoe threw her head back and laughed even louder, "Yes, Sarah Kate. Your favorite bottle of wine has been accounted for. All the liquid refreshments have been delivered. For someone who rarely ever drinks more than one glass of wine or one beer, you are mighty obsessed with liquor, young woman."

"Well, that one glass of wine is important to my image, don't you know," responded Sarah Kate.

"Yes, well," Maggie said with a wink, "being so short and all, it doesn't take much to get her looped."

"I can't help being the adorable petite one in a world of ferocious Amazons," retorted Sarah Kate.

Alex patted her on the head, "We just let you hang around with us 'cause we need a small mascot."

Sarah Kate tried to smack Alex's hand away, "Quit," she squealed.

The teasing continued and the joshing jumped from one to another as the evening went on with friends and family dropping by on their way to or from a walk on the beach or out to the marsh.

When Jonathan showed up with Zelda and Scott, Olivia asked, "What have you done with our children, oh handsome husband of mine?"

He dropped a kiss on her head and reminded her, at some length, about the spend the night party the Tatnalls had planned for their grandchildren and about how there must have been twenty-seven million children there when they dropped Max and Abby off. And each of them in possession of a particularly loud type of squeal he was sure would cause many ears to be damaged for many years to come. His included.

Zelda and Scott, eyes glazed, put their hands over their ears, squeezed their eyes shut and moaned.

Zoe quickly handed them each a glass containing their favorite adult beverage, the first of which appeared to disappear at a rather alarming rate, but the second of which seemed to be consumed more moderately as the zombie type expressions morphed into more relaxed, normal ones.

After a while, amid a few yawns, everyone started saying their good nights.

Emma stood to hug her friends good night and said, "Y'all. I know we're going to be busy and probably won't see one another before the opening. Come over early Saturday morning so we can get dressed together. You do remember what we planned, right?"

The other women all grinned and giggled.

Zoe turned to Emma with her eyebrows raised in question.

"Oh, Aunt Zoe, you'll love it."

And the other Wicked Women chimed in.

"You will."

"Promise."

"And it's going to be huge fun."

"Damned straight!"

Jacob eased out of his chair, "You're gonna have a hard time topping how gorgeous y'all were for the sneak preview, and that's the truth."

"Now that's the livin' truth," agreed Eli.

The women all grinned in return.

The next afternoon while working on a particular tricky piece, Emma moved away from her work table to gaze out her window. Looking across the dunes over the ocean often helped clear the cobwebs away and bring things into focus. It also was a constant source of inspiration and ideas for new designs.

She pulled a small slipper chair closer so she could sit in it with her bare feet propped on the window will. As she got ready to sit, he noticed a red crayon on the cushion.

Holding it in her hand while she sat, she felt her Aunt Elizabeth's presence.

"Thanks for the crayon, Aunt Elizabeth."

"You're welcome, m'dear," Aunt Elizabeth answered. "You haven't remembered yet, have you?"

"No." Emma shook her head. "And you've been toying with me about it, haven't you?"

Elizabeth chuckled, "I suppose I have, yes."

Emma looked down at her silver bracelet and slipped it off her arm. She ran her finger over the engraving on the inside.

Find your crimson and hold on tight.

She smiled as she slipped it back on her arm. Her grandfather Ben made the bracelet and presented it to her on her sixteenth birthday. She'd worn it every day since. All her friends and family were familiar with the bracelet, but few were aware of the message inside. A lovely secret between her and her beloved grandfather. But a secret only one of them knew the full story behind. Ben had never told Emma what it meant. When she asked about it, he told her only that the answer would present itself when the time was right.

Emma tilted her head to one side, "Is the time right?"

"I believe so. Stay seated, child, let me tell you a story."

CHAPTER THIRTY

The story Elizabeth told Emma was from the early days of Whimsey while Ben and Lillith were, in addition to helping Elizabeth, working at their own crafts. Both were still in the early stages of finding their individual voices in their God given talents. And delivering their finest most proud creations - daughters Zelda and Zoe.

Very early one morning, Elizabeth slipped into the kitchen on the first floor. She stood quietly watching her niece paint a nice little still life of a bowl of fruit sitting next to a vase of flowers which she had placed with great care on an old pine table in front on the window looking out over the marsh.

"Very pretty, Lillith."

"Aunt Elizabeth, good morning! Join me for breakfast and a cup of coffee. What on earth are you doing up so early? And down here. This is quite a surprise!"

"I had a suspicion you might be up painting and thought I'd take a chance you might not mind a little company. I've had my breakfast already, but would love a cup of coffee with you, dear. Very convenient having my own fully equipped apartment upstairs, I must say. Otherwise, I fear we would tire of one another quite quickly. Two women under the same roof and all that."

Lillith laughed, "Yes, I suspect you're right, although your roof does cover quite a rather large house, I must say."

"Hmmm. So it does. What do you think, Lillith, have we chosen wisely? Are you and Ben happy here, or do you want a place all your own? Truthfully, now, please."

"Oh, Aunt Elizabeth, we couldn't be happier. You thought of everything when you built this house. Not only do we all have plenty of room, you've planned for the future. And the studio spaces you surprised us with are the loveliest ever. We'll never be able to thank you enough for all you've done. It would have been years before we saved enough money to get married and have our own place without your help."

Elizabeth put her coffee cup down with a thud. "Oh, pshaw. I'm a selfish old woman who wanted your company, that's all."

"Oh, pshaw yourself. Who knew people really said 'pshaw?' You have Annie and Rupert, and you would have been fine."

"Yes, I do have Annie and Rupert for now, but their cottage is almost finished. They'll be moving into it soon, and they'll be able to give all the time they want to their spinning and weaving. We're going to have to find new people to help us keep this house running."

Lillith patted her aunt's hand, "We will. Annie said she would be happy to help us interview some people. And it will remain the smoothly run household it has been with her and Rupert. You have to admit it, Auntie, you are simply brilliant. Your plans are working out to be exactly as we had hoped for all concerned. This is home, and it's perfect, don't you think?"

"I do. Your little painting there, however, is not."

"Is not what? Perfect?" Lillith looked down at her painting and spun around to look at her aunt, placing her hands on her hips.

"Exactly. And don't go getting all defensive. You're not all that wild about it either. Admit it."

Lillith sat down and dropped her chin into the palm of her hand. "You're right. I hate it. But I don't seem to be able to figure out what it is I want to paint. I just know I need to see colors on paper. Glorious splashes of color. But nothing seems to come out the way I see it in my mind, and I hate it. And you know, there's just nothing exciting or fun about painting a dumb bowl of fruit. There's nothing to be done to it to make it more than what it is. And to me, it's just plain and simply boring."

"I have a suggestion."

Lillith looked at her aunt and uttered a tentative "Okay."

"Go look out that window over the marsh and paint what you see."

"Well, how boring will that be? It doesn't change, it's just boring old sea grasses. Sometimes they might look a little browner than they did the day before, and sometimes the water might look a little muddier than it did last week."

Elizabeth followed Lillith to the window and stood beside her, "Lillith, sometimes we don't see the things we're most familiar with at all. We think we already know how things look and expect them to look that way so that's what we see. I want you to clear your mind of the marsh you've seen so many times and see it for the very first time."

"I'll try."

At that moment, a handful of clouds moved aside, revealing a brilliant blue sky and a bright, burning sun above the marsh. Lillith stared, doing her best to see it for the very first time.

"Oh, my. Look at that. The sun's rays mingle with the colors of the flowers and with the shadows under the leaves and branches. Even the blue of the sky is blending with all the other colors to form something I've never noticed before. They form a new color that winds through and around everything else, very subtly, but definitely there. It's like a red, but more vibrant and alive. It's . . . it's . . . oh, what is that color? I know. It's crimson. Why have I never seen it before? How could I have missed it all this time. That's what I want to paint."

Elizabeth smiled and watched Lillith bustle over to the table, muttering to herself, rummaging through tubes of paint, knocking the bowl of fruit out of her way.

Elizabeth put her coffee cup in the sink and said good-bye, although it was clear she had been forgotten. Chuckling as she left the room, Elizabeth paused to listen as Lillith repeatedly mumbled, "Where's my crimson? Where is my crimson?"

As Elizabeth left the house thinking she might enjoy a walk along the beach, she spotted Benjamin strolling up the beach with his hands in his pockets, his head down and appearing to be off in another world. It took calling his name twice to get him to look up. When he did, and caught Elizabeth looking at him, he smiled brightly and waved.

"Mornin'!"

"And good morning to you! You certainly were deep in thought."

"I was, indeed. You know, this beach and this island have offered up a great deal of ideas for some exciting designs. What would you think of a line of sterling shells with a small piece of sea glass worked into each of them in some way? Some would be brooches, some would be pendants."

"Glorious! I think they would be a huge hit!"

"Me, too. I'm going to get into my studio and start drawing up some ideas. First I think I'll drop in and see how Lillith's latest still life is going. She seemed a little dissatisfied earlier."

Elizabeth chuckled, "You may have seen the last of still lifes. I think we're going to see a whole new line of art from your lovely Lillith. If my guess is correct, it's going to be quite exciting."

"Really?! And when did this all take place?"

"Just this morning. You may find her a bit distracted when you go in the house. When I left, she was tossing things left and right, muttering something about needing to find her crimson."

"Her crimson? Well, well, well . . . . ."

Elizabeth left him standing there looking mildly confused as she continued down the beach.

When Aunt Elizabeth finished her story, Emma looked at her with her mouth open and her eyes wide, "Oh, what a wonderful story!"

"I think so, too," said Aunt Elizabeth. "And I'm very happy, Emmaline, that you have found your crimson, not only in the stones I gathered for you, but in simply being back here where you belong among people who love you."

"Thank you, Aunt Elizabeth. I wasn't ready earlier, was I? Even though I thought I was."

Elizabeth shook her head and reached for Emma's hand with her own ghostly one, "No, Emma. You weren't. Your gift is one to be cherished. You would have used it for the fame and fortune, without ever understanding in your heart where the gift had come from. You belong here. Whimsey will nourish you along with your talent. And more - it's time to let go of Hunter Quinn, Emma. You two weren't right for each other, but what happened to him was not your fault. Let it go."

Emma bent over and cried. She cried harder than she knew possible. Long hard wracking sobs that left her drained and exhausted. She cried for Hunter and their sadly mistaken marriage. She cried for the time she had wasted unnecessarily. She wept with gratitude for her talent and for her blessings - and for loved ones who had not given up on her. Once the tears finally stopped, she realized Aunt Elizabeth was gone. She moved from the chair to her bed, pulled a light throw over herself and fell into a deep slumber.

CHAPTER THIRTY-ONE

Mother Nature was in agreement that the day was a special one. She arrived in full splendor.

It was a typical soft Lowcountry day, one of those some people swear is the reason behind southern manners and hospitality, and quite possibly, even the peaches and cream complexion a large percentage of southern women seem to possess.

Zoe arrived before noon to handle a few final touches and enjoy a final turn around her place of dreams while it was still hers. Before she gave it, if only figuratively, to the rest of the world. She did a silent blessing as she walked through, touching things here and there, making minute adjustments for no other reason than to touch these items of beauty which came from the hands and the hearts of the people of Whimsey.

She looked up at one wall on which Eli had stenciled a quote from *Much Ado About Nothing.*

"There was a star danced, and under that was I born."

She thought the whimsical addition of a few quotes and lines of poetry referencing stars was just the perfect touch E'toile had needed. And the idea seemed to have come to both her and Eli at the exact same moment. A moment when she could have sworn she saw a tiny light flash over Eli's head at the same time she heard a little "click" in her own. They enjoyed bringing quotes to one another over the next few days until they were able to decide which they would stencil on the walls. Then they asked a local calligrapher to write all of them down and had them copied onto handmade pale gray paper embossed with pale silver stars with a border of shell pink. These were cut into small cards to be dropped into the E'toile signature bags of the same colors along with items purchased.

On another wall was a piece by Sara Teasdale

"Stars over snow,

And in the west a planet

Swinging below a star--

Look for a lovely thing and you will find it.

It is not far--It never will be far."

~ Night, by Sara Teasdale

Before she knew it, time had flown by and people were stopping by to hug her, congratulate her or ask a question about a particular artist or a piece of their work.

When the caterers showed up, they were able to quickly set up because they had been shown earlier where everything was to be placed. They, too, wanted to join in the festivities and were welcomed.

Zoe was chatting with Lou and Ethan Tatnall when she noticed a drop in the level of noise in the room. Conversation seemed to turn to whispers. When she turned to see what might be the cause, she caught her breath in a gasp.

"Oh, my."

Just inside the entrance stood Emma, Olivia, Alex, Maggie and Sarah Kate.

They were grinning like proverbial Cheshire Cats, but they looked like a vision from another time. They wore vintage dresses in creamy shades of white, along with hats, looking remarkably like Olivia's painting of them hanging to their left. Zoe heard someone quietly whisper, "Our gals are all grown up," and "Lookie there, aren't they beautiful?" And she had to agree.

As they approached her, giggling, Zoe gave them each a hug and called them minxes.

"Yes, that would be us," said Alex.

They each grabbed a flute of sparkling water (it was, after all, going to be a very long day), and made their rounds, visiting with everyone and looking to see what had changed since their earlier sneak preview.

They were surprised by the number of people. They weren't surprised to see that all of Whimsey had turned out, but it would seem a good part of Savannah had shown up as well.

As they elbowed their way through the crowd, Emma and Olivia spotted several of the gallery owners Zoe had introduced them to in Atlanta.

When they reached a photo exhibit that had earlier been set up as Zelda's, they stopped and stepped back.

"Whoa," said Sarah Kate.

Before them was the work of two artists. Teacher and pupil. The black and white images had been arranged to show the same shots from two perspectives: Zelda's and Eli's. The impact of the exhibit as a whole was a major drama of sensations. Once the senses had recovered and upon closer scrutiny, the images elicited moods ranging the entire emotional spectrum. They each, but in very different ways, took the viewer on a journey of emotions from uncontained laughter to unstoppable tears. Each photo was as revealing of the artist as a look into their eyes. How each chose to compose a particular shot was a study in dichotomy. What each chose to hide, or reveal, in their shadows was a bit like a treasure hunt of viewing.

"It's purely and simply exquisite, isn't it?" Zoe asked Emma as she took her hand.

Emma, though nearly breathless, managed to reply, "It's brilliant. It's almost too much, but stops miraculously just short of that. It's perfect. Will you ever be able to bring yourself to break up the exhibit in order to sell the pieces individually?"

"This will be a permanent collection piece. But Zelda and Eli have agreed to sell a very limited edition of prints of some of the photos."

"Some of them? Not all?"

Zoe shook her head, "No, not all."

"Is that marketing wizardry at work or sentiment?"

"I believe," answered Zoe, "it's sentiment that evolves into marketing wizardry. Which will make the artists, and Les étoiles, a great deal of money."

288

"Wow," Emma couldn't move her eyes away from the images. "They're mesmerizing as a whole, but equally so all on their own. How did they do this?"

"I think they've worked together for so many years, they've become quite in sync, but it just never showed up until we started putting things together for the exhibit. No one was more stunned than they were. Your mother is quite proud of the work she's been able to do with Eli. She feels as though he has quite a gift, and it's a talent still young. She believes, as I do, that he's going to be a very big name."

"Wow."

"Yes. So you said."

Emma and Zoe stepped away from the growing crowd wanting to see Zelda and Eli's work and wandered outside.

"You were so smart to handle the opening in just this way, Aunt Zoe. This is so great. Look at all these faces. I haven't seen some of these people in years. And I need to go hug a few necks and get my cheeks pinched a few times. This is just too fun." She spun around and wrapped her aunt in a hug. "Thank you. Thank you for Les étoiles and for everything you've done for all of us."

"Oh, child. Thank you. I'm just trying to make sure we have a Whimsey to still be proud of when the next generations come along. In order for that to happen we have to work at it and nurture it. Take care of it. That way, it will still be all that it is now when your grandchildren come along."

"Wow."

"Emma, we need to work on your vocabulary, darling. It's diminished since you arrived."

"Aunt Zoe! You just keep surprising me. I don't think too quickly on my feet, I guess."

"Oh, bunk. You're the quickest of the quick, but surprises do tend to knock the words out of a body, I suppose. Now, I'm going to go sit down and get off this gimpy leg. I need to catch up with Lou and have a good gossip. You go visit. Have fun." Zoe kissed Emma on the cheek and gave her a little pat on the fanny to get her moving along. She spotted Lou waving at her from across the lawn, pointing at two chairs she had managed to capture for them.

"Before I go join Lou, have you seen your exhibit yet?"

Emma shook her head no.

"Nervous?"

Emma nodded her head yes.

"Want me to go with you?"

Emma took a breath, "No. No, I think I want a few minutes alone. Is that okay?"

Zoe smiled at her niece and patted her face gently, "Completely okay and understandable." She gave her a brief hug before walking away.

Emma walked slowly to the jewelry display discreetly bearing her name. Aunt Zoe had chosen only a few pieces from the amber and turquoise collection which

together they had named "Whimsey Spirits" representing the sun and the ocean. The central piece was the first piece they had done together. There were two bracelets, a large cuff, the other an only slightly smaller bangle.
Additionally, there were a few pairs of earrings and some rings. Each piece crafted with plain and simple lines but large and bold.

While Emma was admiring the exhibit and lighting Zoe had created to show her work at its best, she felt her Aunt Elizabeth's presence. She turned her head towards the light shimmering next to her.

"It's beautiful work you've done, Emma. I'm very, very proud of you."

"I wouldn't have done it without your help. Thank you."

"Oh, pshaw. You would have. Maybe not these exact pieces, but the talent is yours. All yours. You deserve to be quite proud. Now, it's time for you to concentrate on finding your crimson in your life aside from your work. As the saying goes these days, don't blow it."

"Pfffft. Aunt Elizabeth, you are a tonic."

"Bye bye, child. Enjoy your evening."

"Bye," Emma whispered back.

People began wandering up to greet Emma and compliment her on her work. She was enjoying seeing old friends and catching up with their family news. As she turned to walk away to find the rest of The Wicked Women, she bumped squarely into Eli.

"Ooops! Hi." She looked up at him and grinned, "This is so much fun."

"It is. Everything is perfect, I think. Your Aunt Zoe is a genius."

"Oh, yes. I agree."

"And a marketing genius to boot. Even I can figure this out. Anyone buying a single piece of this collection is going to feel cheated if they don't have that killer necklace to go along with it. It's beautiful, Emma. Your grandfather would be proud."

Emma nodded as the tears pooled in her eyes, "He would, wouldn't he?"

"I am, too, Emma. You've come into your own, darlin'." And with that he leaned in to give her a light kiss, which she welcomed by putting her arms around his neck. Surprised, Eli pulled back and looked at her. She smiled, looked deeply into his eyes and pulled him close and kissed him again.

"Emma! Quit kissing that man and come see what Aunt Zoe has done with our stuff, girl! You guys can kiss later."

Eli pulled back a little and looked into Emma's eyes, which were happy.

She nodded again, and said, "Sarah Kate calls."

"And is Sarah Kate right in that we can kiss later?"

"Oh, yes, let's plan on it."

"Wow," he said.

"Wow," said Madeline.

CHAPTER THIRTY-TWO

After Emma joined Sarah Kate and the other girls and they swooned over several exhibits, Emma headed outside toward the food tables. She heard a buzzing around her head and felt a quick little peck on her cheek. She realized it was Earlene, who was now perched on her shoulder.

"Emma?"

"Yes, Earlene?"

"Have you noticed anything different?"

"No," Emma replied. "What do you mean?"

"Look down."

Emma looked down and it finally dawned on her. There was no silver glitter. "Oh, Earlene, does this mean what I think it means?"

"Yes, my dear Emma, from what I've seen here, you've finally got your act together, so no more silver glitter. You might also find your shoes stay where they belong, too."

"I don't know how to ever thank you."

"Well, just don't get too cocky, girlfriend. You screw up and get off track again, and next time, it'll be something worse than silver glitter."

"Oh, I'll remember," Emma said, "And I'll be careful."

"And one more thing," Earlene said, "If you don't latch onto that hunk Eli, I'm going to move in and take him for myself."

Emma laughed, "And I'm sure you could. Don't worry. I'm working on that. And by the way, you look gorgeous!" She smiled at Earlene who smiled back, eyes twinkling - literally.

"Do you like my dress? I overheard you and the other gals planning your look for today and decided to join you. Is that okay?"

"Oh, Earlene, of course it is! We looked for you to ask if you wanted to play along with us. Where were you?"

"Actually, I was right there in the gallery while you were talking, but I had a nasty cold and didn't want you give it to any of you, so I was bundled up and in the toe of one of Sarah Kate's long stockings. I'm in love with those stockings, aren't you?"

"Yes, I am. I never gave much thought to how warm they might be though, truth be told."

"Oh, they're the cat's pajamas! Anyway, I did hear you say you were going to ask me, so I thought I'd just surprise you. So. Tell me what you think!"

Emma looked at Earlene and had to admit - she looked beautiful. She looked more like a fairy than the wicked little pixie she had always thought her to be. Her red hair was down and long, flowing softly down her back in waves, her creamy white cotton dress fell in folds around her tiny feet, and her teeny strappy high heel sandals were the same creamy white as her dress. Her toes were painted a pearly pink.

"Is this going to be your new look, Earlene?"

"HEEEEEE!" she shrieked. "Laws, no. Spoil my image? No way! But it is fun to play every once in a while, isn't it?"

Emma laughed along with her, "Yep. Playfulness is a quality I admire in people. AND pixies!"

Emma and Earlene were grinning at one another when Eli walked up to them, "And may I say you both look dazzling today, ladies?" Eli leaned over to give Emma a kiss on her cheek, careful not to muss the itty bitty little pink one left there by Earlene, just as Earlene flew up to give him a matching kiss on his cheek.

"Hey, handsome!" Earlene greeted him by batting her eyes at him over her pale pink rhinestone cat's eye glasses.

The three of them continued on their way to the food tables, greeting friends and family members along the way.

After finding seats together at a picnic table and enjoying sharing plates filled with a little bit of everything, they spent time watching all the guests. Eli reminded Emma who some of the people were she didn't recognize, along with what they were now doing. Earlene did a good job of filling them both in on the stories they weren't likely to hear from other sources.

Emma had her head tilted toward Earlene when all of a sudden she felt something icy cold running down her back.

"Oh, no! Emma honey, I seemed to have spilled a little bit of my punch on you, sugar. I am SO sorry!" Emma recognized the whiney voice of Reese Prescott.

"Don't give it another thought, Reese."

While Emma stood up and examined her dress to see what damage Reese had caused and to see if it could be fixed, Reese wasted no time. She put her arms around Eli's neck and started nuzzling his ear, "Eli, honey, where have you been? Have you been missing me? We need to get together real soon, you hear. I'll show you a real good time. You know I can, baby."

Eli stepped back and removed Reese's arms, "Reese, you're drunk. Get someone to take you home before you make a bigger fool of yourself than you already have. Come on, Emma, honey. Let's go clean up this pretty dress."

They walked away and Earlene buzzed after them. Emma was sure she heard Earlene giving Reese a raspberry and wondered how she could have disliked the little creature for so long.

When they reached the gallery, Earlene suggested they step into the storeroom where she lived. "There's a mirror and a sink in the bathroom. Come on, I'll show you." When Emma saw the stain on the back of her dress, she didn't know whether to cry or run and find Reese to smack her silly.

"Oh no," she wailed. "This beautiful old dress of Great Aunt Elizabeth's is ruined."

Eli nodded, his face flushed, "The woman is just damned crazy. But not to worry, we're gonna get this dress clean and pretend none of this ever happened. Now, I need some help with this here, Emma. Hot water or cold?"

"I don't know!" Emma wailed again. "I don't even know what's in that punch. I just know it's the ugliest shade of green I've ever seen. Yuck. Who would drink this nasty stuff?"

"It's a Whimsey tradition. The kids always seem to love it, but I think from the smell of Reese's breath, she added a tot or two or several of hard liquor. Maybe some of the homemade stuff you can still find around here if you know who to ask."

Earlene was flying and buzzing, eyes snapping, "Emmaline! Are you crying? No, no, no. Now, honey, don't you dare let that guttersnipe Reese Prescott ruin this day for you! OR that dress. I'll take care of this."

And with that, she started spinning like a dervish. Glitter and sparks and tiny stars flew around the room. It became so bright, Emma and Eli had to close their eyes.

"There. All gone." Earlene was standing on the cold water tap on the sink, hands on her hips and a smug look on her little pixie face.

Emma turned to look in the mirror and the stain from the green punch was all gone.

"Earlene, I love you. Thank you." And she leaned over and gave Earlene a kiss.

"Earlene," said Eli with a grin, "you are a queen among women. Pixies. Whatever. You just rock, honey. Now, are we ready to return to the party?

Earlene hopped on his shoulder for a ride, "We are finer than frog's hair, sugar. Yes, I think we're ready now."

As they walked outside, they spotted Jonathan, Olivia, Max and Abby. Jonathan and Olivia were in lawn chairs chatting while Max and Abby slept soundly on a quilt at their feet. Jonathan waved them over, "Join us!"

Emma hugged her brother and sister-in-law and plopped onto the quilt while Eli slipped into a lawn chair next to Jonathan, "Are you ready to make some music tonight, my friend?"

"You bet," Jonathan said. "How 'bout you? You got that voice of yours in fine fettle?"

"I think so. Your buddy Willie gonna show up and steal my act again?"

They all laughed. "Not that I know of, but Emma might know more about that than I do."

Emma giggled, "Y'all quit."

Olivia asked if any of them had seen the rest of The Wicked Women.

"Speak of the devils, here they come," said Earlene. "Don't they all look beautiful?"

Maggie, Sarah Kate and Alex sauntered over and draped themselves over the chairs, each of them attempting to outdo the others in their extreme "southerness."

"Aftunoon, dahlins, could someone fetch me a mint julip, pretty please?"

"And ah believe ah'll have me a bourbon and branch, honey chile."

"The hell with the branch, just pass me that ol' bottle of Jack and be damned quick about it."

Then they all three laughed and toasted one another with their glasses of iced tea.

"Y'all are too silly for words," said Emma, laughing along with them.

"Can't help it," said Alex.

Maggie added, "It's the dresses. You can't help but be a southern belle wearing one of these."

"And the hats," added Sarah Kate. "Lord A Mercy, these hats, don't you love 'em? Why are women scared to death to wear hats nowadays? They're divine!"

The crowd of friends sat around chatting and visiting with old friends that dropped by. Each of them happy and all of them proud of one another.

As the day moved along, people came and went. It was just as Zoe had predicted with the old timers showing up early and leaving fairly early while the younger crowd didn't show any intention in leaving any time soon. From the looks of some, possibly not ever.

Eli and Jonathan wandered off to meet up with their buddies to get the music going.

As the sun went down and little white fairy lights began twinkling, the sounds of musical instruments being tuned up could be heard in the distance.

Sarah Kate hopped up and squealed, "There's our boys now! C'mon, y'all, lets go see 'em."

The singing and the dancing commenced and was still going strong several hours later.

Emma and Olivia decided to walk around a little and look for Zoe to congratulate her on a successful grand opening before heading home.

They found her inside Les étoiles with Jacob, Scott and Zelda, The Wicked Women's parents, the Tatnalls and a few other Whimsey locals. None of whom seemed in a hurry to go anywhere.

Zoe saw them and waved them over, "Y'all, oh do come over and join us. Isn't this the loveliest gallery opening ever?"

Each of the girls said their hellos and passed around some hugs.

"I'll say," said Olivia. "It's been perfect, but I'm going to carry my tired ol' self home now. Zoe, thanks for hiring Britta to look over all the little ones tonight. Yet another stroke of genius. She and some friends of hers are over at our house with about 20 children and last time I checked, every one of those little ones were either sound asleep or real close."

"And I'm headed home, too," said Emma. "Attending an opening must be harder than throwing one 'cause I'm beat."

Zoe laughed, "I will pay for this tomorrow, I'm sure, but right now, I'm on Cloud Nine with pure joy. You girls go ahead. Nite nite."

When Emma and Olivia reached the bottom of the steps getting ready to go their separate ways home, they heard loud shrieks and screams.

Olivia grabbed Emma's hand, and they ran back to the gallery where they spotted Maggie, Alex and Sarah Kate.

Emma giggled and wondered why they were pretending to be the three "hear no evil, see no evil, speak no evil monkeys" when it dawned on her something was very wrong.

Alex had her hands on either side of her head whispering "What on earth?"

Maggie had one hand over her mouth. Emma heard the word "Whoa."

Sarah Kate had her hands in front of her face yelling, "Holy shit. That silly wench has a punch bowl on her head. Get it off of there!"

Emma ran past them, opened the back door and yelled for help. Several people came running. Eli was the first to get to Reese Prescott who was lying on the floor. The table holding the punch bowls was turned over, and one of the bowls was upside down on her head. He quickly pushed it away and pulled Reese to a sitting position as he yelled, "Sombody call 911." He rolled her over onto her back and began giving her CPR. There were slices of lemon and lime along with a cherry or two tangled in her hair.

"I think I'd like to go back to Atlanta now, please," said Madeline.

A stunned silence was soon replaced with nervous whispers as everyone was wondering the same thing.

Was Reese Prescott dead drunk?

Or was she dead?

CHAPTER THIRTY-THREE

The ambulance arrived quickly, and Reese was transported to the small local clinic.

Chief Ostwalt followed the ambulance from the party, but came back when he had news.

Reese was alive, but she was being treated by Dr. Hank Ryan for alcohol poisoning.

"Course, the question now is," as Chief Ostwalt so succinctly asked, "what the hell was she doing lying on the floor with a punchbowl on her head? No one seems to have seen what happened, but several people have told me how drunk she was earlier. We can only assume she passed out, knocked the table over on her way down with the punchbowl ending up on her head." He shook his head and rubbed his hand across his face. "Dr. Ryan says she's going to be fine. She wants Reese to spend the night at the clinic, but she can go home tomorrow."

Although it was late, many of the guests were still mulling around. Some seemed frozen to their chairs. The need to be with family and community was strong.

Emma felt Earlene bouncing a little on her shoulder and turned her head to look.

"Earlene? You okay, sweetie?"

"This is pretty horrible, huh? And don't think badly of me, Emma, but I really need a cigarette. Do you think anyone will pitch a hissy if I zip away and have a quick smoke? You know how people hate smokers these days."

Emma couldn't help but snicker, "I'll bet if you fly quietly and sneak into the trees at the edge of the property, no one will even notice."

Earlene nodded and did a very slow walk away on her little bitty tippy toes. In the air. Crouched over in an attempt to make herself even smaller. Emma watched her dig around in her itty bitty purse and pull out an itty bitty pack of cigarettes and shook her head in wonderment as an itty bitty little lighter clicked and flashed.

While she watched Earlene slip away, she felt the briefest of kisses land on top of her head. When she looked up, it was into the eyes of Eli, clouded with concern.

"Holding up okay?"

She reached for his hand and guided him onto the picnic bench next to her and nodded, "I'm okay. I think I'm in shock though. It's hard to get my head wrapped around on this. What do you think happened?"

Eli shook his head, "Damned if I know. How does a woman end up on the floor wearing a punch bowl? It's one of those things we'd have a hard time accepting if we read it in a book, you know?"

"True enough."

It was a little after ten o'clock when people finally stared leaving.

Eli took Emma's hand, "Come on, I'll walk you home."

Emma reached up with her other hand and Earlene hopped into it. Emma could feel her trembling. "Earlene, do you want to come with us?"

Earlene looked up with tears on her face, "Can I come?"

Emma smiled gently at her friend, "You bet. C'mon, little partner."

When they reached Zoe's cottage there were a few people scattered around on the porch talking quietly. Emma said her hello's, followed quickly by good nights. Eli said good night and walked slowly home. Emma and Earlene walked up the stairs to bed. While Emma was in the bathroom getting into her nightie, Earlene made herself a comfy spot on the pillow next to Emma's. Both were sound asleep within minutes.

The next morning, Emma awakened to the sounds of snoring in her ear and when she shifted her eyes to the right to see who might be sharing her bed, she giggled when she saw tiny Earlene in the middle of the pillow.

Earlene's little mouth was open and some noises seemingly impossible for someone so small were practically rattling the windows. Pyewackett and Fred, in the big red chair next to the bed, had pushed their heads under the throw pillows. Apparently, Earlene's snoring was bothering them, too.

Emma got up and walked over to the window to look down at the porch. Zoe, Zelda and The Wicked Women were already settled in with their coffee.

Not wanting to take the time to dress, she tossed on a robe and went down to join them.

"Mornin', Women," Emma said. "What are y'all doing here so early, and why didn't you wake me?"

They all looked at her, exchanged looks among themselves and giggled.

Zoe cleared her throat, "Well, child. I was going to do that. However, as I got close to your room and heard those snores, it didn't take me long to figure out I shouldn't disturb you."

Emma stared at her aunt for a few seconds, then looked around at the rest of the women, including her mother, who would not meet her eyes.

Then she burst out laughing and couldn't stop.

One by one, the others joined in.

Once Emma finally got a grip, the only thing she could say was "Earlene."

Everyone looked puzzled.

Emma pointed over her head, snorted and choked out "Earlene."

Zoe turned her head so she was looking at Emma out of the corner of her eyes, "Are you trying to tell us Earlene is in your room?"

Emma nodded and snorted again. She lifted the hem of her robe and had it over her face. Her shoulders shook with laughter.

"Earlene?" Zoe asked again.

Emma nodded and snorted.

As one, the women hopped out of their chairs and tiptoed up the stairs. Zoe opened the door to Emma's apartment, and they all continued, single file, on tiptoe, into her bedroom. The snores were, indeed, coming from the itty bitty redheaded pixie asleep on Emma's pillow.

With eyes wide, hands over their mouths, they backed out and went running down the stairs and back to the porch where they all screamed with laughter until they could hardly breathe.

Finally catching her breath, Zoe said, "Lord A Mercy."

And set them all off again.

After what seemed an eternity, an exhausted group of women returned to their morning coffee and rehashing of last night's party. Since they had learned Reese was going to be fine, they were able to put her out of their minds. They agreed they hated what had happened, and were happy she was okay, but the fact remained she had done more than a few horrendous, mean, and creepy things and would never be warmly welcomed into their hearts.

They chatted only about how perfect the party had been up until what had now become known as, "That Incident Involving Reese and the Punchbowl."

Alex stood, raised her coffee cup and said, "I propose a toast. To our own inimitable Zoe Hamilton." Looking at Zoe with a smile, she bowed, "Honey, you just rock."

Everyone applauded and the toasts continued. After everyone toasted her, Zoe stood, bowed in return, and said, "I never really knew for sure if I'd live long enough to see my dream come true. I'm happy I did. I love each of you more than I can say."

As she was sitting back down, Earlene flew down from Emma's upstairs window and gave Zoe a resounding kiss on her cheek, "I love you too, Zoe." And planted herself on Zoe's shoulder.

Maggie cleared her throat, "Emma, honey, are we all supposed to sit here and pretend we didn't see you kiss Eli Tatnall last night?"

Sarah Kate said, "And, honey, it weren't no little peck!"

Alex laughed, rolled her eyes upward and fanned her face, "Oh, no, it weren't no little peck, honey. It was hot, hot, hot!"

Olivia gave Emma a piercing look, "And, from where I was standing, it looked at though you were the kisser and Eli was the kissee. Just sayin'."

Emma grinned and nodded, "He did seem a little bit surprised, didn't he?"

They fell into laughter again.

Emma walked over to the porch rail and looked out over the ocean for a minute, maybe two. When she turned around, everyone was looking at her expectantly. They were also looking puzzled and concerned.

She gave one decisive nod of her head and let out a big whoosh of air. "I hope there's plenty of coffee. We're going to be here a while. Get comfy, ladies, I want to tell you a story."

CHAPTER THIRTY-FOUR

After they'd all refilled their cups and were settled, Emma continued.

"You know most of this story. To get things rolling, I'll give it a title. Let's call it The Tale of the Mistaken Marriage for lack of anything better. It'll become clear, though, that there are some things you don't know. Before, I wasn't in a place emotionally to share some of this with you, and then, well - then I fell apart and couldn't face things myself, let alone face y'all while telling the story. In hindsight, I have handled things poorly for a number of years. Up until just recently - only the past few weeks - have I even decided to tell you this story at all.

"But, now I'm good. I'm strong. I'm back on the road to being *me.* And, life is good. Hopefully, if I play my cards right, it'll get even better." She smiled mischievously and wiggled her eyebrows.

Zoe moved a chair closer to Emma. Emma looked at her aunt and gave her a gentle smile as she sat.

Maggie spoke up first, "I'm glad we're going to get to hear this story, Emma. I know we all know some of it, but I for one, don't know all of it."

Emma chuckled, "Thanks for helping me get started, guys." She got quiet for a few seconds gathering her thoughts. "I met Hunter during his year in tenure as Writer in Residence here on Whimsey for the Writer's Retreat. He was quite the gourmet and in his spare time, took lessons in Lowcountry cooking from the retreat chef. Oh, how Hunter loved entertaining and hosting dinner parties, sometimes quite elegant, sometimes as simple as steamed shrimp and beer. We got to know one another quite well over these dinners, and became close. He started preparing more meals for just the two of us."

Sarah Kate looked over at Emma, "Was it during this time you decided to get married?"

Emma nodded, "When his term as Writer in Residence ended, it seemed natural at the time for me to move to Atlanta with him and get married."

Emma got up from her chair and walked back to the porch railing. She sipped her coffee and looked out over the dunes. When she turned back around, she cleared her throat. "What I kept from everyone was how the magic of our courtship died without the magic of Whimsey surrounding us. We moved into Hunter's condominium with the understanding it was never meant to be home. It was only meant to be a stopping station. I found it to be cold and sterile. What's sad is that it ended up being the place we stayed for so long. First, because I was waiting for my new husband to show some sort of interest in finding and furnishing our forever and ever nest. The home we would stay in forever, make our life and raise our children.

"The condo was one Hunter bought sight unseen, completely furnished, from a friend who had married and moved to the suburbs. The convenience of a place downtown was perfect for getting to and from the Atlanta newspaper office where he worked and for his quick unexpected trips to the airport while on assignment. He needed a place to crash and mistakenly thought the novel he was writing would come together if he had a home office in which to write it."

Emma walked over to the table to freshen her coffee.

Zelda walked over to stand next to her and took her hand, "Emma, if this is too hard for you . . . ."

"No. It's not," Emma smiled back at her mother. "I promise. I want to do this."

They both sat back down and held hands across the short distance between them.

"I hated the place the minute I saw it. The bleakness of it seemed to wedge itself into our marriage from the very beginning. And I, of course, wanted the type of warm nurturing home I grew up in. Hunter thought all that was hogwash. Four walls and a roof was all anyone needed, he said, and he refused to budge.

"After a year, he finally agreed to start looking around for something, but the appointments I made with realtors never seemed to be convenient, and Hunter failed to show up for most of the showings. When he did show up, it was with a surliness that put a damper on the prospect of a new place almost before walking in the front door.

"After our second year in the condo, I put my foot down. Hunter agreed we were outgrowing the place, and the novel he was supposed to be working on just wasn't coming together. Perhaps a change of scenery would do us both some good, he said. But now he was spending a lot of time traveling. He'd written a series of articles that gained him some fame, and he was being courted by some major news organizations both within the states and in Europe. It was during this time that we decided it would be a good move for us, and for our marriage, to rent a villa in Italy for a month. Our short marriage of only two years wasn't the happy life we had envisioned when we were together back on Whimsey."

Emma took a deep breath. "Wow." She put her head back against the back of the rocking chair.

Olivia popped up out of her chair, "I say we need a little break here, what say?"

Alex nodded, as did Maggie.

"Want me to go in the kitchen and fix us some snackies?" asked Sarah Kate.

Amid the much needed laughter, the women walked into the house and back to the kitchen. Earlene sat on Emma's shoulder with her hand protectively and gently on the back of her neck.

They all fell into a gentle rhythm of passing one another eggs and bread and butter and jelly as they prepared a comfort meal of scrambled eggs and toast.

Maggie spoke up first, "So did you go to Italy? I adore Italy. It didn't help?"

Emma shook her head. "The trip to Italy might have been the opportunity we needed to put aside all the disagreements and differences and reconcile. But at the last minute, I changed my mind during yet another nasty argument.

"Hunter had shouted in anger to make an unnecessary point, and it was the proverbial straw that broke the camel's back. I told him that was enough and that I was giving up. If we couldn't even plan a trip of a lifetime together without arguing, there just wasn't any hope for us.

I told him to go to Italy, but that I was staying in Atlanta, and that it was over for us.

"It was only pride that kept me from telling him I was sorry and hadn't meant it. I wanted to try to recapture what I thought we once had, but couldn't bring myself to be the one to apologize again.

"I remember a long, silent look passing between us, Hunter nodding his head once and leaving without a word. He made arrangements for movers to pick up his belongings. I had no idea where his things were taken, or that he had gone to Italy without me until a few weeks later when my parents showed up unexpectedly to tell her about the accident that had taken Hunter's life."

By now, the women had cooked their meal and finished it. They all sat around the table silently. They knew Emma didn't need their words right now – only their presence.

"So," she continued, "during the year after his death, an apathy seemed to take over. One I wasn't able to shake. I had just started making a bit of a name for myself with my jewelry designs, but now that burst of creativity deserted me. The condo evolved into a big closet, storage bin, and office. One that just happened to have a fridge, a stove and microwave in case I might need to heat up a can of soup and have a glass of cold white wine while working late. Along with a bed to crash on for a few hours sleep between long hours of work. Work that was becoming increasingly harder and less satisfying. The result was that my work was crap.

"But the outcome even harder to face was how afraid I had become to allow myself to feel again, let alone love again. I'd had my heart broken by Eli. No matter that years passed before I realized I had allowed a misunderstanding ruin what we had. Then had my heart broken by Hunter. Top it all off with the guilt I felt about Hunter's death while we were so angry with one another.

"And that's it. End of story." Emma said as she stood up and gave them all a shaky grin.

"Is it?" asked Olivia.

"It is, sweetie, I promise. I'm not hiding anything else. That's it. Well, except I left out the part about running into Alex while I was on sabbatical in Ellijay." She looked at Olivia. "Yes. Sabbatical."

Alex laughed quietly as she looked at the floor and shook her head, "Man, if I had known this story, I would have kept my mouth shut, for sure."

"She pretty much called me every kind of fool imaginable," said Emma. "I didn't realize it then, but I deserved it. And, it was one of the things that helped me get back on track. That and Great Aunt Elizabeth manipulating me back to Whimsey in her own other-worldly way."

A creaking sound brought their attention to an empty rocking chair which had been rocking, but had suddenly stopped.

"I meant that in the nicest possible way of course, Aunt Elizabeth," said Emma.

The chair began rocking again.

Five sets of eyes belonging to The Wicked Women of Whimsey opened wide. Zelda, Zoe and Earlene giggled happily.

"Man, where have you brought me?" asked Madeline.

"Home. I've brought you home." whispered Emma.

To the others, she said, "Okay. So. If I'm going to be completely honest, maybe I do have one more question." Emma was weaving her fingers together in her lap, looking at the floor. "I wish I didn't have to ask this, but if I really want to clear the air, I do. Do you think I'm the worst person you've ever known?"

Surprised, Olivia looked at Emma, "What? What on earth are you talking about?"

Emma looked back, "Because I married Hunter. Knowing I still loved Eli."

"What?" said Olivia. "Emmaline - listen to me. Hunter did care about you - as much as he was capable of caring for anyone. I'm not sure he understood how to love. There was a distance to him, and he worked hard to keep it that way. But now, Emma, it's over. Hunter is gone. Forever. And that was not your fault either. We are all thrilled you finally know you can't live the rest of your life feeling guilty. There's no reason. The fact of the matter is, as harsh as this may sound, you have been given another chance to grab the happiness you deserve. Don't blow it again. Do not blow it again. Do you hear me? I don't want to have to smack you upside that pretty head of yours to get you to pay attention."

Emma's mouth fell open as she stared at Olivia. Her eyes were huge.

"Wow."

Olivia nodded, "Yes. Exactly. Wow."

"When did you get so smart? And bossy?"

Olivia batted her eyelashes and said in an exaggerated southern drawl, "Why, sugah, I don't know what you mean."

Emma closed her eyes and shook her head, "I don't know what to say."

"Don't say anything, Emma. But do, please, think about what I've said. Okay? Promise?"

Emma nodded.

"Okay. Good. Now I have one final question," said Maggie as she raised her hand over her head.

"Yes?" said Emma.

"I'll bet I know what it is," said Sarah Kate.

"Me too," said Alex.

They all turned toward Maggie and waited. After a slight pause and with a wide grin, Maggie said, "Okay, the question is, are you going to jump Eli's bones now?"

Everyone on the porch shrieked with laughter.

Emma refused to answer, but she did wiggle her eyebrows again.

CHAPTER THIRTY-FIVE

The next morning, Eli called Emma and invited her to dinner at his house that evening. She thought *Uh oh,* but said, "Okay."

Eli came to pick her up that evening with a couple jars of his honey, catnip for Pyewackett and some treats for Fred.

"Did your mother bake these little doggie bones?" Zoe asked. "They're adorable!"

"She did. Something new she's trying. Once the dog treats are perfected, she's going to do cat treats."

"She is amazing," said Zoe.

She said her good nights and watched Emma and Eli walk off hand-in-hand.

Emma asked Eli about his trip to Savannah, and he asked about her work.

After a few steps, Eli stopped Emma, "Emma, you're about a million miles away, darlin'. What's on your mind?"

"Eli, could you do me a big favor before we go to your place?"

"Anything you want. What is it?"

"Remember when you told me about Reese's father leaving and blaming her for it? I haven't been able to get that out of my mind. Would you mind going to Dr. Ryan's clinic with me? I want to talk to Reese."

Eli looked at her in surprise. "Are you sure?"

Emma nodded. "I'm sure."

"Emma, do you know what you intend to accomplish, or is this just a fleeting feeling of guilt? I think you need to think about this a bit."

"Oh, Eli, believe me. I have thought and thought about this so much I couldn't begin to tell you. I had almost decided to try to talk to Reese before this happened. Now I feel a real need to do this. It's not just an urge."

"Okay. Then let's go to the clinic. I'll just wait for you, but take as long as you need."

As Emma entered the small building, she spotted a kiosk in the corner selling flowers. There was a small white basket filled with daisies and after a momentary hesitation, Emma bought it.

When she reached Reese's room, she knocked gently on the door before peeking in. Reese was alone and staring out the window. When she turned her head to see who was at the door, Emma saw tears on her face.

"What do you want, Emma? You want to gloat over how I made a fool of myself?"

Emma shook her head. "No, but I did want to stop in for just a minute to bring you some flowers. And, I would like to talk to you if that's okay with you."

Reese looked at her for a few long seconds. "Well, you're here, might as well come on in and get whatever it is off your chest."

Emma put the basket of flowers on the window sill and sat in the chair next to the bed. "Reese, I'm sorry you're in here.

We've never been friends, and that's not right. We're both Whimsey girls, and I'd like to see if we can put all the bad things behind us and start over again. I was hoping we could talk about why things went so bad between us and see if we could make a start at trying to work things out."

"I think you're serious." Reese chuckled and shook her head. "Emma, listen, there's nothing to work out. You were always the most beautiful and most talented and everyone knew the great things you were going to do with your life. You were always perfect, Emma, and I hated you for it. I'm not a real Whimsey girl. I'm not beautiful and I'm not talented like the rest of you. I appreciate you coming by here today, I do. And I'm not even all that surprised. As much as I've hoped you were all show, the truth is you're just a nice person. Still perfect."

"Perfect? You think I'm perfect? Oh my God, Reese. Let me tell you how perfect I am." And proceeded to tell Reese how she had screwed up everything with Eli and with Hunter, how she lost everything when she left Whimsey and all her talent went to hell in a handbasket, and how her life has been anything but perfect.

Before either of them realized it, they were having a real conversation. It wasn't until a nurse knocked on the door to tell Reese Dr. Ryan would be by to release her in just a little while, that they realized they had spent over an hour talking. Reese asked the nurse to give her another couple of minutes and when she closed the door, Reese told Emma she appreciated her coming by. "I don't really know if we can ever be friends, but I'll tell you the truth, I do feel differently about you. And I think I like the feeling."

Emma cocked her head to one side and studied Reese. "You keep saying you don't have any talents. How do you know? Have you ever really tried? Have you worked hard to develop anything you love doing? Your mother is a successful sculptor and I'll bet you were born with talent. I'll bet if you tried, you would find you have some of the Whimsey magic, too. Now that you're not going to continue putting all your energy into hating me in some kind of ridiculous misplaced envy, maybe you'll start thinking about what you want to do. You know what? As soon as you're better, I'm going to help you find your crimson."

Reese said, "Find my what?"

"Oh, don't worry about it now. I'll explain it to you once you get better."

Reese laughed quietly. "I do think you're kinda nutty."

Emma laughed, too. "And you're probably right. I'll see you, Reese."

"See you, Emma. Thanks for the flowers."

When Emma walked out the front door, she found Eli pacing back and forth.

"Hey, you," Emma said. "Sorry I took so long."

"Emma! Girl, you were in there forever. Is everything okay?"

"Let's just say I think we may have just come to a bit of a truce."

Eli stepped back and looked at her. "Really? Wow. That's pretty amazing. Want to tell me about it?"

And so she did. As they walked through town holding hands, Emma filled him in on her visit, and told him Reese would be going home within the hour.

As they approached Eli's cottage, Emma was once again struck by how magical it looked in its perfect dimension sitting in the most perfect spot, as if it had grown there. "I think this place was maybe built by fairies."

"Wouldn't surprise me a bit," Eli said.

Emma followed Eli through the cottage to the kitchen. "What can I do to help?"

"Not a thing, darlin'. Have a seat and a glass of wine. We're eating simple fare this evening. Steak, a baked potato and a salad."

"Perfect!"

They shared stories of the work they had been doing, and Eli asked if Zoe had told her about the photo shoot they were thinking about doing on GalleryLes étoiles.

"Yes! I think it's brilliant! And won't it be a fun thing for you?"

"It will. I'm looking forward to it. I'm hoping to get a few good shots of some of the locals with their work. Including, of course, The Wicked Women, maybe dressed in some wicked theme of their choice."

"Oh boy - they're gonna love hearing this! Too fun!"

After dinner, they wandered to the front porch with their coffee and settled on the glider.

"I could rock in this old glider, look at the Whimsey stars and listen to the surf for hours and hours," said Emma.

"Mmmm. It's nice. I spend a lot of time out here."

When Emma shivered, Eli disappeared inside, but quickly returned with a quilt to toss over Emma's legs. "It still gets cool out here in the evenings, but this should keep you cozy. How 'bout a cup of hot chocolate instead of coffee to go along with the quilt?"

Emma smiled up at Eli, "That sounds lovely."

When he returned carrying a tray with a pot of hot chocolate and two thick mugs which he placed on a table close by, she smiled again, "You, Eli Tatnall, learned well at your mama's knee. This is delightful. Thank you."

"Wait. There's more," With a flourish, he pulled a linen dish towel off a bowl to reveal a mound of fluffy white marshmallows. "Voila!"

Emma laughed, "Perfect!" She popped one into her mouth and another into her mug of chocolate. "Mmmmm."

Eli settled under the quilt next to her. They quietly sipped their hot chocolate and gently rocked the glider as they gazed at the stars over the ocean and listened to the waves break. Emma let her head drop against Eli's shoulder, and he moved himself around to put his arm around her shoulders. She felt him gently kiss the top of her head and felt tears prickling her eyelids with how perfect it all felt.

"I love you, Emma."

"I love you back, Eli. I always have. I never stopped."

"Me, too."

Eli took her mug out of her hands and placed it, along with his, on the table. He wrapped his arms around her, held her tight, and they kissed.

And kissed some more.

Eli leaned back and looked into Emma's eyes as he brushed her hair from her face. "Want another marshmallow?"

Emma snorted and cocked her head. "Well, sure. Okay. But, truth be told, Eli, I was perfectly happy with what we were doing."

"You mean the kissing?"

"Yeah, that."

Eli handed her the bowl, "We'll get back to that, but here, have another marshmallow."

Emmma looked at him and shook her head as she took the bowl from him, "Eli, one of the things I've always loved about you is your off the wall sense of humor. You truly are the craziest man I know." She reached for a marshmallow and when she felt something she felt sure was not a marshmallow, she looked down.

"What . . . .," With her eyes wide, and her mouth open wider, Emma looked down to see a sparkling red ruby with a two diamonds set on either side.

She looked at Eli, "Oh, my."

Emma took the ring out of the bowl, looked at it, then looked back at Eli as he gently took the ring from her and slid down on one knee.

"Will you marry me, Emma?"

Emma put one hand over her mouth, and Eli saw the tears starting to roll down her face.

"Do you like it? I wanted to get you something red so it would match most everything you wear."

Emma nodded. Then she hiccupped.

"Emma? Do you hate the ring? Or do you not want to marry me? Honey? Don't cry. Now, now, darlin'. You're going to wake the neighbors, Emma, and I'm thinking they're gonna think I've hurt your feelings. Darlin', um, I don't want to try to tell you what to do, but could you maybe not sob quite so loudly?"

Emma threw her arms around his neck and between loud laughs and equally loud hiccups with tears still streaming down her face, she squealed. "Yes!"

With both of them now laughing and crying, Eli held her close. "Whew, darlin', you had me worried there for a minute."

"I love the ring. I love you, and yes, yes, yes, I would love to be your wife. I think I've wanted that since I first laid eyes on you when our moms put us in the same playpen so we could get to know one another."

"Wow. Do you really remember that?" asked Eli.

"Well, sure, don't you?"

Eli looked to make sure she was kidding before shaking his head, "I guess my memory's not quite as good as yours.

Eli stood up and took Emma's hand, leading her into the house and up the stairs, as she dragged the quilt along behind her.

She finally dropped the corner of the quilt she had been holding on to as Eli started nuzzling around her neck and unbuttoning her top. She watched his eyes change from blue to steely gray when he slipped her top off her shoulders and stood quietly looking at her.

CHAPTER THIRTY-SIX

That evening, Emma and Eli walked slowly towards Zoe's, excited about telling her their news.

As they got closer, they realized there were quite a few people gathered on the porch. When the group noticed Emma and Eli they burst into a rousing rendition of "Get Me To the Church On Time." The couple stopped in their tracks, surprised and befuddled. Zelda ran down the steps and threw her arms around Emma, "Oh, sweetie! We are all so happy for you both!" And planted a kiss on a very stunned Eli.

Emma looked around at all the happy faces and asked, "What's going on here?"

Scott stepped out of the crowd, spun Emma around in a circle and then shook Eli's hand before also planting a kiss on the top of his head, "We're throwing you guys an engagement party, that's what!

Still befuddled, Emma could only stammer. "But. . .but. . .how did you know?"

Zelda said, "Have you forgotten this is Whimsey, sweetie? Lou told Zoe Eli had taken the ring with him last night, Zoe told me, I told. . .well, you know how word spreads. We all knew what was going to happen."

Emma looked at Eli, who was obviously as surprised as she. He shrugged his shoulders and laughed when she ran up the steps to hugs from everyone as she started showing them her ring.

Zelda walked over to Eli and hugged him, "Oh, Laws. I cannot tell you how happy this makes me. I'm just glad you two are finally getting together. We were all a little afraid for a while that you both might have lost your way. But, it's all worked out. I could not be any happier, son. I know you'll take good care of our Emmaline."

Eli choked up a little and nodded, "Yes, m'am. I want to do just that."

For the next couple of hours, Emma and Eli were hugged, kissed, teased and made over by everyone they'd known since they were babies playing together in that playpen.

Olivia, Sarah Kate, Maggie and Alex arrived and immediately began discussing things like bridesmaid's dresses and matching shoes, flowers and music, wedding and reception venues, wedding cakes and who would catch the bouquet.

Chief Ostwalt cleared his throat loudly. As the crowd quieted, he looked at them, smiled and raised his glass, "I'd like to toast the happy couple. And you all. Here's to Emma and Eli and Whimsey. Let's continue the evening in the spirit of community fellowship and be thankful for the upcoming union of two of Whimsey's own."

He turned and bowed towards the couple, "On behalf of everyone, may I say we all wish you a lifetime of joy. And on behalf of myself, may I say it's about time!"

The crowd erupted into laughter.

It was way past dark when people began to leave the party and head home, waving and shouting their good nights and congratulations as they left.

Pretty soon, the only people left were Emma, Eli, and Zoe. The rest of the family had admitted to being pretty exhausted by the past several hours of excitement and needed to get some sleep.

After sitting for a while, Eli pushed himself out of the rocker. "I think I'll just float on home now. What a great party. Thank you, Zoe." He gave Zoe a hug.

Zoe gave him a peck on the cheek. "Good night, Eli. It's going to be a delight finally having you in the family for real." And she went inside.

Emma and Eli stood quietly with their arms around one another until he finally released her. "Are you happy, darlin'?"

"Oh, Eli. I've never been happier. And I love my ring."

"I'm glad, darlin. Very glad. I love you, Emma."

"I love you back, Eli."

They held each other again and neither of them noticed Earlene sitting quietly on the edge of one of the hanging baskets of geraniums up near the porch ceiling. With a little smile as she smoked one of her itty bitty little cigarettes.

And up at the big house, Elizabeth Calhoun sat on her porch in her favorite rocking chair, grinning, with a glass of wine in one hand and a cigar in the other.

And the stars were bright over Whimsey.

–   The End –

Emma's Iced Latte

2 cups ground coffee

12 cups water

1 cup sugar

1 quart Half & Half *(Emma uses fat free Half & Half even though she thinks that might be an oxymoron)*

1 quart milk

1 Tablespoon vanilla

Brew coffee using 12 cups of water. Pour into a one gallon container. Stir in sugar until dissolved. Stir in Half & Half, milk, and vanilla. Chill. Serve over ice.

Yum.

Optional: Top with whipped cream and shaved chocolate.

Zelda's Breakfast Strata

(Zelda actually got this recipe from her friend John Messer)

12 slices of bread, crusts trimmed

2 cups shredded cheddar cheese

4 eggs

1 Tbs. chopped onion, sauteed or not, cook's choice

1 tsp. salt

1/2 tsp. mustard

1/2 tsp. cayenne

2 1/2 cups milk

Grease a 12x8 baking dish.

Arrange 6 slices bread on bottom of dish. Sprinkle with cheese. Top with remaining bread slices.

In med. mixing bowl beat eggs, onion, salt, mustard, cayenne.

Blend in milk. Pour egg mixture over bread. Cover and refrigerate overnight.

Bake in 325 oven uncovered for 45-55 minutes or until knife inserted in center comes out clean.

Serves 6-8

Zoe's Cappuccino Brownies with Cream Cheese Frosting

For brownie layer:

4 ounces fine-quality bittersweet chocolate (not unsweetened), chopped

3/4 stick (6 tablespoons) unsalted butter, cut into pieces

1 tablespoon instant espresso powder, dissolved in 1/2 tablespoon boiling water

3/4 cup sugar1 teaspoon vanilla

2 large eggs

1/2 cup all-purpose flour

1/4 teaspoon salt

1/2 cup walnuts, chopped

For cream cheese frosting:

4 ounces cream cheese, softened

3 tablespoons unsalted butter, softened

3/4 cup confectioners' sugar, sifted

1/2 teaspoon vanilla

1/2 teaspoon cinnamon

For glaze:

3 ounces fine-quality bittersweet chocolate (not unsweetened)

1 tablespoon unsalted butter

1/4 cup heavy cream

2 1/4 teaspoons instant espresso powder, dissolved in 1/2 tablespoon boiling water

Preheat oven to 350°F. and butter and flour an 8-inch square baking pan, knocking out excess flour.

Make brownie layer: In a heavy 1 1/2-quart saucepan melt chocolate and butter with espresso mixture over low heat, stirring, until smooth and remove pan from heat. Cool mixture to lukewarm and whisk in sugar and vanilla. Add eggs, 1 at a time, whisking well until mixture is glossy and smooth. Stir in flour and salt until just combined and stir in walnuts.

Spread batter evenly in pan and bake in middle of oven 22 to 25 minutes, or until a tester comes out with crumbs adhering to it. Cool brownie layer completely in pan on a rack.

Make cream cheese frosting: In a bowl with an electric mixer beat cream cheese and butter until light and fluffy. Add confectioners' sugar, vanilla, and cinnamon and beat until combined well. Spread frosting evenly over brownie layer. Chill brownies 1 hour, or until frosting is firm.

Make glaze: In a double boiler or metal bowl set over a saucepan of barely simmering water melt chocolate and butter with cream and espresso mixture, stirring, until smooth, and remove top of double boiler or bowl from heat. Cool glaze to room temperature.

Spread glaze carefully over frosting. Chill brownies, covered, until cold, at least 3 hours.

Cut chilled brownies into 24 squares and remove them from pan while still cold. Serve brownies cold or at room temperature. Brownies keep, covered and chilled, in one layer, 5 days.

Zoe's Crab Quiche

Zoe doesn't have time (nor inclination) to make a pie crust and just picks one up at the grocery store from time to time to have in the freezer for when the mood hits.

For the filling, she uses:

1/2 lb lump crabmeat, picked over

4 large eggs

2 cups heavy cream

2 tablespoons finely chopped fresh chives

2 tablespoons finely chopped fresh parsley

2 tablespoons finely chopped fresh cilantro

1/2 teaspoon seafood seasoning

1/2 teaspoon salt

1/4 teaspoon black pepper

1/8 teaspoon freshly grated nutmeg

½ cup coarsely grated Monterey Jack cheese

½ coarsely grated Gruyere cheese

(Zoe often plays around with this recipe and changes things around a little – like the cheeses – try some different things till you find what you like best)

Do this:

Whisk together eggs, cream, herbs, seafood seasoning, salt, pepper, and nutmeg, then stir in cheeses and crabmeat.

Pour into prebaked crust and bake until filling puffs and is no longer wobbly in center when quiche is gently shaken, 40 to 50 minutes. Cool in pie plate on rack 15 minutes.

Bon Appétit ! ! !